A Scandal
by Any Other Name

Also by Kimberly Bell

The Importance of Being
Scandalous

A Scandal by Any Other Name

A TALE OF TWO SISTERS

KIMBERLY BELL

Copyright © 2018 by Kimberly Bell. All rights reserved, including the right to reproduce, distribute, or transmit in any form or by any means. For information regarding subsidiary rights, please contact the Publisher.

Entangled Publishing, LLC
2614 South Timberline Road
Suite 105, PMB 159
Fort Collins, CO 80525

Entangled Amara is an imprint of Entangled Publishing, LLC.

Visit our website at www.entangledpublishing.com.

Edited by Kate Brauning
Cover design by Erin Dameron-Hill
Interior design by Toni Kerr

ISBN: 978-1-63375-889-6
Ebook ISBN: 978-1-63375-890-2

Manufactured in the United States of America

First Edition January 2018

10 9 8 7 6 5 4 3 2 1

To the people who see us better than we see ourselves.

Chapter One

Jasper DeVere tugged at the neck of the scarlet and ermine robe, desperate to have this asinine ritual over. The heat in the antechamber was suffocating. Or perhaps it was just the company. The Duke of Atherton was petulantly sprawled in a chair, scowling wordlessly at Jasper.

The writ of summons to confirm Jasper's new title as Duke of Albemarle required him to be presented to Parliament with the endorsement of a senior peer and a junior peer. While Jasper's outranking of Atherton was hardly a secret, the man was not pleased with having it paraded in front of Parliament as a form of ceremony. Or he could still be bristling over Jasper's twin sister, Ruby, rejecting his marriage proposal. If that was it, he was a bigger idiot than Jasper had initially gauged. Atherton was hardly the first proposal Ruby had turned down.

The Duke of Essex entered, closing the door behind him. He was dressed in the same ceremonial robe, no doubt sweating buckets beneath it. "Looks like we won't be bowing to the cloth after all. The queen is in attendance."

Meaning this nonsense would take twice as long at the minimum. "Why would she bother?"

"Oh, I don't know," Atherton drawled. "Perhaps because you're the first Duke to be confirmed during her reign—and her cousin."

Jasper would love nothing more than to abandon this entire ordeal, and go back to pretending his grandfather was still alive. He didn't want to be the Duke. Not yet. Maybe not ever. He desperately wanted to go back to the days when his grandfather sat stolidly at the end of the breakfast table, anchoring Jasper's world with his resolute presence. Jasper could not be the Duke of Albemarle. He would never be able to fill those shoes.

"…Albemarle? Did you hear me?" Essex was staring at him with concern.

"Hmm?"

"The Black Rod's at the door. It's time."

The House of Lords usher might be there, but it wasn't time—not yet. Jasper shook his head and tossed the black hat and writ of summons onto a chair. The ermine robe followed.

Atherton's eyes went wide. "Albemarle?"

"Tell Victoria I'm sorry." Jasper clawed at the cloak, breaking the clasp in his efforts to get it off. "Something's come up."

"You can't just—"

"Your Grace, please—"

Jasper ignored them all. He opened the nearest door, praying it wouldn't be a closet. It opened out onto a shadowed hallway. He started down the corridor.

Ruby was going to kill him.

He couldn't think about that now, or the disappointment

that was bound to settle onto his grandmother's face. They didn't understand. They mourned Jasper's grandfather with grief equal to his own, but they didn't have to try to *become* him. It couldn't be done, and attempting it would be an insult to his grandfather's legacy. Jasper would find a way to explain that to them, eventually.

Right now, he just had to find a way to escape the building.

A new door opened out onto a wider, brightly lit hall. Out of the corner of his eye, Jasper recognized the impeccable posture and dark-sable coiffure of his twin sister. He pivoted in the opposite direction.

"Jasper?" Ruby's confusion at his flight carried down the hallway.

He pretended not to hear. An exterior door revealed itself at the end of the corridor. He broke into a jog to get there before she caught up to him.

"Jasper DeVere, come back here this instant!"

"What's that, Ruby? I couldn't hear you." He let the high ceiling carry the message back to her.

"Jas, stop!" His sister chased after him, but she was impeded by the constructs of female fashion and good manners. Jasper was impeded by neither.

Outside, a groom was leading a saddled horse toward the stables.

"Pardon me, my good man, but I need to steal that horse."

"What? My lord, you can't—"

Jasper vaulted into the saddle. He could practically feel Ruby's rage behind him. "I'm deeply sorry. Please tell its owner I'll return it eventually. He can forward his complaints to Lady Ruby DeVere."

Ruby caught up with him as he wheeled the mount toward the gates. "Jasper, running away won't bring him back."

"I know."

"Do you? Because you did the same thing when mother and father died."

He didn't want to think about their parents—not on top of everything else. He just needed it all to go away, just for a little while longer. "I can't, Ruby. I'm sorry. I just can't."

Jasper put heels to his horse. They burst out onto the London streets, and he navigated the quickest route out of town at top speed, ignoring the veering carriages and shouting pedestrians. When they reached the outskirts of the city, it still wasn't far enough. He needed more distance. An ocean, perhaps. Maybe that would finally be enough space between him and all the things he couldn't reconcile inside himself.

His grandfather was dead. The larger-than-life man who'd anchored Jasper's world for twenty-six years was gone. He didn't feel gone. His voice still echoed in Jasper's mind, and it felt like, if Jasper just turned fast enough, he might catch a glimpse of the old Duke disappearing around some corner. Everything in London was a reminder.

After hours in the saddle, Jasper amended his ambition from leaving the continent to getting a day's ride outside of London. Neither his backside nor his horse would survive a continental journey, and he'd left the city going west. As far as he knew, there were no viable options for getting to America on foot.

The smartest thing to do would be to assess his situation over a nice meal in a private dining room somewhere, but —since he hadn't planned on making a mad dash out of the city—his lack of funds and luggage were going to prove problematic. He could send for both, but then Ruby would find him. She probably had men scouring the roads looking for him at this very moment. He needed to find somewhere to hide out until he could convince his heart that this was the world now; a world where Edward DeVere, Duke of Albemarle, did not exist.

As his horse overtook a farmer's cart plodding along the road, Jasper leaned over and tried to ascertain his whereabouts. "Excuse me. Could you tell me where we are?"

"Just outside o' Woodley, m'lord," the farmer answered.

"Serendipity!" The world had not completely turned on Jasper just yet. His best friend, Nicholas, had acquired a house in Berkshire after he married his new wife, Amelia, and—if he was not mistaken—it was near Woodley. Since Nicholas and Amelia were off traveling while Nicholas had a break between terms, it would be the ideal place for Jasper to try to reconcile his new situation. "Thank you, my good man. Your assistance has been invaluable."

The farmer answered with a noncommittal grunt. Jasper ignored it in favor of trying to determine which one of these blasted country lanes would lead to Nick's house. All of the tracks looked the same; polite little lines of birch trees surrounded by expansive fields. He found one with a likely signpost and headed down it at a leisurely walk—no sense making haste when he wasn't certain he was headed in the right direction—when the sound of hooves thundering at reckless speed caught his attention.

The Berkshire countryside stretched out, gently rolling hills covered in the bright new grass of spring. Julia's legs itched with the desire to spur her mount and race across them at breakneck pace, but if she did, Nora would be stranded.

"Can't you ride faster?" Julia asked.

"Maids aren't meant to be on horseback." Nora clung to the reins with both hands, her entire body jolting with every step of the horse. "Leisurely strolls? Absolutely. That's quite my speed."

"Well, it's not mine." On foot, Julia looked how Nora did on horseback, lurching along in awkward discomfort, but mounted Julia was unmatched. She could fly across the landscape with wind pulling her hair from her pins, outracing all the sideways glances and poorly veiled whispers. On a horse, Julia wasn't *that crippled Bishop girl*. On horseback, she was the Spartan princess Cynisca, racing to become the first woman to win the Olympic games.

Nora's face went pale. "I'm sorry, my lady. I didn't mean—"

"It's fine." She and Nora had reached an understanding weeks ago. It was a product of Nora's *not* constantly thinking of Julia as an invalid that allowed Nora to slip up, and Julia did not want to go back to the days when Nora treated her as if she were made of glass. "But we should pick up the pace. Tryphosa wants to stretch her legs."

Julia's mount shook her head side to side in agreement. Nora paled even further.

"Unless you think you can make it back to the house," Julia suggested.

It was a straight shot back to the manor, but the sightline to the house would be obscured on the low sides of the hills between their location and the stables. The sun was just beginning to set; plenty of time to get in a good ride and still make it back by dark. If they were at home, Julia would have abandoned Nora without a thought, or more likely never taken her in the first place, but they were visiting Julia's sister Amelia's new estate, and the countryside was new to them both. Julia found that thrilling—it was half the reason she'd decided to wait for her sister's return here, instead of at home—but Nora was possessed of a slightly less adventurous spirit.

"Since I can still see it, I think I can manage. I may not know how to ride, but I am not a simpleton. My lady."

Julia grinned. "Glad to have you back, Nora. Now leave."

Nora hesitated. "It's not proper for you to be riding alone."

"Because I might be compromised? Ruin my chances at marriage?" Julia's raised eyebrow expressed the ridiculousness of that notion.

"Just because nobody is going to marry you doesn't mean they might not try…"

Julia crossed her hands in front of her, leaning in with a grin. "Try what, Nora? Please. Enlighten me."

The maid's face flushed crimson. She grumbled, "You're a devil, Lady Julia."

"That's what they say." And more. She couldn't seem to keep herself from mischief if she tried…not that she tried very often.

"Fine. If some brigand wants to take his chances with you, may God have mercy on him. Get me pointed in the right direction?"

Julia nudged Nora's horse around to face the house. "When you get back, ask if they've had any news from Mia."

"You mean if your sister somehow sent word between the morning post and the evening post?"

Instead of answering, Julia slapped the rump of Nora's mount. It started toward the house at a trot—the poor animal's top speed. The way the maid shouted and carried on, Julia might as well have slapped *her*. Still, Nora didn't

fall off, and she was headed in the right direction.

Satisfied, Julia turned her own mount toward the unexplored countryside. "Shall we, Tryphosa?"

The stocky little bay horse stomped her hoof in response.

Julia scanned the open country. Way off to the left, there was a copse of trees. There might be a stream there. To the right, the thin line of a stone wall snaked along the perimeter of the property line. "Which way do you think?"

This was why Mia needed to get back from her bloody trip. She'd barely been home since she married Nicholas, racing off to this place and that. In her absence, Julia had been reduced to riding with her maid and conversing with her horse. It was all well and good that Mia and Nick were having a splendid time being in love and making disgustingly adorable faces at each other, but couldn't they be in love in England?

Tryphosa tossed her head, jostling the reins.

"Right. Trees it is." Julia clucked her tongue, and Tryphosa burst into motion.

For a moment, everything else fell away. There was only the screaming wind and the pounding thud of Tryphosa's hooves against the packed dirt. The coiling and stretching of the horse's powerful muscles, catapulting them across the world. Julia looped the reins around the pommel and hooked her foot into the stirrup. Tryphosa's gait adjusted underneath her in anticipation. Like she had a hundred times before, Julia let go and bent her body backward over the padded seat of the saddle. The cushioning she'd added supported her back while her shoulders pressed against the churning haunches of the horse. Her vision filled with the blue of the cloudless sky. She stretched her arms out and closed her eyes, letting every part of her relax as Tryphosa's stride ate up the miles.

Julia had barely gotten to melt into the freedom of the open air when a shout nearly caused her to fall off. A streak of chestnut registered in her peripheral vision. A man raced toward her, reaching out. The bloody idiot was trying to gain control of Julia's horse. She pushed herself into an upright position, but it was too late. Surprise gave way to dread as she lost her balance and tumbled over the side of Tryphosa's flank.

This is it. You've finally done it. You've finally taken one risk too many.

The impact with the ground rattled her teeth, but the squelching mud buffered some of the fall. Julia lay very still, doing an internal inventory. There could be weeks of excruciating pain, or she could never recover at all. *Please. Please don't let this be my last adventure.*

Terrified, Julia tried to move her fingers. They fluttered. She tried her toes next, holding back the tears of relief when they wiggled. Her neck wasn't broken. She rolled onto her back, eyes clamped shut in anticipation of the pain. It didn't come. There were bumps, certainly, and there would definitely be bruises—but the dread of spending the rest of her days immobile faded away.

"Are you injured?"

No thanks to you. "I doubt it—I am covered in mud and who knows what else. Did you just shove me off my horse?"

"You've had a fright, I'm sure. Did you faint before or after your horse bolted?"

"Faint? I didn't—" She opened her eyes to a face that would make an artist weep. High cheekbones, full lips— only the square set of his jaw kept him from being too pretty. The dark brown eyes she'd never gotten to see up close, until now. "Oh. Oh, my. You're…"

"Delighted you didn't fall to your death." He helped her up into a sitting position, holding her hand longer than necessity required. "Viscount Bellamy, at your disposal."

Julia knew Lord Bellamy very well. She had peeked at him between cracked curtains and listened through doors every time he came to visit with Amelia. Slowly, she had mined Nicholas for insights into his friend's private life. Alone in her room, within the confines of her imagination, Lord Bellamy had supplanted Prince Albert as the leading role in her fantasy love affairs. But they had never officially met.

Now he was here, holding her hand and staring at her mouth. While she was covered in muck.

"And you are?" he asked.

"You don't know me?" Surely he must have seen her sneaking away at least once, or would recognize her and Amelia's resemblance.

The slow spread of his smile was deliberate—it had to be. It was too charming not to be affected. "I don't, but I would like to."

"I'm Ju—" Oh, God. She couldn't tell him her name and all of the knowledge that would come with it. He didn't know her, but he knew about Julia Bishop. It was a stroke of luck that he hadn't recognized her already, and Julia couldn't stand to watch the interest leave his face. Not yet. "—niper. My name is Juniper. Fairchild."

Juniper? She had lost her mind. And her ability to lie. He would call her out on it immediately.

Lord Bellamy lifted her gloved hand, placing his lips against the butter-soft leather. "It is a pleasure to make your acquaintance, Miss Fairchild."

The pounding of her heart went silent as the world

around Julia stood still. Lord Bellamy's lips were touching her hand. Well, her glove, but it was close enough. No simple accessory would ruin this moment for her. A handsome lord was kissing her hand and telling her it was a pleasure to meet her. Julia smiled at him. It was a struggle to keep it from turning into a girlish giggle, but she managed.

"Let's get you stood up, shall we?"

Before she could protest, he lifted her to her feet. Any moment she would have to move and then he would know, but standing in the circle of his arms with his fingers shadowing her rib cage, it was difficult to remember that. The smoky scent of him with a hint of something fresh and possibly floral intoxicated her. She leaned in to the solid warmth of his chest.

"Are you all right?" he asked.

"Just a little off balance," she lied. She just needed a few moments of delicious closeness to etch into her mind for later, when she could unpack this experience and embellish it to her heart's content.

She took a depth breath. It was jasmine. The teasing floral smell was jasmine.

His arms tightened around her, pressing their bodies close. Lord Bellamy looked down at her. "As I said, I am at your disposal. Use me however you require."

Good heavens. No man should have such a sultry growl in his arsenal. She'd save that memory for later as well. In the meantime, Julia could think of several ways to use him. Her eyes focused on his lips. The lower lip had a slight pout—the product of just a little too much fullness—that begged her to taste it. She bit her own lip. If he would only lean down just a little…

"Help! Someone help me!" Nora's yell broke through the moment.

Lord Bellamy's arms loosened around Julia, and he stepped away. *Damn it all to hell.*

Maid and mount clomped over the hill and into view at a moderate walk. "The beast's gone rogue. Get me off this monster!"

"Oh, for God's sake, Nora." The moment was lost, and it was time to return to the real world. Julia intercepted the not-even-remotely runaway horse and took the reins.

"You're limping," Lord Bellamy exclaimed. "Why didn't you say you'd been hurt in the fall?"

Suddenly, it wasn't over at all. Julia must be precisely the devil everyone said she was, because she felt zero compulsion to come clean and explain the truth. Julia looked down at her skirts, doing her best impression of a mewling miss. "I didn't want to be a bother."

"Don't take another step—you could injure yourself further. Is it your foot or your ankle?"

"My ankle, I think." She widened her eyes with extra innocence.

Up in the saddle, Nora suppressed a choked sound of surprise.

"Perhaps I should have a look, if it's very bad—"

"No!" Julia shouted.

Lord Bellamy took a half step back.

Damn. She hadn't meant to be quite so forceful. "I just…it wouldn't be proper, don't you think?"

As if she cared a fig about propriety. Julia would be more than happy to let him inspect her body in detail, just not her ankle. Above her, Nora coughed excessively.

Lord Bellamy looked between them with squinted eyes before shaking his head. "Well then, you still must get off it at once. Let's get you home. Where are you staying, Miss Fairchild?"

Pure panic sent tingling numbness down to the tips of Julia's fingers. It was too late to claim a blow to the head and pretend she didn't know. "I'm staying with my cousins, Lord Nicholas Wakefield and his wife, Lady Amelia. It's not far."

Lord Bellamy burst into a beaming smile. "What luck! I was headed there myself. I wasn't aware Nick had such a beautiful cousin. I would have insisted he introduce us at once."

Jasper DeVere thought she was beautiful. It was too wonderful to resist. All common sense floated away on the wind. "I'm Amelia's cousin, actually. From Kent."

"That makes a great deal more sense. Any cousin of Amelia's is bound to be lovely, though I doubt even my imaginings could have concocted someone as delightful as you."

A flush spread across Julia's cheeks, and she had to stare at her skirts to keep from bursting into a ridiculous grin. "Shall we—"

"Oh, yes. Let's get you home."

Julia allowed him to help her back onto her horse. Suddenly, she was extremely grateful Amelia and Nicholas hadn't returned yet. They were constantly trying to put a damper on her adventures, and this one was shaping up to be the most diverting of all. She'd tell him eventually, but for now—she was finally getting a taste of the romance she'd always wanted.

Chapter Two

Perhaps Nick and Amelia would understand. It wasn't as if he'd set out to encounter their cousin, or to flirt with her. It was one more instance of serendipity. Practically fated. They were his truest friends—actual friends, not just a society acquaintanceship—and his intentions weren't necessarily dishonorable. He could flirt with a woman without taking her to bed. It didn't happen often, but he was almost certain he was capable of it. He harmlessly flirted with Amelia all the time. That was at least one account in his favor, and in the same family no less.

Not that his responses to Miss Fairchild were entirely harmless. The line of her neck as they rode back to the house was regal perfection, but then an innocent pink flush dusted her cheeks when she caught him admiring her. When she cast her eyes aside in modesty, there was a mischievous twinkle to them and an impish tilt to the corner of her mouth. The complexity of her taunted him. He wanted to know what she was thinking.

He also wanted to know if she blushed pink all over.

Their little party had started down a long gravel driveway, so it was probably prudent for Jasper to stop staring at Miss Fairchild like a randy youth. "I must confess, I had planned on borrowing Nicholas's empty house. I didn't realize he and Amelia were back already."

"They're not. I meant to surprise them by being here when they return." Her cheeks went delightfully pink again. "We're alone for the time being."

He spent a moment with the imaginings *that* brought to life before reason broke through. "I shouldn't stay, then. I'll just wait until the doctor confirms you're in good health, and then find somewhere else. Without a chaperone, it would be quite the scandal."

She looked up from under thick lashes, managing to appear innocent and suggestive at the same time. "I won't tell if you won't."

A fortnight. It would take a fortnight to do everything that look brought to Jasper's mind, and another to start all over and do it again. "I adore secrets."

"I'll go see about sending for a doctor." Miss Fairchild's maid launched herself from her horse in a flurry of skirts and hurried inside, grumbling about wickedness and ruin as she went.

"Don't mind Nora," Miss Fairchild said quickly. "She's just a bit protective."

"As she should be. She has someone very precious in her charge." Jasper waved off the groom that stepped out to help Miss Fairchild down. When she put her hands on his shoulders, he lowered her slowly down each inch of his body. It was devilishly forward, and she ought to have slapped him, but she seemed perfectly willing to wander this path to ruin he was leading them down. If she was amenable to an entertaining diversion, Jasper was game.

That was why he'd come, after all—to escape his present.

He kept his arm around her waist when her feet finally touched the ground and ran his gloved thumb along the line of her lower lip. Her mouth opened, just the slightest of parts, and he repeated the gesture. "What shall we do to occupy ourselves while we're all alone?"

"What *can't* we do?" No guile. No pretense of affront. She wanted him.

Jasper lowered his mouth, slowly closing the distance between them, drawn in by her challenge.

"A doctor has been—" The formal tones of a decidedly butler-ly figure intruded. He cleared his throat.

Miss Fairchild stiffened and the moment was lost. She leaned away from Jasper.

"As I was saying; a groom is getting the doctor, my lady."

So, there were a few limitations to their game. Not to worry. Jasper relished a challenge. "Let's get you settled inside."

He scooped her up, feeling a profound sense of satisfaction when her arms wrapped around his neck. The curves of her pressed against his chest and arm. Her face might be angelic, but beneath all the layers her form was sinful. As they crossed the threshold into the foyer, he murmured against her ear. "You are delightfully luscious, Miss Fairchild."

Her eyebrows raised. "Is that your way of warning me I am about to be dropped?"

"Dropped?" Jasper met her eyes. "I may never put you down."

"I'm afraid you're going to have to, because I need a moment to tidy myself before the doctor arrives."

"You look ravishing." Even the smear of mud across the bridge of her nose and cheek was tantalizing.

"You're a shameless flatterer, Lord Bellamy."

"That doesn't mean it isn't true."

"I didn't say I didn't like it." There was that mischievous twinkle again. They reached the foyer, and she gestured for him to put her down. "Winslow, will you show Lord Bellamy to a room? I'm certain he'd enjoy a bath."

Right. He no doubt smelled like he'd been doing hard labor. His formal clothing hadn't held up very well on the long ride, either. "I haven't any luggage. Do you think Nick would mind if I helped myself to some of his clothes?"

She raised an eyebrow at his lack of luggage, but thankfully didn't ask about it. "I think he'd have to be here to mind, and he's not."

He most certainly was not. Jasper would have to be very careful not to revert to less respectable pursuits. It was one thing to push the boundaries of convention and flirt with a beautiful woman. It was quite another to leap straight over them and ravish a close friend's cousin. "Then I shall see you for drinks before dinner. I promise to be much better presented."

She nodded, and he left her — all the while extremely aware that she was watching him walk every step of the staircase. They would have to be very careful, indeed.

Jasper raided Nicholas's wardrobe while he waited for the bath. If there were any interesting pieces to be had, Nick had taken them with him on his trip. None of the intricate patterns or flashing jewel tones Jasper preferred — just the run-of-the-mill black, brown, and navy of every country lord in Britain. When Nicholas did return, they would have to have a talk. Just because Nick had devoted himself to the respectable pursuit of the law didn't mean he had to look as boring as his profession.

At least they were of a similar size. Jasper might not cut

his usual dashing figure, but the sleeves would fall where they ought to and his shoulders wouldn't be impossibly cramped in ill-fitting tailoring. It was the best one could hope for when one fled the city without any belongings.

The melancholy returned while he bathed. Without Miss Fairchild's alluring presence, the reality of what he'd done set in. He'd left the queen and every other powerful lord of the nation twiddling their thumbs, waiting for a ceremony that couldn't happen without him. It would have been a legendary scandal to be proud of—if he'd planned it. If he'd done it for any reason other than his inability to accept a world without his grandfather in it.

There was no undoing it. The best thing would be to put it from his mind for as long as he could. With deep concentration, Jasper tied his cravat into the deceptively simple arrangement he favored. It took a great deal of effort to make it look so easily done, but it was worth it for the effect. The reflection in the mirror nodded back at him with approval; it was the perfect arrangement for an evening of flirtation.

And there would be flirting. Jasper would inundate Miss Fairchild with a profusion of subtle seductions. It was Jasper's duty, and his pleasure, to entertain his hostess. It added a sense of purpose to his escape that sent a thrill racing beneath his skin. He finished himself off with a dash of Nicholas's cologne—and was immediately paralyzed with memory. It had never registered before that his grandfather and Nicholas wore similar scents, but it registered now as the smell of bergamot transported Jasper back to their last day together.

Laughter shook his grandfather, until it became a hacking cough that shook the bed. The duke gestured and Jasper rushed to pour a glass of water. When he'd calmed from the fit, the duke said, "Don't make me laugh. I'm not quite ready to die yet."

"I would appreciate it if you'd wait another few years." They'd be lucky to get another few days. "Thirty or so ought to do it."

"Enough of that. It's time, and you know it. Now pay attention, because I've got things to say."

Jasper leaned in, clasping the weathered hands that weakened under the ravaging sickness. Hands that had held the world together.

"I'm sorry you didn't get more time. The responsibility of the dukedom isn't meant for the young. You would have had your thirty years, if your father had—" His grandfather broke into another fit of coughing, but it subsided quickly. "He should have had it before you."

"That's not your fault."

"Not yours, either, but that's the way it is. Still, I'm glad you've lived the way you have. You've had adventures enough for twenty men. You're younger than you ought to be, but you won't have nearly as many regrets as you would have. You've lived."

In the mirror, Jasper's face hid the truth of the life he'd led. There were no lines to show for the days on end of debauchery, uninterrupted by sleep or any hint of wholesomeness. Not even lines of grief could find purchase. Even his skin rejected the truth, who he was supposed to be now.

"Are you still glad, grandfather?" Jasper had never learned to be the sort of man who could live up to his grandfather's legacy. The sort of man who did the right thing, instead of the interesting thing.

*J*ulia was not familiar with this doctor. Fortunately, it would be unseemly for Lord Bellamy to be present while she was examined, so there was no need to maintain the farce of the twisted ankle. She could put an end to this visit without ever having to leave her chair by the fire.

The door swung inward and the doctor crossed the plush carpet of her bedroom, hand outstretched. "Miss Fairchild, it's a pleasure to meet you. I hear you've had an eventful—"

"Thank you for your concern, but I will not be allowing an examination." There was nothing wrong with her that he could fix. As an afterthought, she smiled to soften her tone.

"Falling from a horse can cause all manner of complications. You may not feel them at first. You could have a broken bone or strained ligament, not to mention a possible concussion to your brain."

"I am aware of the risks, and my brain is fine. My lady's maid is extremely well-versed in the signs of concussion, fever, and internal difficulties. If anything should arise, she is more than capable of seeing to it."

"My lady, while I am sure your lady's maid is a fine companion—"

Julia let out a deep breath. She may very well have suffered some sort of damage to think she could get away with this kind of deception. "I was born with an exposed spine condition, sir. Unless that is your area of expertise, your services will not be helpful."

The doctor's eyes widened. "But you're an adult."

"So I am. It's a miracle." There was no correlating enthusiasm in her voice. The *miracle* had involved endless procedures throughout Julia's life, not to mention regular invasions of her privacy and patience.

"How was it managed? Did you have a surgeon or—"

"Thank you very much for your time." She stood and ushered him toward the door. His attention was riveted to her limping steps. Julia had endured the fascination of the doctors that her parents hired for her, but she didn't owe this man anything. "I appreciate your concern, but your services are not needed."

"I really should examine you, just in case."

"That won't be necessary." He wanted to see the scar—they always did. One would think the rough patch of skin on her lower back was the bloody Sistine Chapel, rather than the result of painful and repeated injections. Julia didn't allow anyone to see it anymore, not even Nora. She was not some exhibit to be gawked at. "Leave your bill with the butler on your way out."

The door closed behind him, and Julia sat back down to wait. The fire on the hearth reflected in the lacquered surfaces of the desk and armoire. They might as well be the fires of damnation. Any moment Lord Bellamy would burst in, full of affront, demanding to know if what the doctor told him was true. Or perhaps he'd be so offended by the lie that he would just leave without saying anything at all.

The pop of the door latch sounded. Julia squared her shoulders and took a deep breath as the handle turned and the door opened.

"My lady." Nora's skirts brushed against the frame as she stepped in and closed the door behind her. "The doctor is gone."

"And Lord Bellamy?" She held her breath while she waited for the answer.

"Begging your pardon, Lady Julia, but have you

completely lost your mind? Juniper Fairchild? Where on earth…" Nora's complaints died off when confronted with Julia's raised eyebrows. "Lord Bellamy is still cleaning up from his ride. They did not speak before the doctor left."

So the game was still afoot. The dread fell away, leaving Julia with a rapid heartbeat and an overwhelming sense of daring. She could give whatever medical explanation she liked. For the foreseeable future—at least until Nicholas and Amelia returned—she could be Miss Juniper Fairchild and flirt with the outrageous Viscount Bellamy to her heart's content.

"Tell Winthrop that the staff is to call me Miss Fairchild or Lady Juniper from now on. If that is too taxing, they may restrict themselves to 'my lady.'"

"May I ask how long you think you'll be able to keep this up?"

"You may not." Julia's chin lifted with authority. So what if she was operating without a plan? Sometimes a proper adventure had to be improvised. "After you help me decide between the rose silk or the crimson, tell Winthrop what I said."

"The crimson is too bold for an unmarried woman. Why your father lets you order those outrageous colors—"

"The crimson it is." Julia grinned, unable to suppress her excitement. "I feel like being bold."

Nora grumbled as she helped Julia into the dress. "I should have said the pink made you look like a harlot, so you'd be sure to choose it."

"You should have. You're slipping, Nora."

"It's that Lord Bellamy. He makes me nervous. They say things about him, you know."

Oh, Julia knew. They said he was one of the most sought-after lovers on the continent, where he chose to spend most of his time. Men and women alike tried to catch his notice. Only the most remarkable succeeded. And here he was, alone in the country with *her*. Just the thought was enough to keep her awake all night.

Nora stepped back with a sigh. "You're readier than any decent woman ought to be."

"Thank you. Now, go tell Winthrop."

The maid grumbled her way out of the room. Julia checked her hair in the glass one last time, and followed—only to stop short at Lord Bellamy waiting in the hallway outside her room.

He smiled. "Each time I see you, you are even lovelier than the last."

A flush heated her cheeks, and she cursed silently. Sophisticated women did not blush. "I was covered in mud before."

"And you were still more stunning than any woman for miles."

She accepted his arm with a sideways glance. "Oh? You'd already met every woman for miles by the time you got around to meeting me?"

"Every darling one of them. None compared to you on your worst day." He didn't miss a beat.

"You haven't seen me on my worst day."

"Then I hope you'll let me, so that on that day I can reiterate your magnificence."

That produced another wave of warmth across her skin. Julia was going to enjoy sparring with him almost as much as she enjoyed the way he looked at her, like she was some kind of marvel.

At the top of the stairs, all thoughts of flattering glances vanished. If she held Lord Bellamy as tightly as she usually held the railing, he would think her indelicate. If she didn't, and she fell, she could very well meet her death at the bottom of the stairs. And then there was a matter of pace. Having already fallen once today, a second time would be tempting the devil too much for even Julia's reckless spirit. They started down at a much faster rate than the one she set for safe travel up and down steps.

"Perhaps you should go down without me, I think I—" Her fingers clamped down on his arm as she fumbled. Her heart went into a lurch as she pitched forward, but his arm snapped out and hauled her back. "It's all right. I'm all right. I just lost my footing for a moment."

"Well, I'm not all right. I think I just saw my life flash before my eyes, and it wasn't the enjoyable parts." His hands slid to her shoulders, steadying her.

His touch was intoxicating, changing the reason for her rapid heartbeat. "Perhaps we could go a little slower. If you lose *your* footing, we'll both be done for."

Lord Bellamy's eyebrow raised imperiously. "A less confident man might take that as an attack on his athleticism."

"It's fortunate, then, that you're very self-assured." She gave him what she hoped was a teasing smile.

"Very." There was a slight upward curve at the edge of his mouth. "You're quite right about taking it slower—I should have been mindful of your ankle. Hold me tightly. None of this timid grip nonsense. If I still have feeling in my hand, you're being remiss."

Her smile this time was genuine. "All right."

"Let's move to the railing. There's no one here to see that we're not gliding gracefully down the center." His grumbled tones made her laugh.

She leaned into him once she had a firm grip on the railing. "There are only five steps left."

He cast her a sideways glance. "Those could be the most treacherous ones."

"I think we'll manage."

When they reached the bottom of the stairs, her tension disappeared. Until she realized stairs were just one of many complications. She hadn't thought about what having him here would mean—only how to keep him from finding out the truth. There were a number of things she navigated every day that could give her away. Even if they didn't, she would be constantly worrying that they might.

"This was not how I planned the beginning of our evening."

"Oh?" she asked. "I'm sorry."

The edge of his mouth tipped up, giving him away. "Oh, yes. You clearly tried to hurl yourself down the stairs. I didn't realize you were a daredevil."

If you only knew. Every step, every sniffle, every childhood tumble that left her mother gasping, white as a sheet. Any little thing could have been the end. It still could be, though the threat was much diminished now, and for the most part her family had stopped treating her as if she were on the brink of death.

She shook off her dark thoughts. "I like to live dangerously, Lord Bellamy."

"I shall do my best to keep up." His dark-brown eyes shone in the chandelier light as they entered the parlor. "Now, I think we ought to change the subject to what a vision you are in crimson silk."

The damnable heat returned. "Thank you."

"Was your visit with the doctor helpful?"

"Not particularly." She arranged herself on the settee while he poured their drinks. "I've suffered no lasting damage, but there is nothing to be done about my ankle except to wait it out."

"Will you think me a terrible villain if I admit to delight at the idea of being called upon to carry you again?"

No matter how much she enjoyed his touch, it was time to put an end to that particular concept. "Villain? No. Perhaps a bit of a rake, but I should tell you—I don't much enjoy being carried."

"Oh." His face fell. "I'm sorry. I should have asked."

"I do enjoy your company," she rushed to assure him. "Very much."

His smile returned as he took the chair across from her. "How bold of you, Miss Fairchild."

It was a perfect opening. "Does boldness offend you, Lord Bellamy?"

"Not in the slightest." He sipped his drink, watching her over the rim of the glass. "If you don't mind a little boldness in return—what brought you to Berkshire?"

Bother. "Must I have a reason?"

He grinned. "Never. I just wondered. Kent is lovely in spring, and it can't be very exciting to sit in an empty house waiting on your cousin's return."

"Oh, I don't know about that. I nearly died, and a handsome stranger followed me home." She smiled down at her glass. "I can't imagine a more exciting day."

As a connoisseur of exciting days, Lord Bellamy had no doubt experienced more outrageous adventures, but this was by far the most diverting day of Julia's life.

"But you can't have known that would happen. I certainly didn't."

"And you know everything?" she teased. "Fine. I am attempting to escape a scandal. What do you think about that?"

"I think you're in grave danger. Just being near me is a recipe for scandal."

She laughed; if he only knew. "It seems we have that in common, then."

He studied his glass thoughtfully before looking back up at her. A dark lock of hair fell across his brow, and the full curve of his lips stole the entirety of Julia's attention. "May I sit by you?"

Goose bumps of anticipation raised on her skin. "Do you intend to misbehave?"

"Undoubtedly."

"Then, by all means." Julia shifted in her seat, corralling her skirts to make room for him to sit deliciously close.

Like something out of a dream, Lord Bellamy gently lifted her hand and placed it palm upward in his own. Her lips parted at his touch. He stroked his finger across the surface of her skin. She shivered. This was not happening. She truly had hit her head, and she was imagining it all.

If it was a dream, then may it never stop.

Julia's eyelids fell closed as he stroked the length of each finger, each line on her palm. He investigated the bones of her wrist, tracing their outlines. When his thumb snuck under the fabric of her sleeve, circling against the sensitive skin there, she whimpered.

"What foolhardy chaperone left you unattended?" he murmured.

The words barely made sense. None of her imaginings could capture the sensation of actually being touched like this. How could the brushing of hands feel so wicked?

"There's no point to my having a chaperone," she managed.

Any moment, the entire charade could come crashing down. Until then, she needed as much of this feeling as he was willing to provide. Enough to last her a lifetime, as it would likely have to.

"Why is that?" He lifted her wrist to his lips and placed a kiss against it.

"What?" The word left her mouth as a breath. To think she might have missed this.

Lord Bellamy hummed his approval. The kisses continued—the pad of her thumb, the tips of her fingers. Each new feeling drew an *oh* from Julia's mouth. It was everything she'd ever wanted until, suddenly, it wasn't enough. He smiled against her skin. "Why is a chaperone pointless?"

"I'm not…" Julia realized what they were talking about. She'd almost given up the game without realizing it. "I do as I please. My reputation was ruined long ago."

He pressed another kiss against her palm. "And yet, you still blush when I compliment you."

Julia's thudding heart skipped a beat. "There are many ways for a reputation to fall to ruin. Not all of them are…"

"Sensual?"

Julia's breath caught. "Yes."

"That's a shame." He lifted his hand and brushed his thumb against the corner of her lip.

It was truly going to happen. Julia Bishop, society outcast, was going to be kissed by a handsome rogue. Would it feel strange? Would her entire body tingle? Would he attempt to put his tongue in her mouth? If he did, would she like it? She almost wished she hadn't mined Mia for so many details, because then there would be less to worry about.

His fingertips brushed against her cheek, dragging little sparks of pleasure with them as they slid into the hair at her temple. He leaned forward with a mischievous tilt to his lips.

"My Lady, it's—" Nora's voice sounded in time with

the opening door.

Lord Bellamy leaned back, putting distance between them as his hand dropped away.

"For God's sake, Nora!" Julia was going to strangle her. "Were you listening at the door?"

The maid's attention shifted between them. Her mouth tightened with disapproval. "Seems like maybe I should have been. It's almost time for dinner."

"And?"

"And there's a matter we need to take care of, unless you'd like—"

"No!" The last thing Julia wanted was Nora blurting out Julia's chamber pot schedule. No doubt she would find a way to throw in a mention of the leg and back massages Julia underwent for mobility out of spite. "All right. I'll be there in a moment."

Nora narrowed her eyes at them one last time before turning to go—leaving the door open.

"I swear, she was put on this earth to menace me," Julia grumbled and stood up. "I should go."

Lord Bellamy's grin was crooked and impossibly charming as he stood up with her. "I think you'd better. Your Nora seems a very serious sort of woman. But Miss Fairchild?"

The honey of his tone rolled over her skin, making her want to stretch into the sound. "Yes?"

"Come back soon? I'm looking forward to your company for dinner."

As was she. Julia left the room, meeting Nora in the hallway and letting herself be ushered into one of the side rooms in Nicholas and Amelia's house that didn't seem to have any particular purpose.

Nora shoved the chamber pot into Julia's hands.

"We could have done this before I left my room."

"It wasn't eight o'clock before. The schedule says—"

"I know what the bloody schedule says." Julia loathed the schedule, but she knew better than to trifle with it. That was how infections happened, and days spent miserable, trapped in bed. Why did reality insist on ruining what would otherwise have been a perfectly romantic evening? She finished the necessary actions and straightened her skirts. "Happy?"

"Rarely."

Wasn't that the truth. Julia left the maid behind and went back to the parlor, where her dining partner was finishing his drink. "Shall we go in, Lord Bellamy?"

He rose with a smile, putting her hand on his arm once again. "On one condition. You must stop calling me Lord Bellamy. It's only fitting that you use my given name if we're to be partners in danger."

Jasper. Just thinking it sent a delicious shiver through her. She'd whispered it a thousand times alone in her room before they'd met, but now she had the right to say it where he could hear it.

"And you must call me—" Damn.

"Juniper." He rolled it from his mouth with poetry, but it fell like a rock to Julia's ears.

Julia. She wanted to shout it to the frescoed ceiling. She wanted to hear her name on his lips. "I've never liked my name very much."

"What would you like me to call you?"

Darling. Dearest. My love. "I don't know."

"Then I will endeavor to find something that suits you. How do you feel about Chaucer's Thisbe?"

Julia could not have kept the grimace from her face if her life had depended upon it.

"What's wrong with Thisbe?" Jasper asked, as if it was a legitimate question.

"Aside from everything?" She gestured her frustration with the hand that wasn't resting on the crook of his elbow. "She hides while Pyramus stabs himself in the chest. It's ludicrous."

"He thought she was dead—he was overcome with grief."

"He was an idiot. There was no body. I'd like to think the sort of man I'd fall in love with would do a little more investigating before deciding to end it all."

Jasper snickered. "All right. No Thisbe."

"What about Victoria?" Julia asked.

It was Jasper's turn to grimace.

She gasped. "Victoria and Albert have a love for the ages."

If he had unkind opinions toward the royal couple, Julia might have to rethink their entire association. She was a devoted follower of all things Victoria.

Jasper lifted his hands in a defensive gesture. "It would just be a little awkward, since Victoria is a relative of mine."

"You and Queen Victoria."

"Her father and my mother were cousins."

Julia stopped abruptly.

The kinship she felt to the queen could not be understated. Julia and Victoria were only a year apart in age, and they'd both grown up in isolation. Not to mention that Julia was obviously meant to be a royal. She'd spent every spare minute absorbing as much gossip on Victoria and Albert as she could. The idea that she was in a full-fledged flirt with one of Victoria's family members…

"You're in line for the English throne." It was too much to process.

"I mean, it's not a short line and I'm hardly at the front." Jasper winked at her. "And I'm surprised to hear you chose Victoria as your idol. She's very reserved."

"She's *the queen*." Julia shook her head. The entire situation was beyond belief. Julia Bishop, outcast, was having an unchaperoned adventure with Queen Victoria's handsome cousin. It couldn't be more of a dream come true unless Julia suddenly became the regent herself.

"I'm far more interested in you than I am in talking about my cousin."

Julia was wrong. Having Jasper DeVere declare her more intriguing than the monarch was a dream come true — and if there was any justice in the world, she would never wake up.

Chapter Three

Jasper pulled open the door, but stopped at the tug of Miss Fairchild's hand on his elbow.

"This isn't the dining room."

"I know. Since it's just the two of us, I thought we might try something less formal."

Juniper took in the pillows and covered dishes arrayed in front of the fireplace in the small library. Tiny creases formed between her eyebrows.

"You don't like it. Not to worry, I'll just have the footmen—"

"It's fine." She smiled. "It's lovely, actually. I was just surprised."

"You're certain? It's really no trouble to move our meal somewhere else." There was nothing romantic about a fireside picnic if she was only agreeing to it out of politeness.

"Perfectly. Where would you like me?"

Jasper paused, and the corner of his mouth quirked up as he rejected a few of the more vulgar answers that sprang to mind.

She saw it, and blushed.

He waived in the direction of the cushions by the fire as he poured them both wine. "Just there would be lovely, Cleopatra."

Her laughter rang out. "Are you Antony or Caesar?"

"Antony, certainly."

"So it's another double suicide, then." She shook her head as he handed over the glass. "I'm beginning to think you have a very dismal outlook on love, *Antony*."

Jasper frowned, lowering himself to the floor next to her. Perhaps it was recent events coloring his suggestions, but he wasn't about to say so and ruin the lovely mood building between them. "I can't help if the world's famous love stories usually end in tragedy."

Like his parents.

"But why? Why couldn't Cleopatra have demonstrated her love by escaping into hiding and plotting to avenge Antony's death? By going on to live and love again, as anyone who cared for her would wish?" Juniper's animated gestures were delightful. Wisps of hair escaped her pins with the movements, and her eyes lit with intelligence and challenge. "Why should one great tragedy be the end of everything?"

"When you lose someone who means that much to you…" Jasper's throat tightened. He silently thanked his body for the betrayal. She was posing a philosophical question, not asking for a glimpse of his grief.

But Juniper looked at him, eyes wide with interest. "What?"

"It's nothing."

"It's not nothing. When you lose someone who means that much to you…"

Jasper sighed. "The world feels wrong. Like it's

corrupted itself, by having the audacity to go on without that person in it."

"You've lost someone recently," she said softly.

He nodded and took a swallow of his wine. Everything he touched was going to turn melancholy. He was terrible company.

"Is that why you came here? To escape it?"

"Yes." Another swallow. Jasper wished he'd had a less indulgent youth, so the wine would be doing more potent work now.

"Then I shall help you," she declared. Juniper lifted the lids off dishes, and started loading their plates. "I know a thing or two about avoiding misery. So we'll speak no more about tragedy. In fact, you're going to tell me about your most amusing grand adventure."

Jasper looked at her—really looked. There wasn't any trace of pity in her face. If anything, she glowed with challenge even more than before. "What makes you think I've one grand adventure, never mind enough to choose from?" he asked.

She popped a piece of cheese into her mouth and stared him down.

"You are a famous reprobate, *Jasper*. I am owed at least one tale to compare to the outrageous stories I've read in the papers. They can't all have been true."

The truth was, most of the gossip rags didn't do his exploits half the justice they deserved. And just like that, Jasper wasn't thinking about how nothing could ever be right again without his grandfather in the world. He was sifting through every raucous memory, trying to find the best one to light her eyes with laughter.

He leaned back, resting his arm across the seat of the settee behind them. No matter how lovely of a distraction it might be, there wasn't a single story Jasper could tell Amelia's sheltered cousin while still maintaining the pretense that his intentions were harmless. "Why don't you tell me about one of your adventures instead?"

"Not a chance. I will not fall for your prevarication, and even if I wanted to, I haven't had any adventures."

"I don't believe that."

"Regardless, it is the truth."

Jasper sighed. "My stories would shock you. They are not for genteel company."

Her eyes narrowed, glinting with challenge. "Who was your most surprising lover?"

He nearly choked on his wine. "Juniper—"

"Come on, out with it." She leaned back with a siren's smile. "You don't need to use names, if you value discretion."

Jasper bought himself time by reaching for the laden plate she'd set aside for him. Reminiscing about his exploits, tantalizing them both with provocative imagery, was exactly what he needed. What he wanted.

But he couldn't seduce Amelia's cousin. It wouldn't be right. Unfortunately, his dinner companion did not share his caution.

"I heard you spent time in Bucharest with a crown princess who had some unusual habits."

Nadya. "She isn't the crown princess. She has three older siblings."

Juniper's smile was all triumph, but then a blush dusted her cheeks and she looked away when she asked, "Is it true what they say?"

"That she likes to tie people up?" Jasper sipped his wine. He could have both. If he was careful, if he kept himself in check, he could have this distraction without doing anything dishonorable. He could. "Yes. But, since that particular habit was what drew us to each other in the first place, I don't count that as surprising."

Her eyes went wide. "You enjoy being tied up?"

Jasper smiled. "I enjoy most things, in the right mood."

Pink turned to bright red. She snuck a look at him before darting her eyes back to the fireplace. They appeared to have reached the limit of her daring, because she changed the subject, but there was still a smile at the corners of her lips. "So, if the princess was not surprising, who is?"

Jasper chose a morsel from his plate and offered it to her. She hesitated, before closing her lips around it, brushing the edges of his fingers. "You are."

Juniper took a heavy swallow of her wine. Her cheeks were delightfully pink. "We're not lovers."

He heard the unspoken *yet* lingering at the end of her assertion. It pulled at him, but he kept a tight rein on his impulses. He would not betray Nicholas or Amelia's trust—not without at least giving them warning of his intentions. Words only. There was no harm in words. "A love doesn't need to be consummated to make two people lovers."

"Do you mean to pretend you love me?" Juniper scoffed.

Jasper took her skepticism for the opportunity that it was. He shouldn't make love to her with words. Instead, he chose a light tone. "Would that be so ridiculous?"

"We've only just met. You couldn't possibly love me."

He pressed his hand to his chest with full dramatics. "You wound me. Romeo and Juliet only knew each other—"

"Fiction! More of your fatalistic dolts. No." Juniper shook her head, drinking more of her wine. She leaned back with her wineglass, narrowing her eyes. "Tell me, really, who was your most surprising lover?"

The way the firelight played across her hair, catching

strands of gold and lighting them up, fascinated him. The words came out of him of their own volition. "You're beautiful."

She threw a roll at him. "You really won't tell me."

He laughed and took a bite out of the projectile. "I would rather find out how you've managed to avoid adventure all this time."

"Innate talent."

They spent the evening that way. Juniper blushed the sweetest shade of pink and continued to demand details of his love life and adventures. Jasper lavished her with compliments and occasionally admitted to some of the tamer exploits of his past. While they talked, they shifted closer together. By the time a pile of empty plates surrounded them, she was leaning against his chest, and his arm rested across her shoulders on the settee seat.

Jasper lifted another spoonful of treacle pudding.

Juniper groaned. "I'll burst."

"That seems highly unlikely."

"We've eaten enough for a small army!"

"Just one more?" It was too tempting, watching the way her lips closed over the spoon.

"One more."

"And one more glass of wine."

"Be honest with me—are you the devil in disguise?"

They'd already crossed more lines than they should have. Jasper had hoped the wine would dull his senses and make him less aware of her, but all it had done was sabotage his resolution to behave. "If I was, I'd like to think I wouldn't be so easy to figure out."

"Maybe it's a clever ploy to divert suspicion."

"But you're far too quick to be fooled." His fingers came up and traced the curve of her jaw just under her earlobe.

She let out a shuddering breath. "Jasper."

Time stopped around them. Her pulse raced beneath his fingers. Just one touch, and then he would say good night. If he kept it to just one, he could go to sleep with the feel of her against his skin and be satisfied. She leaned into him. His hand moved into her upswept hair, down the column of her neck. He traced the line of her collarbone. *Enough.*

If he didn't stop there, he wouldn't stop at all. "We should probably retire for the evening."

"I—" Her brow creased into a frown. "Truly?"

"Truly. It's very late, and the staff will start to wonder." Jasper felt like an utter ass. He stood and offered her his hand.

She accepted it silently.

He didn't want to leave the evening this way, but he had no choice. If they spent another moment together, it would go too far. Still, her obvious confusion lodged an ache in his chest. It was as unlikely to dissipate as the other protests his body was currently lodging at the idea of walking away from her.

"It has been a singularly enjoyable evening." He lifted her hand to his lips, lingering as he held her eyes.

"For me, also."

"Sleep well, Penelope." Jasper left her behind, heading for the terrace and a much-needed walk in the cold night air.

<hr />

"My lady? You need to get up."

Julia groaned and rolled over, burying her head in an overstuffed down pillow to block out Nora's voice.

It didn't work. "Come on, now. You know as well as I do, you have to get up."

"My head hurts."

"A lot more than that will hurt if you don't handle the necessaries."

Julia groaned again and rolled back over. She swung her legs over the edge and accepted the chamber pot Nora was holding out. "I hate today."

"Hopefully it doesn't hate you back, my lady."

It definitively hated her back. The wall of windows overlooking the rolling green hills—something Julia had adored when she first saw the room—were now sending vicious beams of sunlight straight into her eyes. She closed them again. "Why does my head hurt so much?"

"Could be God is punishing you for your wicked ways." Nora started arranging the pillows and straightening the sheets now that Julia was off the bed. "Or could be you stayed up late and drank too much wine."

Julia slid the chamber pot under the bed and tried to take a step toward her dressing gown. A sharp, stabbing pain shot through her hip. She winced. "I think it's the first one."

Sitting on the floor during dinner had been a mistake. She'd *thought* it would be well worth the trouble, but then Jasper had bid her good night, calling her *Penelope* as he went. It was an apt choice. Penelope had spent ages waiting for Odysseus. Julia wondered how long she would end up waiting for Jasper.

"Want me to call for a bath?"

"I just had one after the ride yesterday."

"They help with the aches, and don't try to tell me you don't have any. I saw your face."

She sat on the edge of the bed, digging the heel of her

hand into her hip and thigh. "I can't miss breakfast. If I miss breakfast, Jasper will think—"

"I could give two figs what Lord Bellamy thinks." Nora raised her arm to yank the pull. "You're having a soak, or you're staying in this room. What will it be?"

"You do know you work for me, right? Not the other way around."

"Actually, I work for your father. Shall we ask him if you ought to take care of yourself, or go chasing after some rake?"

A lot of good the chasing was doing—she couldn't manage to catch him. Julia let her body slump back onto the brocade coverlet. "I take it back. I don't hate today. I hate you."

Nora smirked. "I'm heartbroken."

"Fine. I will be your willing hostage, on the condition that you must take a message to Lord Bellamy telling him I won't be down for breakfast, but I look forward to seeing him later."

Nora blinked at her.

"Those are my terms."

The maid nodded, leaving Julia alone with her headache and her confusion. The latter had kept her up half the night, until she'd fallen into a very troubled sleep full of confusing dreams.

Why hadn't Jasper kissed her? He enjoyed her company, and he was attracted to her—he'd said as much. Was it something she'd done? Had she ruined it somehow? Breakfast would be long over by the time Julia soaked the ache out of her leg. What if he thought she was angry with him? She was, a little, but it would be embarrassing for him to know that.

Damn every boy in the Berkshires during her childhood.

If any of them had been able to look past her disability for even a second, she'd have something to go off in the flirting department and would know what the trouble was now. While she was glaring at the ceiling, no doubt giving herself a lifetime of frown lines, Nora returned with an answering message from Jasper.

"He says that he hopes you are well, and asks if everything is all right."

Why don't you tell me, she wanted to reply. Obviously, Julia wasn't the one driving their flirtation or she'd be reliving her first kiss right now instead of trying to dissect her confusion. "Is that all he says?"

"He also says you're a ridiculous girl and you should listen to your maid more."

Julia glared at Nora, but her heart wasn't in it. She was too busy trying to solve the puzzle that was Jasper DeVere. He'd obviously wanted to kiss her. He was perfectly attentive. She hadn't sensed any reservations from him, beyond the irrefutable fact that he hadn't kissed her. Perhaps he just needed some encouragement.

"Tell him I am perfectly well, I just feel like languishing in bed for a while."

"I'm not paid to ferry messages to your paramours."

Julia turned to the kitchen maid filling the bath with water. "Letty, please tell Lord Bellamy—"

"For God's sake. Fine. If only to save poor Letty from your wickedness."

Letty did not look like she'd just been saved. If anything, she looked disappointed. She was a pretty girl. Undoubtedly, she had more experience flirting with men than Julia.

"Letty," Julia asked. "What would you do if you knew a man was interested in you, but you couldn't get him to misbehave?"

Nora stopped dead at the door. "Lady Julia!"

"What? I'd ask you, but you'd probably just start quoting scripture at me. Letty is a free woman. She can say what she likes."

The kitchen maid blushed beet red. "I—I'm sure I don't know, my lady."

"Of course you do," Julia encouraged. "If you were trying to snag a charming suitor, what would you do?"

Letty slid a sideways glance at Nora, before staring at the floor. "I suppose I might…try to get him alone, my lady?"

That was exactly what Julia needed—more time alone with Jasper. He had wanted to kiss her. With enough time in each other's presence, it would happen. "Nora, also ask him if he'd like to accompany me on an adventure this afternoon."

No sooner had Julia submerged herself in the tub than Nora returned with a scowl that should have turned Julia to stone. "He asks what happened to your innate talent for avoiding adventure."

Julia couldn't help the grin that split her face. "Tell him I'm trying to remedy that, and I need his expertise in the matter."

The two maids shared a glance.

"Go on. Tell him." Julia was feeling much more optimistic when Nora left again. She hummed as she swished her fingers through the water, pondering possibilities for the afternoon. There were a number of things she'd imagined doing if she ever had a proper suitor. The question was, which one should she pick?

The closing door announced Nora's return. "I swear on my mother's grave—"

"What did he say?"

"He asks what manner of adventure he should prepare for."

It didn't matter that Nora's tone was flat and disapproving—Julia could imagine the wicked glint in Jasper's eye and his teasing tone in perfect detail. "Tell him it's a secret, and if he wishes to know what kind, he should meet me at the boathouse at one o'clock."

"What the devil do you plan to get up to at the boathouse?" Nora demanded.

Julia didn't answer. Instead, she held out the washing cloth in a wordless request. Nora could disapprove all she wanted. Julia had an opportunity to achieve her goal and fulfill some of her long-held fantasies. She intended to take that opportunity.

A romantic outing on the lake would be the perfect place to continue what they'd started.

Chapter Four

With very little to go on, Jasper walked down to the lake. The intrigue of their messages this morning had turned into an anticipation that was almost electric across his skin. He couldn't deny the appeal of her request for his adventure expertise any more than he could allow himself to give it to her. He might never be the heir his grandfather deserved, but he would be a good friend to Nicholas and Amelia. He would not cross that line.

Last night, Juniper showed him that there were limits to her boldness. He could use that to help keep them within the bounds of propriety, if only just. Barely would be good enough. It was all he had any hope of achieving.

The building Jasper arrived at was small and charmingly weathered. Inside, two simple rowboats sat overturned on the dock. He nudged a tarp with the toe of his boot. A puff of dust rose and something scurried into a dark corner. If her adventure involved staying here, he was woefully overdressed.

Juniper cleared her throat. He turned to find her standing

in the doorway, clutching a satchel to her chest. The hood of a buttercream bonnet framed her face, highlighting little flecks of gold in her eyes.

"Now do I get to know what you're planning?" He hoped this was just a convenient meeting place.

"I'm going to sketch you."

"In here?" Jasper looked around again, suppressing a shudder.

Juniper laughed. "No. On the water."

The water. Presumably, in one of these boats. Even worse. Under normal circumstances Jasper would refuse—he did not associate with boats or bodies of water—but Juniper's expression stopped him. Her eyes sparkled and her face was flushed. She was impossibly excited.

That made one of them.

After last night, he refused to ruin something that clearly brought her joy. It was just a lake. A small one. Practically a pond. And the boats were enormous, he told himself as he looked them over. Easily room for both of them. Maybe a third person.

As he tried to talk himself into the magnificence of the rowboats, a problem presented itself. They were on the dock. On dry land.

"I don't suppose you've put one of these boats in the water before."

"I—" She looked around, frowning. "Oh. I didn't realize they'd all be put away. They've always just been ready before."

"Not to worry. I'm sure I can manage it."

As it turned out, he could not manage it. The boats were heavy and cumbersome, and they disapproved of Jasper as much as he disapproved of them. After half an hour struggling with the infernal things, Jasper's jacket was ruined, his sleeves were rolled up, and he was sweating profusely. The first boat had slipped his grip and fallen sideways off the dock. It was now resting peacefully on the bottom of the lake. If getting in the water weren't one of Jasper's worst nightmares, he would be tempted to join it.

Jasper had learned a great deal from that first boat. For one thing, they were as heavy as the devil, and he supremely doubted anything with that kind of weight would float. He had also learned that there was a trick to maneuvering the angled bottom without losing control of the vessel, which he was now applying to his liberation of the second boat. If he ever went home, Jasper resolved to give whoever handled these matters on his estates a raise.

"This was a terrible idea. We don't need to do this." Juniper had alternated between fretting and offering suggestions. It was her observations that had revealed the easiest method of circumventing the boat's tendency to roll sideways out of Jasper's grip. She'd also offered to help, but Jasper's pride had not allowed him to accept.

"Oh, no. You wanted a romantic boat ride on the lake, and you're getting one." His grip slipped, and the infernal vessel crushed his toes with a force that compelled some of his more creative curses. Thirty minutes ago, Jasper would have given up. Now, it was a personal vendetta. He was a peer of the realm, heir to a duke, and twelfth in line for the throne. He could launch a goddamn boat.

The boat landed in the water with a splash—upright— and he scrambled to catch it before it floated away. Against all odds, it did not immediately sink to the bottom. Seeing it in the water was one of the single most satisfying moments of his life.

Securing the vessel with a rope, Jasper stood up and

stretched out his arms. "Isolde, your armada awaits."

Her smile outshone the sun. "Does that make you Tristan? Are we about to fall madly in love during our voyage?"

"We'd better. That jacket I borrowed was one of Nicholas's favorites."

Jasper grabbed two oars and tossed them into the bottom of the boat. He carefully handed Juniper down, cringing at the way she casually risked her life. While she settled herself on the bench, he took a deep breath. It was a small lake. He could see the bottom.

Nothing bad was going to happen. Even if the boat somehow capsized, he wouldn't be trapped inside it. He wouldn't drown. He was not his parents, and he wasn't six years old anymore.

With his eyes closed for courage, Jasper stepped in. The wobbling of the boat almost undid him, but he made his way onto the bench by feel. When he opened his eyes…it wasn't so bad. The bench felt solid beneath him—and it ought to, it weighed a bloody ton. Juniper's beaming face was across from him. He could do this.

Jasper untied the line. They were officially free-floating.

"Should we put the oars in the locks?" Juniper suggested after a moment.

It sounded sensible enough. Jasper fit the handles against the curved metal arcs set into the sides of the boat. "Like this?"

"Have you never been rowing before?"

"Of course I have. Every Englishman rows." Except Jasper didn't. He didn't row, and he didn't swim, but telling her that would lead to too many questions from his exceedingly observant Isolde, and he'd already ruined their picnic last night.

It was just rowing. Jasper was a DeVere. How hard could it be?

He thought back to every lawn party he'd ever been to, mimicking the motions of the men who *did* row as he dipped the oars into the water and pulled. The boat leapt away from the dock out into the sunshine. Juniper clapped her hands and looked at him like he'd just put the stars in the heavens.

For that, he would row until his arms gave out.

With relatively few further mishaps, they managed to end up in the middle of the lake. It would have been as satisfying as successfully launching the boat, if it weren't so bloody terrifying.

"All right," Juniper announced. "Now relax and let me sketch you."

Relax. As if that was possible with the water surrounding them. Jasper sat back and pretended, doing his best impression of a lounging demi-god. Preferably one who was immune to drowning.

"I should have brought some fruit. Something to eat, at least." Juniper situated herself, taking off the bonnet and shaking out her hair. She lifted her face to the sun for a moment, and suddenly his only thoughts where of how beautiful she was—until a small swell rocked the boat.

"When did you start drawing?" He gripped the edge of the boat until his knuckles went white, forcing his tone to be as casual as he could manage.

"I hardly remember. It was one of the few things I could do without—" Juniper's eyes flew wide. They were fascinating eyes. *Focus on her eyes, not the water.* "Without being a complete tyrant to my tutor, so I've always favored it."

"Tell me more about this tyranny." *Tell me anything,*

just keep talking.

Juniper laughed. "I'm afraid I've always been a bit headstrong. I never played what my music teachers wanted me to play. I always skipped ahead and picked my own lessons."

"What did they want you to play?"

"Boring, slow tempo songs."

"But you like a faster pace."

She looked at him, and the glint from last night was back. "Yes, I do."

It was a mistake. She responded to his flirting so readily. Jasper ought not to do it, but something in her called to something in him, and when she looked at him like that, he couldn't think about any of the things that were haunting him. Not his grandfather, not the depths of the lake around him. He couldn't think about anything but saying something to make her blush, or smile, or bring that impish twinkle into her eye.

Another swell slapped the side of the boat, sending a few drops of water over the edge and onto Jasper's arm.

Right and wrong be damned—he was not going to make it through this outing with his sanity if he didn't distract himself, and Juniper Fairchild was a delicious distraction. "Does that mean you intend to sketch me quickly? I rather hoped you'd take your time admiring me."

He had lied about the rowing, and he was not relaxed. That much was obvious as Julia pulled out her sketchpad and charcoal stick. The tension he was trying to hide compelled her with the way it sat just beneath the

surface of his face. He looked frightened, and yet defiant
at the same time. Like he was under siege, but refused to
surrender. The defiance called to her even more than the
corded muscles of his forearms as he leaned back against
the bow of the boat.

She shouldn't have enjoyed watching him on the dock
as much as she did, but there was something about seeing
him so completely out of his element that brought a flush
to her entire body. Jasper was a creature of decadence
and ballrooms. Seeing him roll up his sleeves and strain,
seeing the way his muscles shifted underneath his shirt as
it became transparent with sweat, took her breath away.

He took her breath away still, soaking up the sun and
trying to pretend he wasn't wholly uncomfortable. Every
time it seemed like he might forget his surroundings, the
water lapped at the boat and he turned to stone from
the tension of it. Julia sketched the impossible beauty of
him, but she also sketched the struggle. There was more
to Jasper DeVere than a famous name and a perfect face.
She wondered how many people knew that. She wondered
how many people he allowed to see it.

"You know, you could have drawn me in the house when
I wasn't covered in filth."

"I could have, but it wouldn't have been nearly as
entertaining."

He let out an inelegant snort. "You enjoy watching me
make a fool of myself?"

"I enjoy seeing you without your armor." Julia
immediately wanted to take it back. It was too honest.

Jasper didn't seem to notice. "If by armor, you mean
Nicholas's coat, I'm flattered."

Julia pressed her lips together and took another risk.
"Flattered enough to remove a bit more?"

His eyes slid open like a jungle cat—slow, with disturbing intensity. She felt like a trembling mouse that had accidentally caught his attention.

"For…for the drawing," she stuttered.

"Liar." But he pushed himself forward and started pulling his shirt from his waistband.

Julia's mouth went dry.

He didn't take his eyes off her as he lifted it. Slowly, the muscles in his torso and chest were revealed, each chiseled line flexed into stark relief. Julia was certain he was doing it on purpose, and she hoped he never stopped. When his shirt finally rose high enough to block out his stare, she took a shuddering breath. Good lord. Whoever had thought up Jasper DeVere, deity or devil, they had an excellent imagination. He was a masterpiece.

Then he was balling up the shirt between his hands and piling it behind his head as he laid back against the rail of the boat. His crooked smile taunted her. "How disarmed would you like me, Isolde?"

Her brain stopped working. It just quit on her, completely. All she could process was the sensuality of his pose. It was the posture of a man stretched out for a lover to admire him. The lines of his legs extended across the boat toward her. Tan skin and the shadow of dark hairs. Crisp white linen against the dark strands of his hair and his long fingers disappearing into the folds—

His hands couldn't be behind his head. They *shouldn't* be. She looked at the bottom of the boat, but it was empty except for her satchel and bonnet. "Jasper?"

"Yes?"

"Where are the oars?"

"The—" He lurched into a sitting position and whipped around.

They spotted the first one at the same time, drifting away sluggishly. They found the second a moment later—headed in the other direction. He must have let them go immediately for them to be that far away. Neither of them had noticed.

"Well, that complicates things." Julia couldn't muster any irritation, though. There were worse things than being trapped alone with a handsome man.

Jasper was not quite as calm. His knuckles blanched as he gripped the sides of the boat. "If we don't do anything, will we eventually drift to shore?"

Julia looked down at the barely moving water. "Maybe? It would take a very long time."

Beneath his tan, Jasper went pale.

She reached out, covering his hand with hers. "Don't worry. We can just swim it. It's not very far."

"I…uh…" He was shaking his head, looking at the water. "I don't swim."

"You don't?" Good Lord. No wonder he was terrified.

"No." There was so much tension in the word. The tendons in his neck were beginning to stand out from the strain.

He couldn't swim—and he'd let her drag him out into the middle of a lake. Jasper DeVere was a saint. Or an idiot. Maybe both. "All right. Don't worry. I can swim just fine, and I'll—"

"Do not leave me in this boat alone." He gripped her fingers. His eyes met hers in a plea. "Please."

"I won't leave you." She promised. "I'll get in and tow the boat to shore."

He shook his head. "You can't."

Julia looked around them. They were a few hundred yards from land. Without something to propel them in the right direction, they could be out here until Nora set to looking for them. Since that wouldn't be until after Julia failed to show up for the four o'clock regimen on the schedule, it could be hours until someone located them. Ignoring the schedule was not an option, and they'd sunk the other boat that would have come to rescue them. If someone had to swim it, it might as well be her.

"I'm afraid we don't have much choice."

Jasper was still shaking his head. "You'll get tired. And you're injured! You'll drown and I won't be able to…I won't…"

She'd lost him again. "I'll be holding on to the boat the whole time. If I get tired, you can pull me back in."

He took a couple deep breaths that made his chest rise and fall beautifully. Julia tried not to get distracted—one of them needed to focus. When he spoke, he sounded like himself again.

"This is highly embarrassing."

"It could be worse."

"Oh?"

"You could still be wearing your shirt." Julia looked down to disguise as much of her blush as she could.

Jasper's laughter bounced off the floor of the boat, and drained some of the tension out of Julia's muscles. He was back.

He nodded, looking at her and very pointedly not looking at the lake. "So, you're going to get in the water."

"Yes. I just…need you to undo the buttons on my dress. And my corset laces."

The predatory look flirted with the edges of his expression. "Really."

"Dresses and petticoats get very heavy when they're waterlogged," she rushed to explain.

Jasper held up his hands. "You'll receive no argument from me."

"And I need you close your eyes while you do it."

"Now, that's not very fair."

It wasn't fair at all. He'd been more than generous by allowing her to ogle his form under the weak guise of art, but Julia couldn't let him see her in just her shift no matter how much she wanted to. The scar on her back might not be visible, but her foot would raise immediate questions.

"Please?" she asked.

"Of course." Jasper immediately ceased protesting and closed his eyes, but not before sending her one last predatory glance. "I am a gentleman, after all."

Julia was all too aware. If he were less of a gentleman, as she had hoped, she would be stripping down in front of her paramour, instead of the charming enigma who refused to kiss her.

Chapter Five

The tiny buttons on Juniper's dress were a godsend. Focusing on them let him stop focusing on the water and how much of it there was, and how very far they were from the shore. It hadn't seemed like much at all when he was rowing out to the middle, but now it stretched out in an endless expanse that seemed to grow larger every time he looked at it.

When the buttons were undone, he closed his eyes. It heightened the sensation as he let his fingers trace the laces of her corset, untying them with deliberate precision. With each loosened tie, a new section of her back was exposed—the warmth of skin radiating through the thin fabric of her shift.

"Jasper?"

"Hmm?"

"Is that all of them?"

"I think so." He ran his thumbs the length of her spine, pushing the thick weave of the corset away with his fingers. When he reached the indent of her waist, she jumped away.

"Your eyes are closed?" she asked.

"As promised."

The rustle of cloth filled his ears. Jasper's imagination supplied the vision of petticoats and undergarments sliding off her hips and landing on the bottom of the boat. "You should know, this is a special kind of torture."

The only response was two thuds against the boards.

"What was that?"

"My boots." Her voice was barely audible. "I'm going to get in now."

"Do I need to do anything?"

"Lean to the left until you hear the splash."

She might as well have asked him to hold a pit viper. "Is the boat going to tip over?"

"It shouldn't. Just balance out my weight."

Heaven help them. The boat started tipping right, so he leaned left. There was a lurch, followed by a splash. Jasper's heart stopped. "Juniper? Juniper!"

He gave up keeping his eyes closed and leaned over the right side of the boat.

A blond head surfaced, darker now for being soaked, and Juniper sputtered as she wiped water from her face. "I'm all right."

"Well, I'm not. Please don't go under again."

The woman had the audacity to giggle. "I'll try not to."

"I'm not kidding. If you go under, I'm jumping in after you. And then when I drown and die, it will be your fault."

"Head above water, I promise." She walked her hands along the rail of the boat until she reached the back and started kicking her legs, moving the boat forward.

He couldn't watch. He couldn't. He peeked behind him and caught the flash of a perfectly rounded buttock flexing beneath Juniper's ineffective, waterlogged shift. Perhaps he could find the fortitude to watch a little.

"Are you looking?" she demanded.

Damn. "…Maybe."

"You promised!"

"I thought that was just while you were in the boat," he lied. Jasper didn't have to suppress his grin because she couldn't see his face. "Your backside is flawless, by the way."

The splash of the kicks lost their rhythm for a moment. "Keep your eyes forward."

"As you wish."

They made steady progress toward the shore. Without the distraction of Juniper's curves, Jasper was forced to contemplate his situation. He'd broken down in a panic in front of the woman he was trying to impress. He hadn't embarrassed himself this thoroughly since he'd propositioned Lady Melton at age thirteen. And yet, he wasn't embarrassed—he was grateful. Juniper had simply rescued him rather than judging him. Of course, there was still plenty of time for her to ridicule him once they were safely ashore.

The splashing stopped.

"Is everything all right?"

She let out a deep breath and her head rose above the edge of the rail. "It's shallow enough for me to touch the bottom now."

Sweet deliverance. Relief rushed through him in a wave, followed immediately by guilt. Jasper started stripping off his boots.

"What are you doing?"

By way of an answer, he crossed himself and rolled over the side into the water. The panic sprang up in an overwhelming burst.

"Jasper!"

His feet touched the ground, and his shoulders broke the surface. "Well, that was awful."

"Then why did you do it?" she demanded.

"You've rescued me enough for one day. I thought I'd try to be of use."

She shook her head at him. "We didn't both need to get wet."

"You should hardly be dragging boats around with your ankle. Besides, wet looks so good on you. I got jealous." He didn't need to look to know she blushed. Jasper grabbed hold of the boat and started towing it behind him with a smile.

As he squelched through the mud and dragged the boat ashore, he realized he was the only one squelching. He spun around—to make sure of what, he didn't know. That she hadn't collapsed in the mud? Been dragged back to the depths by some fanciful lake monster?

Juniper was standing in the shallows with the water lapping around her hips. With her hair plastered flat around her face, her eyes were impossibly large. Water adhered her shift to her body, rendering it all but useless.

Jasper blinked. "You're breathtaking."

"You're not supposed to be looking." Her arms came up, crossing over her chest and blocking out the view of her breasts.

"Sorry," he answered softly. He'd thought something had happened to her.

Her smile was small. Private. "Up the shore and turn around."

Jasper turned away from her. "I feel like we should discuss this. Negotiations might be in order."

"What happened to being a gentleman?"

"Highly overrated. Who needs it?"

Her laugh rang out like bells across the water. "Walk up the shore, please."

He started walking, calling over his shoulder. "You're missing out. My ungentlemanly talents are world-renowned."

"So I hear." Light splashes sounded behind him as she left the water.

"I've already seen most of what there is to see."

"Then you should be content in your good fortune."

"Never." If he glimpsed Juniper undressed a thousand times, he would still want the one thousand and first.

After a moment, she said, "You can turn now."

Jasper turned. She'd eschewed the other layers and just put on her dress. It was sticking to her damp curves with tantalizing precision.

"You're going to cause a riot." He reached into the boat and handed her his shirt. "Here."

She ran her eyes the length of his bare chest and waterlogged trousers. "What will you wear?"

"My irresistible masculinity."

She choked a laugh as she pulled the shirt over her head. "Well then, you should be well covered."

Jasper chose not to ruin his boots by putting them back on, so he traversed the lawn in bare feet. Juniper walked beside him, swallowed up by the billowing fabric of his shirt. They were a ridiculous pair, but there was something so intrinsically right about it, something that resonated satisfaction through him. When he reached for her hand, she looked up at him with a question in her eyes.

"I almost drowned. I'm feeling quite vulnerable."

She looked down with a laugh. "Liar."

He pushed open the door off the terrace with her fingers threaded through his. The halls leading to the foyer were empty, and they almost made it through the ground floor of the house without causing a fuss—until they ran smack into their absent hosts at the foot of the main staircase.

Jasper hadn't realized how closely Juniper resembled her cousin until he saw Amelia standing there; a brunette version of his dripping companion. There were small differences—Amelia's face was rounder, and her eyes were darker brown, but there was no denying their relation. She was frowning up at the much taller, dark-haired figure of her husband. Nicholas was looking down at his wife with the embarrassingly besotted expression Jasper suspected he'd worn his entire life. How Amelia had failed to notice it for so long was a mystery of the universe, but she certainly noticed it now. Her expression softened to a doughy ridiculousness of her own, and Jasper felt a warming sensation in his chest. He'd helped make that happen.

Then Nicholas ruined it by spotting them.

"What in the bloody hell?" Nicholas took in their disheveled states with a scowl.

"You're back!" Jasper did his best not to sound disappointed.

"You're wearing my trousers," Nicholas countered.

"Why are you wet? What is Jasper doing here? Hello, by the way." Amelia rushed to her cousin and Juniper's hand left his as they embraced each other. "Is everything all right?"

Juniper answered her cousin with a beaming grin. "Perfectly."

A storm was brewing on Nicholas's face, and Jasper had no intention of facing it half-dressed and dripping, or of subjecting Juniper to one of Nicholas's conservative diatribes in their present state. "Why don't we tell you

both about it after we've changed?"

"Jasper—"

"Oh, I owe you a boat," he called over his shoulder as he reclaimed Juniper's hand and led her up the stairs. "And two oars. See you at tea—and not a moment before!"

For the second time that day, Julia ended up in a bath. However, she agreed to this one with significantly less resentment. For one thing, she smelled like lake water. For another, instead of being anxious to see Jasper, she could lean back against the copper tub and relive their afternoon. He'd told her he intended to hide out from Nicholas until tea time, so she had a few blissful moments to relive her adventure.

It wasn't the idyllic rendezvous she'd envisioned when she sent him out to the boathouse, but in some ways it was better. He was clearly terrified of the water, but he'd gone anyway. Because she'd asked him. And the way he'd looked at her when she was standing in her shift—if it was the last thing she did, he would look at her like that again, and next time she would not make him walk away.

"Nora, the water's getting cold. Could you get some more to heat it up a little?"

"Of course. I live to haul kettles up and down the stairs."

"You're a ray of sunshine." Julia rested her head against the edge of the tub.

Nora opened the bedroom door and gasped, hand on her heart. "Lady Amelia. You gave me a fright."

"I'm sorry, Nora. Is my sister decent?"

"No, but there's no force on heaven or earth that's going

to change that."

"I can hear you," Julia called.

"Can you? So, when I told you it was a bad idea to go gallivanting off with his lordship—"

"Go away, Nora."

As Nora left, Amelia came in and sat on the bed. "You should be nicer to her, you know."

"Then she'd be forced to be nice to me, and we'd both be miserable."

"So, this gallivanting." Amelia stacked a pile of pillows behind her back. Not a short visit, then. So much for waiting until tea. "What is going on?"

Oh, you know. Just desperately trying to engage a known rake in a scandalous affair. "Welcome back, by the way. How was your trip?"

"Don't change the subject."

Julia should never have wished her sister would come back. Not having to explain herself had been delightful.

"What's going on with you and Jasper? Why were you soaking wet? Why is he even here?"

"Well, I was out riding, and we came across each other…"

"And you get on famously, just like I always said you would." Amelia was beaming with *I told you so* pride.

"We do, but there's a slight complication."

Amelia's smile dropped away. "What complication?"

Julia cringed in advance, knowing what was coming next. "I told him I was Miss Juniper Fairchild."

Amelia blinked at her. "Who the devil is Miss Juniper Fairchild?"

The woman I could have been—would have been—if not for my spine. "Your cousin. From Kent."

"We don't have a cousin in Kent."

"We do now."

"But surely…how did you explain your back and the schedule?"

"He thinks I limp because I turned my ankle. I figured I would think of something for the rest of it when it came to that."

"Oh, Julia." Amelia sighed, the same way she'd sighed whenever Julia had gotten herself in too deep with some scheme or another. "How do you get yourself into such trouble? If you'd only — "

Julia sank down until the water covered her ears and she was staring at the ceiling. Amelia's answer was just a distorted warbling of sounds. Julia smiled — until a palm flattened against her head and pushed her all the way under. She came back up flailing and stuttering. "You're hateful."

"Very. So." Amelia returned to her pillow nest. "What happened today? Why were you all wet and wearing Jasper's shirt? Are you lovers?"

"No," Julia sighed. "Not for lack of trying. The bloody man has an incredible knack for *not* kissing me."

"Julia!"

"What? Don't pretend you didn't seduce Nicholas with dishonorable intentions."

Amelia ignored that. "What happened today?"

The pink flush that crept over Julia's skin was not from the hot water. "I asked Jasper to row us around the lake while I sketched him."

"Like we used to imagine we would do with our imaginary, perfect future husbands."

Julia started to sink back down under the water.

"I will dunk you again," Amelia promised.

She sighed. "I just wanted to know what it would be like, once."

"And?"

"And Jasper has never rowed before, he let go of the oars, and apparently, he does not know how to swim."

A laugh escaped Amelia. She pressed her hand to her mouth. "It was a disaster? I'm so sorry."

It hadn't been, though. It had been perhaps the greatest afternoon of Julia's life. Nothing so exciting had ever happened to her. Again, she wished it had involved kissing. But it was progress, and what's more—she felt closer to him. They shared something now that was just theirs. No one else could claim any part of it.

Amelia was watching her face. She sighed. "Oh, Jules."

Julia stood up and stepped out of the bathtub, wrapping the towel around her body. "It was just a row around the lake. Don't get all sentimental about it."

"You're falling for him."

"Don't be ridiculous. I fall for everyone in my imagination. It doesn't mean anything."

"But this isn't imaginary. This is really happening."

"He doesn't even know who I am."

"While we're back on that subject…" Amelia scooted over, making room for Julia. "Why on earth did you choose *Juniper*, of all names?"

Julia tossed an embroidered pillow at her sister. "I was halfway through telling him my actual name when I realized I couldn't. It was the first 'Ju' name that came to my mind."

"What an unfortunate time to lose your silver tongue. Goodness, what are we supposed to call you? Is there a single good nickname for Juniper?" Amelia broke down in giggles again. "Juney."

"No."

"Niper?"

"They will never find your body."

"Really, I could pick whatever I wanted and claim we've called you it since childhood. This is the sort of power you've placed in my hands with this ridiculous lie."

Julia groaned. Twenty years of being the dominant force in their relationship was about to be paid back all at once. "As long as you go along with it."

Amelia's eyebrows raised and her mouth pursed in a dreadful similarity to Nora's favorite expression. "You could just tell him instead."

She couldn't. Every time Julia thought about it, a sick feeling rose up in her stomach. "He wouldn't like me as… *me*."

"Why not? From where I was standing, it seemed like he liked you just fine."

It seemed that way to Julia, too, but the idea of telling him was terrifying. "I just need more time, Mia. I'm not ready to risk it yet. Will you ask Nicholas not to give me away?"

Amelia sighed. "You know we'll do anything for you, but we're awful liars. You should tell him before we mess it up on accident."

She should. She *would*. Just not quite yet.

Chapter Six

The writing desk in Jasper's room was small, but large enough for the single sheet of paper centered on its walnut surface. He held the pen, inked nib suspended above cream vellum. So far, he'd only managed two words.

Dearest Ruby,

A day's worth of distance wasn't enough to get out what he needed to say. There might not be enough time in their whole lives, but he had to say something. She deserved something. Instead of the words that would slice his heart to shreds, he wrote about his day and trusted she would be able to read the meaning in them.

Today I rowed in a boat on a lake. It was exactly the catastrophe you would expect—a young lady had to jump in and push me to shore. You would have found it quite comical.

If she was capable of finding anything comical at the moment.

I'm sorry for the way I left. I know you expected better of me. You always do.

It was all he could manage. Everything else came too close to the knot that closed up his throat.

Give my love to Gran and to

Jasper's hand shook as he realized what he'd been about to write. He took a deep breath to steady it as he crossed out the words.

Give my love to Gran. and to

Be well,

Jas

He hesitated, pen poised over the post script. There was always a danger in giving Ruby too much information. In the end, he threw caution to the wind because that was his way.

P. S. —If you need to reach me, send word to my solicitor in London. He won't tell you where I am, but he can get word to me if necessary. Please don't try to find me.

It wasn't enough, but it was what he could give her. Jasper folded the page over on itself and headed out of his room to put it with the outgoing post.

"Jasper!"

He turned at the top of the stairs to find Nicholas

coming from the opposite hall. "Hullo, Nick."

"I need a word with you."

Undoubtedly, but better now than after Juniper joined them. Nicholas in a temper wasn't the most careful with his words.

"Study?"

Nick nodded. Jasper followed his silent march down the hall and through the dark walnut door of the ground-floor study.

When it closed behind them, Nicholas whirled on him. "What in the bloody hell are you thinking?"

Jasper didn't need to ask what he was referring to. "She's a delightful woman."

"She's Amelia's—a member of Amelia's family. Of my family, now."

"Nothing untoward has happened."

Nicholas stared him down.

"I mean it. I have been behaving myself quite admirably."

"You two were barely dressed."

Jasper poured them each a glass of port. This conversation would clearly require something stronger than tea. "That was an unfortunate circumstance, but not in any way planned."

"Are you trying to tell me you *aren't* pursuing her?"

"It's complicated. I'm trying not to, but I've still got a pulse, Nick." Jasper took a quick sip, barely tasting the fortified wine as it passed his throat. "Nothing serious has occurred."

"You're unbelievable."

"Oh, come on. I promise to behave myself. Where's the harm?" He leaned against the edge of the desk and tried to lure Nicholas back to the lighthearted friendship they usually enjoyed.

Nicholas refused. "The harm? The harm is what if she gets attached to you? What if she takes you seriously and develops feelings for you?"

The thought generated a warm flush just under Jasper's skin that had nothing to do with the wine. "I would be quite flattered."

"And she will be devastated, because you don't mean it and this..." Nick shook his head. "This cannot end well."

"Maybe I do mean it," Jasper said quietly.

"Excuse me?"

"Maybe I do mean it." His voice was louder, more confident, the second time. "Maybe Miss Fairchild is special. In fact, I know she's special. Maybe she's the woman for me."

"I'm not kidding, Jas. Take this seriously."

"I am. Are you?" Being near Juniper, hearing her laugh, made Jasper feel a rightness that had been missing for a long time. He wasn't in the habit of analyzing his feelings, so he couldn't say for certain what it was. But why couldn't it be love? Stranger things had happened.

"No! Why would I?"

"Maybe Miss Fairchild is the person I've been waiting to meet my whole life." The idea was taking root. Their story had a great deal of romance to it. He'd run off to the country in a fit of grief, saved her life on the hillside, and then they would fall madly in love to the backdrop of the rustic English countryside.

While he crafted the ballad in his mind, Nicholas stared at him like he'd lost it. "You're incredible. I've always known you only have a passing acquaintanceship with the truth, but that you would be willing to fabricate this kind of justification—"

If Nicholas truly *could* read his mind, he'd know none of it was fabricated. Perhaps a little embellished, but fully truthful. "I have never needed to justify myself."

"—purely so you can continue to pursue Jul—Juniper with lascivious intent."

"My intentions are not lascivious." That was where he deviated from the truth. It was only circumstantial interruption that had kept Jasper from kissing Miss Fairchild senseless, and his resolve to keep things between them purely a flirtation was crumbling further by the hour. But it was more than just a physical attraction. Jasper wanted her smile. Her sweet blush and the unexpected edges to her conversation that snuck out and revealed the vicious wit beneath. There was nothing lascivious about that. That was pure.

Nicholas's glass connected with the surface of the table like a gunshot. "She's important to me, Jas. She's important to Amelia."

Jasper stood his ground. "She's important to me, too."

"I think you may actually mean that," Nicholas admitted softly.

Relief eased through Jasper. He did not like being at odds with Nicholas. "I do."

He needed Juniper. He needed her blushes and her laugh. Without them, he would be forced to think about what he'd run from. Jasper looked up, wanting to explain at least part of that to Nicholas, but his friend's face stopped him cold.

Where Jasper normally found the curving lines of a half smile, Nicholas's face was all tense edges and censure. "Unfortunately, I don't believe you'll still mean it in a fortnight."

And there it was.

He wanted to hate Nicholas for saying it, but how could he when it was the truth? Jasper was unreliable. He couldn't be counted on not to change his mind—to not run halfway across the world on a lark. The same reasons he wasn't fit to carry on his grandfather's legacy were the same reasons he couldn't have Juniper. Jasper DeVere couldn't be counted on.

Not an admirable quality in a husband, or in one of the most powerful lords of the land.

When Julia opened the drawing room door, she stopped short. Amelia was reading a book on the settee while Nicholas and Jasper played chess in front of the windows. Nick mumbled something under his breath and they exchanged a laugh. Julia told herself to be calm. Amelia had promised Nicholas wouldn't tell Jasper before Julia was ready. She trusted them. They were her family.

"You two look cozy."

"Hardly," Nick answered. "I'm fairly certain Jasper cheats."

Amelia looked up from her book. "Everyone beats you at chess, darling. You just don't have a very diabolical mindset."

Nicholas turned to his wife. "Didn't you swear some sort of loyalty to me in front of witnesses? I think there were rings involved…"

"All I swore was to take you as my husband. There was nothing about bolstering your ego."

"So that's why we eloped to Scotland. I'm certain an

English ceremony would have covered that."

"You caught me. That was the only reason." Amelia returned to her book with a smile.

"Well, I give up." Nick toppled his king. "You'll have to challenge one of the ladies if you want to keep playing."

Jasper turned to Julia. "Do you play?"

Julia Bishop did—with great skill and absolutely no mercy. The question was, did Juniper Fairchild? "A little. It's been a very long time. Will you teach me?"

On the settee, Amelia fell victim to a coughing fit.

"Are you all right?" Jasper asked.

"Fine, fine," she said. "Cousin *Junie*, I could swear you played more often than that. I remember you being quite good."

"You must be mistaking me for someone else." Julia settled herself in front of the board.

"Perhaps. My sister and I play so often, maybe I just assumed everyone does."

"That could be." *Leave it alone, Amelia.*

Jasper reset the pieces on the board. "I still haven't met the mysterious Lady Julia."

"No. No, you have not," Nicholas agreed.

"I doubt you ever will," Amelia said. "Julia's quite the recluse. Very socially inept, I'm afraid."

"But extremely adept at chess," Nicholas added.

"Quite."

Julia would strangle them both. "I've always found cousin Julia to be very charming."

"You're just being kind." Amelia turned to Jasper. "Cousin Juniper has the temperament of a saint. Always believing the best in people."

Jasper frowned. "You've only ever had glowing things to say about your sister before, Mia."

"Really?" Julia leaned in. "What sort of things?"

"That she was beautiful, and clever, and talented. She sounded like a woman of remarkable character."

That was more like it.

Amelia stared straight at Julia and said, "I exaggerated."

Nicholas chimed in. "Don't be unkind, Mia. She's like that sometimes."

Thank you, Nick.

"But then other times, it's like she's an entirely different person."

A slow death would be too good for Nicholas Wakefield.

Jasper's attention was bouncing between the three of them, his brow furrowing. This was it. He would figure it out. Everything would be ruined, all because Amelia and Nicholas thought they were clever.

"They're being deliberately cruel," Julia explained. "And I don't think *cousin Julia* deserves it one bit."

"She deserves it a little bit," Amelia mumbled.

"I must admit, after everything you told me, I harbored a small infatuation for the mysterious Lady Julia," Jasper said.

The thud of Julia's heartbeat drowned out everything else.

"But perhaps I'm just partial to all the female members of your family." He smiled at Julia. "Shall we play?"

Julia was more than happy to agree.

"This piece is the king. If you lose your king, you lose the game."

"Fascinating." Julia had no trouble pretending to be distracted and inept. She was far too busy marveling that Jasper DeVere had thought about her as she really was.

They played three games, and Julia managed to lose every single one without arousing Jasper's suspicion. It was worth it to be able to sit across from him and watch the way the light played across his face as pondered his next move. Or as he tapped the bridge of his nose when he was thinking about making a sacrifice play. Or smiled gently when he successfully trapped her king.

This was what Amelia had. Julia had envied it throughout their childhood, watching her sister sit across from Nicholas while he looked at Mia like she was the only person that mattered in the world. Julia knew what it felt like now and no one could take it from her—no matter what happened.

"Perhaps chess just isn't my game," Julia announced.

Amelia made a vulgar snorting sound.

"Shall we do something else?" Jasper asked. His fingers brushed across hers on the table, tracing the lines of her knuckles. "Maybe something…just the two of us?"

The flush rose up under Julia's skin. Her attention was riveted to his slow exploration of her hand.

"Jasper." Nicholas's voice held a note of warning.

Jasper's hand pulled away like she'd burned him. It hovered in midair as he frowned down at it. When he withdrew it fully, his expression shuttered into a polite neutrality. He stood up from the table. "Excuse me a moment. I think I'd like to take a walk alone."

When he was gone, Julia turned on Nick. "What did you do?"

If he had ruined it, if he had told Jasper after promising he wouldn't, she would never forgive him.

"Someone is going to get hurt, and it won't be Jasper. It never is." Nicholas's mulish expression told her everything she needed to know. He'd said something to Jasper.

Bloody, interfering ass. "Thank you for your unsolicited opinion."

Julia went after Jasper. If she stayed, she would throttle her brother-in-law. He had no right, and he ought to know better. Julia made her own decisions. She did not allow anyone, no matter how well-meaning, to limit her. Perhaps Jasper would hurt her. Perhaps someday she would lose her footing on the stairs, or one of the infections that laid her low would finally be the end of her. The idea that she should wrap herself in cotton and hide away from life because of what *might* happen was ludicrous.

She turned the corner of a sculpted hedge and found Jasper contemplating his reflection in the water of the lake. "Jasper?"

The light shifted across his face as he turned. His initial smile at the sight of her crumbled into a frown. "You shouldn't have come. Your ankle—"

Damn you, Nicholas. Bugger her ankle, and whatever this nonsense was. "What are you doing out here?"

He sighed and returned to his reflection. "Trying to decide if I'm a terrible person."

Julia stepped forward, her skirts blending with the fabric of his trousers in their watery mirror. "Are you?"

"I think maybe I am." His eyes closed. The lines of his face were tortured and tense. "It was never my intention to mislead you."

"Have you?" It would be the wrong time to laugh, no matter how much Julia appreciated irony.

"I'm not certain I can offer you what you deserve."

"And what do you think that is?"

"An honorable courtship."

If he'd been looking, Julia's relief would have been obvious. He was out here worrying about not being able to make her an honorable offer? That, at least, she could fix. If it was time for their flirtation to end, it would be because she chose to end it, not because of Nicholas's interference. And maybe, just maybe…

"Jasper, if anyone is guilty of misleading, it is me." She took a deep breath. "I am not Amelia's cousin."

"What?" His eyes flew open.

She took a deep breath. "My name is Julia Bishop. I am—"

"Amelia's sister." Realization dawned on his face. "They were teasing you, during our chess game."

"Yes." Julia held her breath.

His shoulders dropped and the tension fell away from his body. "Why did you lie?"

She frowned at him. He had to know—how could he not? "You were flirting with me. I just wanted…I wanted it to keep happening a little while longer."

"I would have flirted with you anyway."

"Would you have, really?" Her throat was tight, but the question escaped anyway.

"Yes." No hesitation, no attempt to avoid her eyes. Everything about him screamed the truth.

She let the euphoria of the moment wash over her.

"But it doesn't change the situation." He shook his head, pacing as his hand drove furrows through his hair. "If anything, it makes it even more complicated. Amelia is utterly devoted to you. If I led you on somehow, or couldn't deliver on the promises my flirtation has made—"

Amelia might be devoted, but she had her own life now; her own love affair. Julia deserved one, too.

She put her hand on his arm to make him stand still. "Jasper, even if you did ask me to marry you, I would be forced to refuse you. I am not a suitable spouse for anyone, least of all the heir to a dukedom."

"But Nicholas—"

"Is very sweet." Julia could think of a few other words to describe Nick just then. "But he has unrealistic notions about my prospects."

"He wants the best for you."

"The only person who knows what's best for me is me." Julia took a deep breath. Boldness had never been difficult for her, but this was different. "Jasper, do you care for me?"

"Yes." It seemed like that was all he would say, but then he added, "You constantly surprise me, and I find myself wanting to know everything about you."

"Then what, precisely, is the complication?" She would love nothing more than for him to learn it all.

"I'm not known for my constancy. What if it doesn't last? At some point, I'll have to go back to London, and I don't know what will happen to us then."

"I can guarantee it won't last. I've known that since I met you." She could at least ease his mind on this. "You and I are not destined to end up together. It didn't stop me inviting you here unchaperoned, and it won't stop me from wanting to continue what we've begun."

"Are you certain?"

"My future has never been certain, Jasper. Quite the opposite." Crickets chirped in the setting sun as she searched for the words to make him understand. "I choose to live in the moment, and I'd like to spend this moment with you, for as long as it lasts, if you're interested."

He took her hand in his. "Even if it doesn't last?"

"Even though it can't," she corrected.

"Julia Bishop, are you asking me to embark on a scandalous affair with you?"

The thud of her heart beat in her ears. Her name on

his lips. *Hers*, not anyone else's. This wasn't some fantasy in her room anymore. He hadn't run from who she was and he wasn't looking away. "I am."

He lifted her hand to his lips and placed a kiss against her knuckles. "I accept."

Chapter Seven

Jasper had never slept so well in his life. Julia had tempted him all night long in his dreams, and the compulsion to roll over and find her in his sleep again was strong. But the flesh and blood woman was just a few halls away, and Jasper had never been content to dream when he could experience something in truth.

She was exceptional. From the boldness of her lie to the frankness of her confession. There was something remarkable about the way she embraced the present—her wholehearted pursuit of the present echoed his own beliefs. The future was not guaranteed. At any moment, a carriage could careen off the road and destroy it all. Fretting over tomorrow was wasted energy, and letting today pass by could be a grave error.

Julia Bishop deserved the love affair to end all love affairs, and Jasper DeVere was just the man to give it to her.

He was whistling when he took the stairs two at a time and practically skipped his way into the dining room. The whistle died off when he saw only Nicholas at the breakfast table. Jasper's attention shifted between the breakfast table and the footman waiting at silent attention next to the sideboard. Perhaps it wasn't too late to leave.

"Jasper."

...Perhaps it was. Jasper accepted a seat at the table and nodded his thanks when a cup of coffee and a laden plate were set in front of him.

After a long moment, Nicholas asked, "Did you sleep well?"

An olive branch. "I did, thank you. Your home is very relaxing."

Nicholas peered over the edge of *The Morning Post.* "You and Juniper took dinner in your rooms last night."

Ah. Not an olive branch—an ambush. "We did. It had been a long day—and I think you mean Julia."

The sound of Nicholas's exhaled breath dominated the room, and robbed his expression of its sternness. "Oh, thank God. She told you."

Jasper grinned. "How long did you think you were going to be able pull off a lie of that magnitude?"

Nick took a bite of toast, shaking his head. "The Bishop sisters are going put me into an early grave."

"Does this mean we're friends again?"

"We were never not friends, but—are you still pursuing Julia, now that you *know* she's Julia?"

"I am." Jasper tried to ignore the slight inherent in the question, but he couldn't. What sort of man Nicholas must think he was; willing to throw over a beautiful, intriguing woman purely because of a circumstance of birth? An edge crept into his voice. "Will that be a problem?"

"I don't know!" Nicholas pinched the bridge of his nose and finally, for the first time since he'd arrived, looked like Jasper's friend and not some disapproving uncle. "This

whole thing is just… I don't know, Jas. It's difficult for me to process."

"What's difficult about it?"

He pinned Jasper with a knowing scowl. "You and I have done a great deal of troublemaking together. I have detailed knowledge of your intimate exploits."

"And…"

"And I don't want to think about those details in relation to *my relation*."

Jasper tried to put himself in Nicholas's shoes. If Ruby suddenly took up with one of his more hedonistic friends, then he— No. His brain immediately went blank, refusing to contemplate it. "I see the problem."

"You do?"

"I do."

"Then you'll give up pursuing Julia?"

"No." That wasn't something he could do.

"But you just—"

"I like her, Nicholas. More than I've ever liked anyone, and martyrdom is not in my nature, but I will be more understanding of your difficulties."

"Oh, thank you." Nicholas's tone was full of sarcasm.

"Any time. We are friends, after all." They were, and would continue to be. It was a weight off Jasper's mind. Nicholas would continue to be surly and difficult, but their friendship would survive. Jasper hadn't quite realized how important that was to him. "So about the eldest Bishop, what can you tell me about what she likes?"

"No. I will not help you seduce my sister-in-law."

"It must be difficult to live such a conflicted life."

"What can I say"—Nicholas raised his coffee cup in a toast—"I'm a complicated man."

"You're a wonderful one," Amelia announced as

she entered the dining room. She dropped a kiss on her husband's cheek on the way to her chair. "Don't get up."

Jasper stood, taking his seat when she did. "I thought married women luxuriated through the morning, taking breakfast in bed."

"And miss all the excitement? I'm surprised I didn't find you two battling to the death with butter knives."

"The morning isn't over," Nicholas warned.

Amelia ignored him. "Jasper, I don't think I ever thanked you for sending us Giovani."

"It's entirely my pleasure. I couldn't let a great chef go to waste, and I travel too much to make proper use of him."

"Don't thank him, Mia. Moments ago, he was grilling me for advice on seducing your sister."

Amelia's eyebrows rose at *sister*, and Jasper nodded confirmation that he knew. Her happy laughter spilled across the table. "Why did you ask Nicholas? What would he know about it?"

"Excuse me." Nick discarded *The Morning Post*. "I know things."

"About me, certainly. But Julia? I sincerely doubt it."

Jasper gave Amelia his most charming smile. "Where might you stand on helping me woo your sibling?"

"That depends on your intentions, Lord Bellamy. Perhaps we should take a walk after breakfast." Her eyes twinkled behind her teacup. "But first, I'm starving and I am woefully behind on news. While I eat breakfast, tell me—how is your sister?"

Devastated, no doubt. Angry. Terrified. Mostly angry.

Amelia saved him from having to answer by continuing to chatter. "I usually catch up on her exploits through the society papers, but Nicholas and I decided to make it a news-free holiday. No papers, no interruptions."

"I was attempting to get up to speed on the country's goings on, but then my wife insulted my prowess." Nicholas tapped the closed paper while he arched an eyebrow at Amelia. She brandished her fork at him in a mock threat after she emptied it of eggs.

They didn't know.

Jasper should tell them now about his grandfather, but he couldn't bring himself to do it. Eventually it would be inescapable, but for right now he could pretend like everything was exactly as it had been. He could imagine the old duke was still sitting at his own breakfast table in London, perusing a copy of *The Post* and teasing Jasper's grandmother, much like Nick and Mia were doing right now.

"I apologize for nothing," Amelia was saying. "Hiding behind the paper when there is perfectly decent company to converse with is rude."

Jasper added a bit of fuel to the fire. "Weren't you always complaining about your father doing that?"

"Now, wait one second—"

"Maybe I'll invite your sister out for a visit," Amelia said. "I'd love for us all to be together again."

Damn. "I'm not certain that's a good idea."

"Why not?"

"Ruby is lovely, truly, but she turns into an entirely different person when she thinks I might be pursuing an attachment. She can be quite cold, and I wouldn't want Julia subjected to that."

"Oh. Well that's unfortunate." Amelia frowned. "I wouldn't want that, either."

Somewhere in England, Lady Ruby DeVere's eyes were narrowing as she sensed her brother perverting the truth. Ruby would be cold, but it wouldn't have a thing to do with Julia.

*ulia made it downstairs just as breakfast was finishing. She'd thought she and Jasper might spend the day together, but apparently that was a foolish expectation. He and Amelia disappeared almost immediately after with their heads bent together, whispering furiously. They didn't cast so much as a backward glance at Julia and Nicholas.

"It looks as though we've been abandoned," Nick said, stating the obvious.

"What do you think they're up to?"

"Betraying the laws of nature and good sense."

Julia peered at him. "I do believe marriage is making you less agreeable than usual."

His eyebrows raised as he set down his paper. "Marriage suits me very well."

"Then why are you such a crank?"

"Oh, I don't know." Nick leaned back, arms crossed over his chest. "Perhaps it's a side effect of being disappointed in my closest friend."

"Jasper hasn't done anything untoward."

"I wasn't talking about Jasper."

"I—" For once, Julia didn't have a clever quip. "You don't mean that. About our friendship."

"Don't I? Jasper and I are close, but I've known you almost my whole life. You were there for every triumph. Every disappointment."

"Most of them over Amelia."

"Yes, most of them were. You were the only person I could be completely honest with for years. What did you think that made you?"

A fool. They'd been close, certainly, but she'd always thought…well, she was the sister of the woman he was in love with. A captive audience. She didn't exactly make or receive social calls, so she was infinitely available whenever he needed to cross the field between their houses and unburden himself. It cast a different light on their relationship to know that was how he thought of her.

"How have I disappointed you?" she asked quietly.

Nick sighed. "You're an extraordinary person, Julia. Anyone would be lucky to know you. I'm disappointed you thought Juniper Fairchild was necessary."

"You know why I feel that way."

"I do, and that's why I went along with it. But just because people have been cruel in the past—"

She choked out a wry laugh. "The past?"

"And will undoubtedly be cruel in the future, it doesn't make them right. It doesn't make Julia Bishop someone who should ever be ashamed of who she is."

A sniffle snuck past as Julia wiped the corner of her eye. "If you keep making speeches like that, you'll be a member of Parliament in no time."

Nicholas laughed. "I have to make it through becoming a barrister first. Your sister isn't helping."

"Amelia loves the idea of you becoming a barrister."

"The idea of it, perhaps. She also loves traveling the continent. And having me home every night. And every morning. And occasionally in the afternoons."

Julia held up hand. "That's quite enough. I don't need to hear any of that."

"And I don't need to see Jasper DeVere strolling bare-chested through my foyer, but here we both are."

She cringed. "I see your point."

"Do you?"

"You would prefer it if I were more discreet in my adventures with Jasper."

"I would prefer you didn't have adventures with Jasper at all," Nicholas grumbled.

"But?" It definitely sounded like there was a "but."

"But since I know that's extremely unlikely, I'll settle for plausible deniability when your father comes to tear my head from my shoulders."

"Papa wouldn't hurt you. He likes you."

"Not *that* much. He lives for you and Amelia."

It was true—their father spoiled them horribly. He'd purchased this estate and a house in London for Amelia and Nicholas as a wedding present. He'd always moved heaven and earth to give Julia anything she wanted. Almost anything. There were some things even a devoted father and a great deal of money couldn't buy.

"Fair enough," Julia agreed. "I will do my best to keep you clear of my father's wrath."

"Thank you."

Julia grinned. "What are closest friends for?"

"A question I ask myself constantly."

After breakfast, Nicholas left to finish up some paperwork and Julia found herself completely alone. Even Nora was scarcer than usual. The next time she caught sight of anyone was at the midday meal. Jasper walked into the dining room with a cat-in-the-cream smile, as if he hadn't spent the entire day colluding with her sister.

"You look very pleased with yourself," she accused as he sat down across from her.

"I am very pleased with myself. You're going to be pleased with me, too."

"Am I?"

"Very." He winked at Amelia, who was sitting next to him and doing a terrible job of pretending not to be listening.

"Why is that?"

"Just wait and see." Jasper turned away and struck up a conversation about continental politics with Nick.

Julia didn't give a fig which prince of where had done what. She wanted to know what Jasper and Amelia had been up to. For the rest of the meal, every time Julia looked in Jasper's direction, he smiled like he had some great secret—because he did. She didn't, and she hated it. To add insult to injury, whenever she brought it up, Amelia and Jasper pretended as if she hadn't spoken at all. Nicholas just shrugged.

"I despise you both," Julia announced when the plates were cleared away. "Now do I get to know?"

"Very soon," Jasper told her.

"You're impossible!" she cried.

He just laughed and held out his hand. "Come on."

"Where are we going?"

"You are going to ring for a bonnet and a cloak, since it's a bit chilly today."

"It is not."

"It will be later this evening."

"Is this surprise is going to take that long?"

He kept silent.

"You're *still* not going to tell me?"

He led her down the halls, toward the foyer. "Your patience will be rewarded shortly."

What patience? "I don't believe you."

He just smiled. They stayed that way, standing in the middle of the foyer, him grinning and her glaring, during the entire wait for Nora. Of course, the maid wasn't about to let her disappear for hours on end without a fight. Before any of Julia's items were handed over, Nora insisted on strong-arming her into the parlor for a private discussion.

"You cannot go," the maid insisted.

"I can, and I will." The merits of Jasper's mystery adventure raised significantly in the face of Nora's disapproval.

"You'll miss the four o'clock schedule."

"Forget the bloody schedule."

"Lady Julia," Nora warned.

A normal day—that's all she was asking. One day where she didn't have to think about the various ways her body could disappoint her, but that wasn't Julia's life no matter how many Jaspers showed up to flirt with her. "What can we do?"

"You can stay here."

Julia scowled at Nora. "What *else* can we do?"

The maid stared at her for a long moment. With a sigh, she admitted, "We can do it now. That should hold you over until eight, but you must be back by then."

"Then let's get to it." Eight o'clock was ages away. She could have the whole afternoon and most of the evening with Jasper. When the schedule was appeased and Julia was properly bonneted with her cloak draped around her shoulders, she dispatched Nora and returned to Jasper and the foyer.

"Now what?" she asked.

"Now we walk twelve steps."

"Your big surprise is the driveway?" Julia was not impressed.

He gave her a sideways look, full of mischief. "My surprise is the high-perch phaeton in the driveway."

Something about the way he said it made her skin

start to tingle, but she wasn't ready to give in yet. "You mean *my* high-perch phaeton. The one I brought with me."

"The very same."

Sure enough, Julia's carriage was waiting at the bottom of the stairs, with her matched bays in the traces. "I take it we're going somewhere?"

"We are."

She let the last of her frustration go when Jasper handed her up into the driver's seat. It was difficult to stay cross with a man who had the sense to know no one else drove her phaeton. His hand brushed against her thigh with promise as he handed her the reins, and his excitement for the adventure started to transfer to her. Just because it wasn't her plan didn't mean it couldn't be fun. "Do I get any directions at all, or should I just strike out into the wilderness?"

He came around and vaulted into the seat beside her. "South, if it pleases you."

"If it doesn't?"

"I think it will."

There was that tingle again. Julia clicked to her horses, and they were off with a bouncing lurch of springs. The gravel of the drive crunched beneath the phaeton's wheels. Jasper leaned back against the upholstery and stretched his arm out behind her. She leaned into it, the closeness of him shifting her the last of the way toward accepting his mystery outing.

When they reached the road, Jasper gave her directions one turn at a time. Before long the breeze and the sunshine drained all concern from her about where they might be going. When he suggested she turn left at the fork heading into town, it came back in the form a dull ache in her stomach. "We're going to the fair."

"We are." There was that pleased look again. "Amelia mentioned they were having one, and I thought it might be nice to stroll around and make everyone wildly jealous."

"Amelia told you to take me to a fair?"

"She mentioned it in passing, but what could be better?" His smile was boyish in its utter delight. "I've never walked with a pretty girl at a fair. It seems a grave oversight, and I can think of no one better to correct it with."

The small relief Julia felt that her sister wasn't sabotaging her disappeared in the face of reality. "I'm not certain this is a good idea."

"Why not?"

What he described sounded lovely. Unfortunately, that wasn't how it would turn out. No one would be jealous watching Julia walk with her awkward gait. If she were lucky, they would only whisper and stare. If she weren't… "Isn't a small-town fair a little rustic for your tastes?"

"Nonsense. I enjoy mingling with the common man every now and then."

That made one of them. Still, he looked so pleased with himself. Julia didn't have the heart to ruin it. Perhaps a miracle would occur and no one would notice her at all. Maybe Jasper's presence would intimidate them too much for them to cause a scene. He did cut a very regal figure, even in the clothes he'd borrowed from Nicholas.

"Well, then." She pasted an exceedingly wide smile onto her face. "Let's mingle."

The village green was alive with activity. Temporary shops were set up in stalls arranged in haphazard order.

There were food vendors, trinket sellers, men who proclaimed their products could work miracles, and even a pair of competing Punch and Judy puppet shows. The livestock brought for trade were penned at one end, away from the games, and there was a large space in the center where men were challenging one other to various feats of athleticism.

Jasper threaded her fingers through his as they walked, and for a moment she thought everything might turn out all right. Then, about ten steps into the crowd, the first person stopped to stare at her. Five more, and two women leaned together whispering.

Jasper didn't appear to notice, making running commentary about the more aggressive hawkers and pointing out stalls that caught his attention. "Do you want a meat pie?"

"We just ate." A man pulled his child back as she passed and Julia cringed.

"Refreshment, then?"

"No, thank you."

"I've got it," he announced. "I'll win you a prize."

She smiled in spite of the other fairgoers. She squeezed his hand—the one that had never once tried to pull away from hers. "You really don't need to."

"I think I do. It's a requirement, when one goes walking at a fair with a beautiful woman, to exhibit proper displays of masculine aptitude."

"I think you're plenty apt, but I've heard those ring games are a cheat."

Jasper would not be deterred. Within moments, he was lobbing away at a trio of wooden targets. Julia cheered when he got the first target, losing herself in his determination. He was actually quite talented, and it wasn't long until he was bowing and presenting her with a folded paper flower. "Your prize, madam."

They moved to the next booth and Julia added an orange to their winnings when she correctly picked the fastest kitten in a race. People pointed and whispered when she walked away, but she kept her eyes firmly on Jasper's handsome profile. He'd braved the water for her and she would brave this for him. It was enjoyable, when she managed to block out everyone else. She managed it completely after Jasper towed her to the puppet show. He heckled the puppeteer until the man jumped up red faced and furious to tell him off, and Julia could hardly breathe from laughing when they were made to leave.

"Lord Bellamy, I'm beginning to think you spend more time at fairs than you let on."

"Nonsense. I am merely inspired to great heights by my lovely company."

The blush rose in her cheeks, but for once she didn't mind...until she noticed they were heading past a booth lauding its vast daguerreotype collection of freak show figures. The crowd was packed five deep with people waiting to step inside and ogle the unusual. *It never stops.* No one in that group was paying any attention to her, but the excitement of the day and the strain of so much attention caught up with her all at once. "I don't see how this day can get any better. Why don't we go back?"

"Already? I worked up quite a thirst enraging that puppeteer."

"Let's get a bottle of something and take it back to the phaeton, then. We could go for a drive." Evening was coming on, and getting lost on a quiet country lane with Jasper would be the perfect ending to the day.

They walked back in the direction of the vendors

hawking food. Jasper looked down at her and she smiled, but out of the corner of her eye she saw a child pointing. He saw it, too. Looking around, his frown turned into a scowl as he finally noticed how many people were paying undue attention to them.

His hand tightened on hers. "Of course. I don't need anything else. Let's go to the carriage."

Julia kept her chin high on the way back, even when the last couple they passed didn't bother keeping their voices lowered.

When they were ensconced back in the phaeton, she took the reins and let the road erase everything except her and Jasper. People were cruel and horrible, and they didn't deserve a moment of her distress. They weren't worth a bit of her time or happiness. The carriage flew down the country lanes, wind whipping her hair until she'd lost her bonnet and the pins. As the miles dissolved beneath them, she looked over to see Jasper's knuckles white on the wood of the phaeton.

Julia pulled off beside a bubbling creek and took a deep breath. She leaned back against the soft leather of the seat and watched the setting sun. The air was cool around them, breeze whispering through the leaves above them. When she looked back at him, Jasper was staring at her.

"I enjoy fresh air." Julia could feel herself blushing.

"I can tell." There was a huskiness to his voice that set her senses alight. "I'm sorry about today. I didn't realize it would be like that."

She smiled. "I had a nice time, actually. It was much more pleasant than I thought it would be."

"I'm glad, but I should have realized it might not be pleasant at all. I ruined the afternoon on the lake yesterday, too. It seems I can't do anything right around you."

"You didn't ruin anything. I'm just sorry I made you do it. I didn't realize—"

"That I would lie about being an expert rower?" His tone was wry.

"Why did you? If you'd told me you were afraid, I wouldn't have asked you to go."

"Why didn't you tell me why you didn't want to go to the fair?"

Touché. Julia looked out at the water glinting in the setting sun as it raced over the rocks.

He leaned back and plucked a leaf from a branch drooping near the edge of the carriage. "You make me wish things were different. That I was different. I wanted to be the sort of man who could have a romantic afternoon on the lake with you."

The same reason she'd let him take her to the fair. "The lake *was* romantic."

Jasper squinted at her. "It was a comedy of errors."

"Maybe a little," she admitted. "Why have you never learned to swim?"

"I'll tell you, but not today."

"Why not?"

"It's not a happy answer, and, if you'll let me, I still plan to salvage this excursion."

Julia looked around. They were in the middle of nowhere. "Are we going somewhere else?"

Jasper's lips curved up in the sensual, crooked way that set her pulse to racing. "Not that I know of."

"Do you…are you…"

His raised eyebrow teased her. "Am I what?"

"You're going to kiss me," Julia blurted.

He lifted her hand, pressing his lips to each knuckle in turn. "Am I? I thought I'd kissed you already."

It almost made her forget what she'd been trying to ask—almost. "You know what I mean. Not on my hands, or my cheek."

He tipped her chin up with his fingers, and then she really did forget everything she'd been trying to say.

Chapter Eight

He shouldn't be kissing her. Not today. The whole point had been to make up for ruining their rowing adventure — to give them both a day of lighthearted romance — but the fair had been even worse than the lake. He should have just taken them home. But Julia had taken it all in stride, walking down the green with the dignity of a queen. The plan was to take things deliciously, torturously slow between them, but Jasper didn't want to end their evening on a sour note, and he'd spent a great deal of time thinking about exactly how he would kiss her when the time came.

The first touch was whisper soft. Jasper brushed his mouth lightly across hers — once, twice. When she sighed, he leaned closer. The gentle resistance of her lips against his was exactly as he'd imagined it. Full, with just a little bit of challenge.

The taste of her drew him in. He chased its essence as his hands threaded through her hair and her chest pressed against his. He wanted more of it. He wanted all of it.

Julia's fingers dug into his shoulders, pulling him closer still until there was no space left between them. There was still *too much* space left between them. Jasper pulled her onto his lap.

"Is this all right?" They hadn't discussed the limits of their affair.

She answered by pulling his mouth back to hers.

Compared to the evening air, her hands were hot through the linen of his shirt. Everywhere she touched him, he burned. She shifted against his lap; searching for better angles, making demands. The padding of her skirts did nothing to lessen the delicious torture of feeling her move against him.

They needed to slow down. It would be all too easy to lose themselves in each other's bodies right here in this carriage. The press of her hips against his cock was already making him lose track of things he ought to be remembering.

The evening breeze teased their skin and the phaeton creaked beneath them as they explored each other with hands and mouths. Her hands slipped inside his jacket, molding to the lines of his abdomen through his shirt. He traced the edge of her bodice, dragging his fingertips along the smooth swells of her breasts. Her foot moved against his calf. He filled his hands with her hips, caressing the full curves

"Darling. Darling, wait." He framed her face with his hands. It was meant to keep her at bay, but he couldn't stop himself from dipping in and stealing another kiss. And another. She had the most tempting lips.

"You say 'wait,' but your kisses say 'come.'"

She had no idea. They said exactly that. Jasper would love to feel her come apart in his arms, brought to ecstasy from just his kiss.

He groaned. "We mustn't let ourselves—"

Julia put her hand on his thigh.

How was a man supposed to cling to reason with that kind of temptation? Every nerve in Jasper's body focused itself on that one point of connection. On the possibility. If her fingers shifted an inch… Jasper swore under his breath and gave up. Responsibility had never been his talent. "Just tell me when to stop."

Jasper twisted, leaning Julia back against the side of the carriage. His leg found a home between her thighs, the heat of her surrounding him and driving him mad with promise. Her skin was flushed from the perfect column of her neck to the soft swells of her breasts, pushing up over the neckline of her dress. He knelt down, teasing his tongue along the edge of her bodice. Julia shifted her hips against his thigh.

He lifted her arms, crossing them above her head. He dragged his fingertips down the length of her—elbows, arms, breasts, waist. At her hips, he tugged, pulling her tighter against him. The rise and fall of her chest hypnotized him. "You are exquisite."

"I *feel* exquisite," she answered.

"As you should, always."

The look in her eyes would haunt his dreams. She was the most sensual woman he had ever seen, and she still had every piece of her clothing on—which was for the best. Without their clothing, they were one deep breath away from Julia losing her virginity on the seat of a phaeton. While Jasper would like nothing more than to bury himself in her sweet heat and feel her shudder around him, he held himself to a higher standard than that.

"How do you feel?" She reached out, running her hand

up his thigh, closing her palm over his manhood.

Two things happened simultaneously. The first was delirious, aching pleasure. Every molecule of Jasper's being wanted to surge forward and bury itself against her. His hips did flex a little, pushing against her hand and reveling in the sweet pressure of her touch.

The second thing would have been comical, under different circumstances. Julia's gold-flecked eyes had widened as far as they could possibly go. The flush dropped out of her face, only to come back tenfold. Her body went stock-still.

An argument began within Jasper. Julia was an intelligent adult, capable of making her own decisions. She was clearly willing and she knew her own mind. Jasper had never been more willing in his life. By the normal standards of Jasper's moral code, there was no reason he shouldn't give in to what they both wanted. And yet.

She hadn't said stop, but she was clearly out of her depth. Jasper couldn't forgive himself if they moved too quickly. Julia deserved romance. She deserved to be certain—not moderately petrified. He wouldn't take her like this. Not in a hurry, on the side of a road.

Jasper lifted her hand by the wrist—cursing himself with every breath—and brought it to his lips. He kissed each fingertip, each line. Every crease and satin-soft inch of skin. "I think it's time for us to head back."

"What?" Julia pulled her arm away, coming back to life. "Why?"

"There is such a thing as too much of a good thing."

She shook her head. "That's ludicrous."

It was anathema to Jasper as well. He had committed his life to indulging in all things to the fullest. Choosing self-denial now was deeply disconcerting, but he had to do it. There was a great deal more seduction required before he could make love to Julia without feeling like he'd been careless with her. "I'm sorry. I think we should go back. Amelia and Nora are probably beside themselves with worry."

Coward. Using her sister and her maid as an excuse was a new low.

"I thought you were going to—we were going to—" She looked around, confusion creasing her brow. "You were going to make love to me."

He couldn't pretend she was mistaken. "It wouldn't have been right."

"Right according to who? Not me."

"I'm sorry. I just… I want to be a better man than this. Will you wait? Will you take it slow with me?"

It was not the image of Julia looking up at him with passion in her eyes that would haunt his dreams. It was the way she looked at him then, as if he'd betrayed her most sacred of trusts. "Fine."

He disentangled them, settling into the passenger seat and handing her the reins. Julia didn't speak to him again the entire drive back. He could tell himself she just needed to focus on the rapidly darkening road, but the stiffness of her shoulders and her mouth declared that a lie. He didn't attempt to make conversation.

They pulled up to the gray stone of Nicholas's country house in silence. She didn't wait for him to help her down, murmuring "good-night" as she climbed free of the phaeton.

"Good-night," he replied.

Jasper watched her hurry away from him with her uneven steps and disappear into the house and realized he had been correct about one thing. Doing "the right thing" felt exactly as unsatisfying as he'd always suspected it would.

*J*ulia barely saw the halls as she stumbled down them. Thankfully, most of the house had retired for the evening. Tears filled her eyes and distorted everything around her. It didn't matter—she knew where she was going. All she had to do was hold in her emotions until she could get there. The door to Amelia's bedroom appeared through the watery haze. Julia pushed it open without bothering to knock. The strip of light coming through the open door fell across the bed, lighting up Mia's face.

"If Nicholas is in here, I hope he has clothes on," Julia said.

"Why would I?" Nicholas growled from under the covers on Amelia's other side. "I am sleeping with my wife."

Julia turned her back to them. *Don't cry yet. Not yet.*

There was a muffled discussion that escalated into a muffled argument. It ended with Nicholas putting on a dressing gown and announcing, "I guess I'm sleeping in my own room, then."

"I love you," Amelia called after him.

Julia didn't catch his reply. When he was gone, she kicked off her shoes and climbed onto the bed next to her sister.

"I'm also naked," Amelia warned.

"You, I can handle." Still, Julia stayed above the covers all the same. She scooted herself in next to the lump that was her sister.

Amelia shifted until they were nose to nose. "What's wrong?"

Then, they came. A flood of tears followed by great, gulping sobs. She couldn't stop them. She didn't even understand them. Jasper hadn't wanted to make to love to her—he was hardly the first. Most men didn't even bother to speak with her. It shouldn't matter so much.

"Jules? Tell me."

"We were kissing, and it was wonderful, and I wanted more and he just kept kissing…so, I touched him."

Amelia's hand came out of the covers to rub the sleep out of her eyes. "Touched him how?"

Julia gave her sister a look. "Do I ever do anything in half measures?"

"Oh my God." Mia buried her face. "Then what happened?"

"He told me we should go home."

"No!"

"Yes. He even used you and Nora as an excuse." No matter how convincingly he claimed to want her, he obviously didn't. Otherwise she wouldn't be lying next to her sister right now. "Why doesn't he want me, Mia? I know he likes me."

Amelia's eyes narrowed in thought. "When you touched him, how did it feel?"

"It felt natural. It felt like the right time to make my intentions known and—"

"Not philosophically," Amelia interrupted. "I mean, what did *it* feel like?"

"Mia!"

"What! If it was hard, he was…enjoying himself. Was it?"

"Yes."

"But he stopped you."

"Yes."

Amelia thought about that for a moment. "Did he say why?"

It was enough to make Julia want to scream. "He said

it wouldn't be right and that he wanted to be a better man, whatever that means."

Mia's lips curled into a ridiculous smile. "It means a great deal."

"Oh, come off it—both you and him." Julia flopped onto her back, staring up at the darkened ceiling. "It's lovely to *say* I deserve some kind of storybook romance, but if I have to wait for the circumstances to be perfect, I'm not going to end up with any romance at all."

"That's not true."

"Oh, really? Am I sprawled out naked with a handsome viscount right now?"

"That's not the only kind of romance." Amelia pushed herself up into a sitting position, holding the coverlet to her chest. "Did you enjoy the evening before that?"

Julia was aware of what her sister was trying to do, and she refused to play along. "I'm going to die a virgin."

"He cares for you, and he's attracted to you. He *wants* to sleep with you. If that's what you want, too, then find out what's stopping him and fix it."

Julia punched at the pillows behind her head, plumping them. "I came in here to bawl my eyes out and slander Jasper, not be given sound advice."

Amelia laughed. "My apologies. How dare he respect and care about you—the bastard."

"That's more like it."

"May I have my bed back now?" Amelia asked. "If the crisis is past, I'd like to release my husband from his exile."

Julia wasn't quite ready to leave yet. "How would you do it?"

"Seduce Jasper? Well for starters, I wouldn't have married Nick." Amelia dodged her sister's elbow, giggling at her own imagined cleverness.

"I don't want to seduce him. I want him to seduce me, but if I *had* to be the one to do it—how would I go about it?"

"Are you certain that's what you want?"

Julia's brow furrowed. "Why wouldn't I?"

Amelia sighed. "Well, for one thing, making love means getting undressed in front of him. You barely let Nora see you without stockings and a dressing gown, and dressing you is her job."

Being naked with Jasper. Being naked *in front* of Jasper. Julia's arms crossed over her chest. "People make love with their clothes on."

"Not people like Jasper. Jules, if you're not ready—"

"I'll figure something out." If she had to, she'd find a way, but Amelia was wrong. They'd practically made love tonight, and all their clothes had been in place. Something could certainly be managed. She could make it fun—like a game. "You said 'for one thing'. What else?"

It was Amelia's turn to become uncomfortable.

The silence stretched out while Julia waited for an answer. "Mia?"

"Some of his tastes might be…" Amelia's hand rose, as if she could pluck the word she was looking for from the air. "Advanced. I wouldn't want you to get in over your head."

Julia raised her eyebrows. "What if my tastes are also advanced?"

She *had* to convince Jasper to make love to her. There might not be another chance.

"Then, I suppose, keep doing what you're doing," Amelia said. "A week ago, you hadn't even met him. Now you're groping each other in carriages. I'd say things are headed in a desirable direction."

The weariness in Amelia's tone meant that was all the

advice she was willing to dole out at the moment. Julia sat up and slid off the bed. "You can have your husband back now."

Her sister answered with a happy hum.

Julia closed the door and started the long walk to her bedroom, taking a circuitous route to avoid passing by Jasper's door. The thick carpet runner muffled her steps as she wandered through the darkened hallways. Her relationship with Jasper had progressed quickly, but it wasn't quick enough for Julia. He'd admitted to coming here for an escape, and his lack of luggage implied he hadn't exactly had a plan when he decided to come. Any moment, something could call him back to London and she'd miss her chance. He'd already admitted he didn't know what would remain between them when that happened.

It wasn't just the chance she'd miss. These last few days with Jasper had been some of the most delightful days of her life. Not everything had gone to plan, but, compared to her usual routine, her time with Jasper was downright magical.

She had to convince him to stop putting limits on their time together. They only had so much of it, and Julia wasn't willing to miss out on anything.

Chapter Nine

Julia did not come down for breakfast. She was noticeably absent around the house all morning, and Jasper heard a rumor she'd taken the midday meal in her room. She'd been upset last night—reasonably so—but in the clear light of morning, with their passions cooled, Jasper had hoped to be able to have a more detailed conversation with her about it. Instead, he spent his day stuck with Nicholas, who had nothing nice to say to anyone.

"Have we lost Amelia, as well?" Jasper asked, tossing his book onto the sofa cushion beside him. There was dismally little to do in the country without one of the Bishop sisters to breathe life into the mundane.

Nicholas did the same, abandoning his heavy legal tome and leaning back against the armchair he'd taken by the fire. "Probably. Any time Julia has a crisis, all our lives skid to a halt."

"A crisis? What happened?"

"You tell me. When Julia came back from your drive, I

got ousted from my bed and my wife has been distracted ever since."

Jasper was the crisis. Of course. It was hardly the first time, but it was only one of a handful of times he felt truly awful about it.

They fell back to silence until the butler arrived looking more straight-backed than usual. "Lord Wakefield, Lady Ruby DeVere has just arrived. I wasn't told to expect her, but under the circumstances, I've had her luggage taken upstairs. I hope that is acceptable."

Oh, hell. It was not acceptable to Jasper. He closed his eyes and assessed his options.

"Of course. Thank you, Winslow. Did she go up with her luggage or is she waiting?" Nick asked.

"She asked me to see if you were otherwise occupied."

"Show her in, please." When the butler left, Nick turned to Jasper. "Did you know your sister was coming?"

"No." Perhaps, if he left the drawing room immediately, he could slip out and be clear of the house by the time she entered.

"Jasper." His sister's perfectly articulated consonants cut through the room. "I have to say, I'm disappointed."

Too late.

Nicholas jumped up at her entrance. "Lady Ruby."

Jasper resigned himself to the situation, but remained seated. "I would expect no less, dear sister."

The true heir—to anyone who paid attention—of the Albemarle legacy came into view in a perfectly tailored traveling gown of cream and apricot stripes. It was impeccable, just like her dark-sable coiffure. In spite of himself, Jasper admired that. Even on what must have been a hastily planned trip out of London, his sister never let her armor slip.

Ruby smiled at their host. "Nicholas. I'd say it's a pleasure to see you, but under the circumstances I'm afraid I cannot."

"Circumstances?" Nick asked.

Ruby turned a raised eyebrow in Jasper's direction as she took the chair Nick offered. "Have you managed to leave your friend in the dark?"

He'd have liked to leave him in the dark a little while longer.

"He's been traveling." Jasper pinched the bridge of his nose to preempt the headache he knew would start building any moment. "I told you not to look for me, Ruby."

"Fortunately, I don't answer to you." Ruby turned back to Nicholas. "Our grandfather passed. Jasper is the Duke of Albemarle now, but rather than face it, he has chosen to run here and pretend that nothing has changed."

Nicholas froze in the middle of resuming his own seat. "Jas?"

"I didn't want to talk about it." Or think about it. He just wanted to find a nice quiet room—hell, even a boathouse— to disappear with Julia and forget about the world.

He just wanted time to deal with it before he had to accept it.

"Would you mind if I had a few moments alone with my brother?" Ruby smiled at Nicholas. It was not a comforting smile. Neither was the request. Lady Ruby DeVere never caused a scene. Politely asking Nicholas for a private moment was a premeditated maneuver designed to allow Ruby to speak freely. Free Ruby was a terrifying creature to be at odds with.

"I'll give you a thousand pounds to stay, Nick."

Nicholas stood up. "I do not need your money, and I

rather suspect you deserve whatever she means to say to you, Jas."

Traitor. Nicholas bid good day to Ruby and left Jasper alone with his twin.

"You walked out on the queen," she whispered through clenched teeth as soon as the door closed. As if the words were too foul to be said at full volume. "You walked out on *me*."

The second part was the only part Jasper cared about, but even if he might change the way he'd gone about it, he couldn't take it back now. "The queen will survive. As will the dukedom."

A muscle in Ruby's jaw twitched. "How would you know? How would you have any idea what it takes to run an estate the size of ours, or what it can survive?"

"It'll manage. It's been around for centuries, and we both know you've been doing most of it for years anyway."

"The estate runs under the careful stewardship of men who trained for decades to carry the weight of that responsibility!" Ruby leaped up, bristling with unrest as she paced the floor. No doubt she'd been stewing every minute that had passed since he rode away from her at Parliament. "You should have been learning from him as soon as we left the schoolroom, but he went easy on you—"

"He went easy on both of us."

She pressed her fingers hard against her forehead and took a breath. "How many acres of farmland are going unplanted because the Duke of Albemarle hasn't decided what to plant or which fields to leave fallow?"

Now she was just being ridiculous. "Surely there's someone who handles—"

"Sixty thousand," she announced, cutting him off. "Enough to send England into a famine when those crops aren't harvested in the fall. That's how important it is. That's why a duke decides."

A thread of worry—or maybe it was guilt—began tugging at him. "See, I knew you've been handling it."

"It is supposed to be handled by you!"

And that was the reality. They didn't need Jasper. They only wanted him because tradition dictated that the duke should preside over the decisions. He had no expertise to offer. He was not in any way qualified, and the idea of sitting at his grandfather's desk, making the decisions his grandfather used to make, was too much. Jasper wasn't ready to face it yet. He needed more time.

"No."

"What?" The pause had thrown momentarily Ruby off her tirade.

"If it's that important to England, do it without me. Whatever you decide is fine."

She bent toward him, their twin faces inches apart as she punctuated every syllable. "This is not *my* responsibility. I am not the heir. I cannot inherit the dukedom. This is something you have to do yourself."

"Then it won't be done."

It was a shame Ruby couldn't inherit. She would have made an excellent Duke of Albemarle. While Jasper had devoted his life to fleeting pleasures that distracted him from memories he didn't want to recall, Ruby had thrown herself wholeheartedly into the family legacy. She had the decades of training by his grandfather's side, and she had the will to use it. But the dukedom didn't just need a figurehead to sacrifice on the altar of duty—it needed a *male* figurehead.

"What do you want?" she asked abruptly. "What will it take to get you to do this?"

"Time."

It was the one answer she didn't want to hear, but it was the only honest one Jasper could give. In time, the pain of losing their grandfather—the greatest man Jasper had ever known—would fade a bit. He'd be able to sit still without wanting to smash everything in a room. He would be able to unpack the memories without the need to scream at God and the universe trying to tear its way free of his throat.

"Time is the one thing I can't give you," Ruby answered. "If I thought it would just be a week, or a month…"

But it wouldn't be. Jasper had run from his parents' deaths for years. He was a boy of six when the accident happened, and a man in his twenties before he could take a breath without the weight of what he'd lost pressing in on him. Ruby knew. She'd spent her whole life watching him run.

"I can't be the duke Grandfather was."

"It doesn't matter. Just be the duke you can be."

The Duke of Albemarle was a leader of the British Empire. One of the finest titles held by one of the finest families in the finest country in the world. Jasper would not sully generations of great men by doing the job badly. Better that he stay Viscount Bellamy and leave it vacant. He couldn't disgrace the Dukes of Albemarle if he never took the title.

Ruby's chin lifted and her shoulders squared. "You will accept your responsibility. Until you do, I will be here—dogging your steps day and night."

It was the last thing Jasper needed. He was trying to forget, but Ruby would insist on reminding him every chance she got.

"You can't stay," he told her.

"You're not in charge of that decision."

And Nicholas would side with her, damn him.

"Then I'll leave." Jasper stood up, intending to do exactly that.

"I'll follow," Ruby promised.

He tried one last tactic. "Grandmother is grieving."

"Grandmother told me to come. She told me not to return without you." Ruby's voice broke a little on the last bit.

What a sad pair they were. Jasper was content to be left alone, to pursue his life on his own terms. Ruby dedicated her life to being a perfect lady and a dutiful member of their family. If she were more like him, they would all be lost.

"I can't give you what you want, Ruby."

"I think you can."

There was nothing left to say. She would hold her ground and he would hold his. It was one of few things they shared besides their looks—stubbornness. Jasper turned to go, intending to change into riding clothes and find Julia for a much-needed diversion.

Ruby followed.

He left the drawing room and went up the stairs, and she was still on his heels. "Surely you don't mean to literally follow me through this house."

"It seems the surest way to make sure you don't disappear again."

The sympathy he'd felt faded and irritation took its place. "I'm going to my room to change. I think you can ease off a little."

Ruby smirked. "It would hardly be the first bedroom window you've snuck out of."

So be it. If she thought she could embarrass or annoy him into coming home with her, she was sadly mistaken.

He opened the door to his room—and stopped short.

Laid out across his bed, in stockings and a whisper-thin chemise, was Julia. Her hair was loose, spilling across his pillows, and the dressing gown she'd no doubt worn on her trek through the halls was draped across her feet. She was stunning.

She also had horrible timing.

Behind him, Ruby cleared her throat. Jasper lifted his arms, trying to block her view and afford Julia some measure of privacy, but it was too late. Julia's face lost all color and she jumped to drag the dressing gown over her body.

Ruby's tone was the coldest he'd ever heard from his sister. "I almost believed your sad story about needing time. Tell me, did you find someone to warm your bed *after* you ran away from inheriting the dukedom, or were you running to her the whole time?"

"Ruby—" Jasper turned, trying to explain.

"I bet you told *her* you're the Duke of Albemarle. How else would you get a well-bred woman to play your whore?"

"Julia isn't—"

"Jasper?" Julia's shaky tone came from just over his shoulder.

Shit. He spun again. "I wasn't keeping my title from you. I just…wasn't ready to talk about it."

Julia nodded. He couldn't take his eyes off her, or the unnatural stillness she'd achieved.

"Isn't what?" Ruby continued, oblivious to the fact that she was no longer Jasper's primary concern. "Isn't well-bred? I wouldn't think Amelia would let you install some trollop in her house, but who knows with the kinds of company you keep."

While he watched, Julia took a deep breath and stepped

around him. "My name is Julia Bishop. I assume you're Jasper's sister, Lady Ruby?"

Ruby blinked. "I am."

"It's lovely to meet you. I'm sure you and your brother have a great deal to catch up on, so I'll leave you to it." Julia gave them both an overly wide smile and pushed past Ruby out into the hall.

Jasper moved to do the same. "Julia—"

"Let her go." Ruby grabbed his arm. "Unless you want me following you and extending this despicable drama to the entire household."

For Julia's sake, he stayed, but his mind was racing. She'd forgiven him for last night, that much was clear. God, she looked delectable in that chemise, but he'd ruined it— just like he'd ruined every other overture Julia had made.

"I suppose I shouldn't be surprised," Ruby was saying. "Philandering is your chosen method of dealing with grief— or anything else for that matter."

Jasper didn't answer, his attention still on the place where Julia had disappeared around a corner. Her quiet, shaky 'Jasper' echoed in his ears. She'd needed something from him, some kind of assurance, and he hadn't been able to give it to her. He couldn't give any of them what they needed. He wasn't enough.

"I can't go down there." Julia tossed yet another dress onto the floor. "I can't."

Amelia picked it up and handed it back to Nora. "Unless you can develop a legitimate malady in the next five minutes, you have to."

"I have a permanent legitimate malady."

"One that you haven't insisted for your entire life doesn't stop you from doing anything."

Julia rejected another dress. It was futile to even look—she didn't own anything appropriate for dinner with the sister of a Duke. Especially not one who had just witnessed her utter humiliation.

"I think you'll like each other," Amelia encouraged. "You were afraid to meet Jasper, and look how well that's gone."

Oh, God. "Lady Ruby and I have met."

"You have? When?"

"Earlier this afternoon."

Amelia beamed. "See, then. There's nothing to be nervous about."

"When I was sprawled across Jasper's bed in my underclothes." Julia squeezed her eyes shut, unwilling to witness her sister's reaction.

The *whoosh* of skirts as Amelia sat down suddenly was unmistakable. As was the strain in her tone. "Oh, Jules. In front of a duchess's granddaughter?"

Julia abandoned the dress hunt and sat next to Amelia on the bed, letting herself fall backward against the mattress. "Obviously, I didn't expect her to be there."

"When I suggested you keep doing what you've been doing—"

"Don't. I feel ridiculous enough already. I don't need a lecture."

The expression on his face when he came through the door would have been less shocked if she'd slapped him. Up until that moment, Julia had imagined the worst thing that could happen would be for him to politely suggest she put some clothes on, and send her on her way. The rejection would have been devastating, but she'd prepared herself for the possibility.

Oh, how her imagination had failed her.

Not once had she considered that a member of his family would be with him. That she would meet his *sister* while frantically trying to cover herself. Not to mention the other thing.

"He's a duke, Mia."

"Nick told me." Amelia laid back and rolled onto her side. "Does that change things for you?"

No. *Yes.* Julia resisted the urge to roll and face Amelia. If she did that, her sister would know. The distance between Julia and Jasper's stations was not small, but when he'd been just a Viscount, she could pretend that it wasn't insurmountable. She was an earl's daughter, after all, if an unpopular one. It was not so far of a leap.

If she admitted that, she would have to admit that she'd thought about the leap. That she'd allowed herself to consider the possibility of something more than temporary. She hadn't considered it for long, or with any sort of seriousness, but she had considered it—and now he was a duke. The distance between them was impossibly vast.

"I'd make a terrible duchess," Julia answered.

"I think you'd make an incredible duchess," Amelia retorted. "You're already vain and spoiled. Imagine what you'd do with some power."

"Invade the continent, probably."

"I've always wanted to own France." Amelia laid her hand on Julia's shoulder, but Julia shrugged it off.

It would take more than banter to undo the events of the day.

"What am I going to do, Mia?"

Amelia pushed herself up off the bed. "For starters,

you're going to get dressed. Once you look suitably fabulous, you're going to do the only thing you can do— brazen through it and be amazing."

Easier said than done.

Amelia held up a mass of midnight satin. "When were you expecting to need this?"

"You never know."

Mia considered it. "It's pretty. You could—"

Julia sat up, taking the dress from her and handed it to Nora. "I can manage on my own. Why don't you go get dressed?"

Amelia looked down. "I am dressed."

Oh, good heavens. "Do you even have a lady's maid? Nora, go with Mia. Find her something suitable, and don't listen to any of her protests. She has never paid any attention to fashion."

Once they were gone, Julia assessed her wardrobe with a critical eye. Nothing would erase the impression she'd already made, so the question was—did she want to apologize for it or flaunt it? She pulled out a dress in deep green. As ball gowns went, it bordered on the simple, and it had a somber feel. It was the sort of demure choice she *ought* to make.

Julia set it aside, returning to the black. It was an impractical dress; too immodest to be appropriate for mourning, too *black* to be appropriate for anything else. She'd commissioned it in a flight of fancy, imagining herself entering a ball to whispers behind fans, with black silk and white diamonds flashing in a feminine mimicry of the men's eveningwear.

It was the sort of dress a mistress would order.

She was still holding it when Nora returned with a quiet close of the door. "All sorted, my lady. She's got a nice gold chiffon that's never seen the light of day. It's perfect."

"I've decided on the midnight silk. And diamonds. Lots of diamonds. We can borrow some from Mia if we didn't bring enough."

Nora opened her mouth, but closed it again without saying something. She stayed silent the entire time she helped Julia dress and pin her hair. By the time Julia was adding the diamond drops to her ears and Nora was securing the clasp on the five-row necklace, Julia couldn't take it anymore.

"Whatever you want to say, just say it."

"I don't need to," Nora answered. "You already know."

Julia turned to face her instead of continuing their conversation via the mirror. "This is the path I've chosen, Nora."

The maid's hands stilled against her shoulders. "Because you want it, or because you think it's the only path open to you?"

It was Julia's turn to be robbed of words. It was an unkind question when it *was* the only path open to her, and Julia refused to be ashamed of her willingness to take it. "Thank you, Nora. That will be all for tonight."

She wasted a bit more time checking and rechecking her hair in the mirror to make sure she would arrive just before dinner was announced and save herself from as much of the necessary cocktail conversation as possible. When the chimes of the clock rang out, it was time to make her entrance.

There were no fans and no whispering, but the conversation in the drawing room lurched to a halt when Julia stepped inside. Nicholas raised his eyebrow at her and Amelia had to struggle to hide her smile, but it wasn't their reactions Julia was looking for. Lady Ruby's expression had gone curiously blank, except for a slight widening of her eyes, and Jasper... Jasper looked like he wanted to devour her.

It gave Julia the confidence she needed to smile. "I apologize for my lateness. What did I miss?"

Nicholas crossed the room and handed her a drink. Under his breath, he said, "Are you up to something, Bishop?"

"Perhaps I am."

The door opened and Winslow saved her from further inquiries. "Dinner is served, my lord."

Nicholas offered his arm to Lady Ruby, and Amelia winked at Julia as she followed them out. That left Julia and Jasper to go into dinner together. He offered her his arm but, instead of taking it, Julia pushed the door closed.

"About earlier," he started to say.

Julia pressed a gloved fingertip to his mouth. She traced the edges of his lips, watching them part under her attention. "Now is not the time, but we do have things to talk about."

"We do."

"Tonight, after everyone else goes to bed."

The rise and fall of his chest underneath his jacket picked up pace. "Julia—"

"Tell me I look nice, Jasper."

He stepped forward, circling his hands around her waist. "You look ravishing."

They leaned into each other, midnight silk brushing against the black velvet of his dinner jacket. Julia stood up on the tips of her toes, just high enough to reach his bottom lip. She took it between her teeth and tugged, scraping it gently as she pulled away.

"Now take me into dinner," she ordered.

His hands tightened on her waist, and she thought he might refuse. To be honest, she hoped for it. She hoped he would say "dinner be damned," push her up against the door, and finish what they'd started in the carriage. But instead he took a deep breath that he let out in a half laugh, half moan and did as she asked.

Just before they reached the dining room, Jasper leaned down and kissed the delicate skin beneath her ear. "Until later," he whispered

It sent a shiver of anticipation across her skin, but for once she didn't blush.

"Everything all right?" Nicholas asked when they entered.

Julia smiled. "Just a bit of trouble with the clasp on my necklace."

Lady Ruby arched an eyebrow. "It's a Rundell, isn't it?"

"It is. Thank you for noticing." *I might be your brother's trollop, but my jewelry has a pedigree at least as good as yours.*

"I have a few pieces from Rundell and Bridge, but I've never known them to have faulty clasps."

Julia let the footman pull out her chair while she thought of her response—and realized that she didn't need one. Let Ruby imply whatever she liked. Hell, let her suspect the truth, if it pleased her. Julia picked up her wineglass, smiling at Jasper's sister over its edge, and said nothing.

Ruby frowned, but didn't pursue an answer. She turned and struck up a conversation with Nicholas instead. Julia gave a silent cheer. She could do this. She could play the part of the shameless mistress. If she was honest, it was exhilarating.

Unfortunately, fate had other plans for Julia. As the

footman placed a bowl of soup in front of her, a familiar ache started behind Julia's eyes and up the back of her spine. It was terrible timing for so many reasons. She needed to be bold. She needed to be in control. She needed to *not* collapse in agony while Jasper's judgmental sister looked on with interest. Why couldn't there be just one bloody day where none of her problems revolved around her health?

Julia pressed her fingers to her temples, trying to will away the oncoming migraine. It had never worked before, and it wasn't working now. She pushed her chair back, mumbling her excuses and stumbling out into the hall before she embarrassed herself twice in one day.

The door opened and closed behind her.

"I'll be fine, Mia."

Jasper's voice sounded behind her. "What's wrong?"

Of course. It was foolish to think she'd be allowed to maintain an air of sophistication for even an hour. "Go back in to dinner. It's nothing."

The pain buckled her knees, and she grabbed the wall for support.

Jasper was there in an instant, wrapping his arms around her. "It doesn't look like nothing."

So much for her brief role as a temptress. "It's a migraine. They're a side effect of my condition."

"What can I do?"

The pain brought nausea with it, forcing her to breathe deeply and steadily to keep it under control. "Help me get to my room."

Together they traversed the stairs and down the halls that led to Julia's room. After she was ensconced in the shadowy haven of her bed, he leaned close. "Are you comfortable? What do you need?"

Too many things, none of which were in his power to give. "Just Nora, and then you should go back down to dinner before you're missed."

"I don't care about being missed."

Another wave of stabbing pain, and the accompanying nausea, rolled over her. When she could open her eyes again, Jasper's face was hovering over hers with concern. She tried to set him at ease, but she could tell it wasn't successful.

"I think I'm going to need to postpone our talk." If only she had told him to take her against the door instead of taking her into dinner. It could be days before she had another chance.

He pressed his hand to her cheek. "I'll be waiting."

Chapter Ten

The following day was unbearable. Jasper had nothing to do but wait, feeling completely helpless, while Julia continued to suffer through whatever had befallen her. Amelia said it was just a headache, albeit a strong one, but Jasper had never seen a headache that could buckle someone's knees.

To make matters worse, Ruby was still following him like a diligent debt collector.

"Go away, Ruby."

"Go home, Jasper."

He sighed, tossing the morning paper onto the cushion. He didn't care what was going on in London or the world—he cared about what was going on upstairs. About when Julia would be all right again.

"You like her, don't you?" Ruby was peering at him from the opposite sofa, making no pretense of having anything else to do besides stalk him.

"Of course I like her." What an asinine thing to say. Julia was very likeable. And delectable, when she wasn't being brought low by some unseen force. Even when she was, really, but it was hardly the right time to appreciate her finer physical features.

"Bring her with you, then."

Jasper's eyebrows rose, and he focused his full attention on Ruby. "Excuse me?"

"If she's what you need to help you accept grandfather's passing, bring her with you. She certainly has the spirit to be your mistress." Ruby leaned forward. "I'll even smooth the way for her in town, if you'll come back."

If it was anyone else, Ruby's offer would be intriguing. But because it was Julia, Jasper's hand clenched of its own accord. "You will not speak of Julia with disrespect."

"On the contrary, the fact that I think she can keep your interest is one of my higher compliments."

"It's not like that."

Ruby laughed. "It's always like that with you. If they're attractive and at all clever, you can't help yourself."

It wasn't true. Maybe it had been, but it wasn't true anymore. Jasper had helped himself, against all odds. There was more to him and Julia than the usual thing. How much more, he still wasn't entirely certain—but he knew enough to know it was different.

Suddenly, he couldn't stay in Ruby's company a moment longer. All his nerves were on edge and his patience was stretched far too thin. If he didn't get out of this room and out of this house, he was going to break something or say something he regretted. He stood up and Ruby stood up to follow him.

"Ruby, I swear to God, if you don't give me some time to myself, I will not be held responsible for what happens."

She stopped. "Promise me you're not going to disappear."

"As if my promise means anything to anyone." As if he had any intention of leaving Julia without any explanation.

"Promise it," she insisted.

"I promise."

As Jasper passed into the hallway, Nick was coming the other direction. "Jasper. Perfect. Put on riding clothes. We're going out."

"We are?"

"We are. Don't argue, just do it."

It suited Jasper fine. He let Nick call for the horses to be saddled while he bounded upstairs to change his clothes. As furious as Ruby was, she hadn't been too furious to bring some of his own belongings with her. Jasper was back down in the foyer in record time, leading Nick out into the drive.

"If I didn't know better, I'd think this ride was your idea," Nicholas joked as he struggled to keep up.

"I'm tired of being stuck inside." Jasper hustled them out the door and onto their waiting horses. He couldn't help the sensation of the walls closing in around him. He needed to be out and moving. He needed to be on an adventure. "Are we going anywhere in particular?"

"I thought we could just ride for a while—and talk."

Jasper's hands clenched on the reins. There were only two things Nick could want to talk about. One of them was lying upstairs, possibly in agony. The other, Jasper had no intention of talking about. "Let's go to Woodley. They have a pub, don't they?"

"Yes, but—"

With a nudge, Jasper urged his mount into a sprint, but it made no difference. Racing at top speed didn't soothe him the way it did to Julia.

Hooves thundered and then slowed as Nicholas caught up to him. "I assume you did that because you know we can't talk at a gallop, and you're trying to pretend everything is fine."

Jasper avoided Nicholas's eyes. "Everything is fine."

"The hell it is. No one has ever been in this big of a hurry to get to Woodley, least of all you." Nick stopped his horse in the middle of the road. "What is the matter?"

"Nothing. I just need…I need…" He didn't know what he needed.

"Your grandfather died."

It dropped like a cannonball between them. Jasper stared down the road without really seeing anything.

"You're not handling it well."

Clearly. "Is there a good way to handle it?"

"Probably." Nick directed his horse forward, filling Jasper's view. "If there is, this isn't it."

Jasper scrubbed his hand over his face. "I can't do it, Nick. I'm not ready to be him."

"No one ever is."

The pity in his furrowed brow was too much. Jasper nudged his mount around Nick's and started down the road again.

Nick kept pace with him. "I wasn't ready when I found out my father was losing his mind."

"It's not the same. You have your brother, Phillip."

"The same way Ruby has you."

Not the same — at all. Phillip Wakefield was a paragon of lordly virtues. Jasper DeVere was a reprobate, and that was only when the people doing the labeling were feeling kind.

A cricket chirped on the roadside, punctuating Jasper's refusal to continue that line of conversation. Eventually, Nick asked, "Why Woodley?"

"I feel like getting into a fight." It was the truth. He couldn't do anything about his grandfather. He couldn't get his sister to leave him alone. He couldn't help Julia. He couldn't do anything worthwhile, but Jasper *could* coerce someone twice his size into taking a swing at him so he didn't have to think about any of it.

"Don't you normally get yourself out of these moods by—" His horse stopped. Nick turned it again so he could see Jasper's face. "That's it, isn't it? Normally, you'd find someone to disappear with for a few days and get it out of your system…"

"But the person I want to disappear with is Julia. Even if you and Amelia would accept that, Ruby would find a way to follow me."

Nick closed his eyes, shaking his head. "Again, why Woodley? I'm a respectable landowner in this county now. We can't just go around causing trouble."

Jasper clucked both of their horses back into motion toward Woodley. "Did Julia tell you about our visit to the fair?"

The pause before Nick's answer stretched out. "She didn't have to."

Right. Nick had grown up with the Bishop daughters. He'd probably seen plenty of abhorrent townsfolk behavior.

"How did you handle it?" Jasper asked.

"Ignored it, when we could. Tried to use the Wakefield name as a buffer, when I could." Nick looked at him. "How did you handle it?"

"Well," Jasper looked down the road where Woodley was just coming into view. "I stewed over it for a day or two, and now I've drafted my best friend into heading back with me to pick a fight."

Nick turned his focus to the end of the road. "After we've done that, you're going to talk to me about your grandfather."

"All right." As they drew up in front of Woodley's premier—and only—drinking establishment, Jasper silently prayed to get knocked unconscious before that happened.

"How do you feel?"

"Like I'm in a cloud." Julia kept her eyes closed. There was a very real possibility if she opened them, her headache would come back. After many agonizing hours, she'd managed to restrict her world to the fluffy down of the pillow and the soothing coolness of Amelia's silk sheets. "How do *you* feel?"

Amelia brushed the hair away from her face. "Soft white sheep cloud or storm cloud?"

She cracked one eye, just barely. "Dense. Gray. But I don't think it will rain."

"Do you think there will be clear skies in a few hours?" Amelia gave her an overly wide smile.

Julia was immediately suspicious. "Why?"

"We've been invited for dinner." The mattress bounced as Amelia turned to face her. "By the Hathaways. Please don't make me go alone."

"Who are the Hathaways?"

"Apparently, they're our neighbors."

"And they invited you for dinner?"

"Us. All of us. But if you're not feeling well enough, we can stay home."

Julia opened both of her eyes. The apocalypse didn't immediately descend upon her bedroom. "We can go. They really invited us? By name? Did they say why?"

"To welcome us to the area."

"Well, that's friendly."

The sheets rustled as Amelia burrowed her way farther into the bed. "It's odd, is what it is. I thought our bad reputation and my bad behavior while I was engaged to Montrose would save me from this sort of thing."

"You're impossible."

"But you'll come?"

"Of course I'll come." A log on the fire popped, and it miraculously did not send pain shooting through Julia's temples. She really was feeling better. "I can't turn down my first-ever invitation to a dinner party. What sort of message would that send?"

"The blissfully antisocial kind? Come on, Jules. Pretend to be sick for me."

Julia threw back the covers, pulling them away from Amelia in the process. "Go away. I have a dinner party to plan for."

"Are you certain? You've missed a great deal of excitement due to your headache. But if you'd rather not hear about it—"

Julia turned, unable to resist gossip. "What? What is it?"

"For starters, the entire staff knows Lady Ruby DeVere thinks you're a harlot."

"What!"

"Hand of God," Amelia answered, raising her own in an oath. "That nosey upstairs maid I hired heard the shouting when you were in his room."

Bloody typical. "One more reputation I don't deserve."

"You deserve it a little."

"I'd like to deserve it all the way, or not at all."

Amelia nudged her. "It gets better. This morning, she tried to bargain with Jasper by offering to sponsor you in London as his mistress."

"That can't be true." Julia would bet all her pin money that Ruby DeVere would like nothing more than to never see her again.

"It is. I had that from a very reliable downstairs source."

In Nora's absence, Julia got up and went to open the windows herself. A soft breeze blew through the room, sending the curtains swaying and taking the sickbed feeling of the room away with it.

"Of course, hearsay has blown it way out of proportion," Amelia admitted. "I caught a scullery maid telling the cook you were *already* Jasper's mistress, and that's why he came out here in the first place."

Julia was only half listening. All this talk of mistresses reminded her she'd been on the verge of something very promising with Jasper before they'd gone in to dinner. If not for her headache, some of those rumors might have come true last night.

"Stop it," Amelia said.

"Stop what?"

"You're looking gloomy."

"Maybe this is just the face all wrongfully accused harlots wear."

"Speaking of harlots, last night Nicholas asked me to—"

Julia threw her hands up, begging for mercy. Some things, she did not need to know. "How long do I have to get ready for this dinner?"

"Enough time for a bath. Nick and Jasper managed to get themselves into a pub brawl in Woodley."

"What!"

Amelia nodded emphatically. "They went for a ride, and came back filthy and quite pleased with themselves. Lady Ruby is beside herself. I've got Nora seeing what she can do about the bruises."

"A pub brawl. What on earth. Why?" Julia really had missed a lot while she'd been stuck in bed.

"I tried to get Nick to tell me, but he started talking about 'a code among men'? I stopped listening when he started going on about Spartan warriors."

"Honestly." It was as much feigned indignation as Julia could muster. She hadn't been able to keep her eyes off Jasper when he was flushed and perspiring from wrestling their boat into the water. She could only imagine what he looked like coming back from a fight. The thought of it hurried her through preparations for the dinner and had her waiting in the foyer to catch a glimpse of him.

Unfortunately, a bath and Nora's ministrations had done their job a little too well. When Jasper came down the stairs in another borrowed set of Nicholas's evening clothes, Julia couldn't detect any sign of his ferocious afternoon activities.

Five of them, with three women in formal attire, meant taking two carriages. Despite her attempts to arrange it differently, Nick thwarted her and Julia was forced to give up her hope of riding with Jasper alone.

"Do you think they've killed each other?" Julia wondered. "The carriage would stop if it came to blows, wouldn't it?"

They followed behind the DeVere carriage, and Julia had kept up a steady stream of pondering. It helped keep her from being nervous. Her first invitation to a dinner.

Nicholas shook his head. "Jasper and Lady Ruby are as devoted to each other as you and Amelia. They just show it differently."

"They argue like sworn enemies." Julia pressed her face to the glass, trying to see ahead of them.

"How long will we have to stay, do you think?" Amelia also looked out the window, but not with excitement.

"Unbelievable. And here I thought we had no friends because I destroyed our reputations at birth," Julia said.

Amelia shook her head. "Convenient scapegoat. In fact, people wanted to be friends with us, but I've been writing them hateful letters to make sure they never made the attempt."

"This whole time, sabotaged by my own sister." Julia threw her hand against her forehead and flopped dramatically across the carriage bench.

"It's true. I've actually received loads of dinner invitations, I've just never gone because none of the hosts seemed very interesting."

"But the Hathaways piqued your interest." Julia let her eyes go wide. "They're very exciting, those Hathaways."

Amelia joined the game. "I heard they served the fish before the soup once."

"I heard they robbed a mail coach once."

"It's probably too late for me to decline on both your behalves." Nicholas leaned back against the bench, shaking his head.

Julia leaned forward, tugging on his arm. "Come on, Nick. Play with us."

Nicholas stared at them both. And then, in his most pompous Lords of Wakefield voice, he said, "I heard the Hathaways once ate in a public dining room."

Amelia and Julia went wild.

"Scandal!"

"Mayhem!"

"Surely not."

They were still at it when the coach rolled to a stop. Nicholas had to stifle them with his very sternest tone. The groom helped them down, and the nerves Julia had been distracting herself from started up again. Would they ask about her limp? What if another headache came on? What if something worse happened? What if they hated her? She followed Nicholas and Amelia to the door under a cacophony of worries.

When they reached the entry hall and were introduced to their hosts, Julia received an immediate answer to one of her questions.

Amelia leaned over to discreetly whisper, "Is that…"

"Yes." The face was different, older, but there was no mistaking it. It was the same face that had sneered at Julia all through childhood. The same face that had rallied all of the women in what passed for society in Julia's neighborhood to boycott any store that allowed Julia to shop there.

Lady Hathaway was the previous Miss Prudence Northam, daughter of Lord and Lady Northam, neighbors to the Bishop estate, and all around awful human being. She knew Julia and Julia knew her—and they definitely hated each other.

Chapter Eleven

"We're the real reason for this asinine invitation," Ruby said in a lowered voice. "The question is, which DeVere are they after—me or you?"

Jasper couldn't argue with Ruby's assessment. The introductions made it painfully obvious as Lord Hathaway fawned all over him and his sister.

"We're absolutely delighted you accepted our invitation. Absolutely delighted," he was saying. The marble floors echoed with his assertions.

Jasper inhaled through his nose. "Nicholas accepted it, actually. You sent it to him."

"Right, right. Wakefield's a good man. Neighbors with my wife growing up, isn't that right, Pru?"

The thin brunette's smile fell short of her eyes. "Our estate was near the Wakefield's and the Bishop's, both. You probably don't remember, but we were both at Lady Amelia's engagement party. To Lord Montrose, that is. I don't recall being invited to the second one."

A tense silence fell over the entry hall.

Amelia's chin lifted. "There wasn't a second one."

"What party was this?" Ruby's interest did what manners should have, intimidating Lady Hathaway into silence.

Unfortunately, Jasper was immune to Ruby's intimidation and not inclined to let the dig pass. "The one where I punched Amelia's fiancé—the awful one, before she married Nick."

Behind him, Julia snickered. Nicholas developed a sudden cough.

Lord Hathaway's nervous glance flitted from guest to guest. "You're very close with the Bishops, then?"

"Very," Jasper agreed. "We think of Nicholas and Amelia as family—don't we, Ruby?"

She sent him a bored scowl, but she played along. "Indeed, we do. We were guests at their wedding. The only guests, in fact. My grandmother can't wait to have Amelia back at the London house."

Lady Hathaway's skin paled noticeably.

Jasper could have kissed his sister. Whatever else was between them, his sister was marvelous at wielding the family influence.

"Hopefully, we will all think of each other as family someday. Let this dinner be the happy beginning," Lord Hathaway announced.

Not bloody likely.

"I hope you don't mind—we invited my brother to round out the numbers. Lord Bellamy, Lady Ruby, may I present Mister Frederick Hathaway." He stepped back with a sweep of his arm, like he was presenting a new carriage, revealing a youngish man of unremarkable looks.

"And this is my wife's sister, Lady Julia Bishop," Nicholas was saying.

"A pleasure." Frederick Hathaway's obsequious attention to Ruby's glove made their intentions obvious. His lack of interest in meeting Julia made them more so.

Ruby yanked her hand back with a tight smile.

Lady Hathaway's drooping curls tipped at a curious angle and her eyes narrowed. "How good of you to come, Julia. I know it must be…difficult, for you to get out."

"No, not particularly." Julia kept her face smooth and her voice impassive.

Amelia's eyes narrowed dangerously.

Nicholas's instinctive Wakefield aversion to unpleasantness took over. "Is there more to the house, or just the foyer?"

"Oh! Where are our manners?" Lord Hathaway shot a glare at his wife.

"Where, indeed," Amelia mumbled.

"Let's stop loitering, shall we?" Lord Hathaway swept his arm in a welcoming gesture. "There are drinks in the drawing room."

In the drawing room, Jasper found himself and Nicholas monopolized by Lord and Lady Hathaway while the presumably marriageable Mister Fredrick Hathaway did his best to secure Ruby's affections. Given the daggers she was glaring at Jasper every chance she had, Jasper suspected he would not be attending a wedding anytime soon.

When Lord Hathaway made the mistake of engaging Nicholas in a discussion of the law as it related to landowners, Jasper saw his chance. A good brother might have gone to rescue Ruby, but she'd made it perfectly clear only one thing would put him back in that category to her mind. Besides, she was more than equipped at fending off unwanted suitors. Julia, however, was alone, perusing paintings on the wall by the door.

A footman left the drawing room, and Jasper wrapped his arm around her waist and snuck them both out into the hall in the servants' wake.

She looked up at him expectantly as he maneuvered them into an alcove. "May I help you with something, Lord Bellamy?"

"In fact, you may." He covered her mouth with his. All day and all night, he'd been wanting to do that. Fighting hadn't done a thing to diminish wanting to be close to her, and watching that awful Hathaway woman taunt her had only made it stronger. He coaxed her lips apart, asking for and receiving her soft moan.

Their tongues danced. Her fingers teased the hair at the back of his neck. He covered her hand with his own, closing her grip. Jasper pressed her tight against the wall, breathing in the smell of her, reveling in her taste. He filled his senses with her, and some of the tension he'd been feeling eased out of them.

He drew back with kisses, making each one softer and more teasing than the last. "I missed you."

"So it seems." Julia's breasts rose and fell hypnotically as she regained her breath. "I heard you were in a brawl today."

Jasper nodded.

She reached up to cup his chin. "You're still as pretty as ever."

He buried his face in her neck and laughed. "Julia…"
"Yes?"

It wasn't the right time to tell her that something was happening to him—between them—that he'd never felt before. Not here, in this awful house with its rude hosts and its fading wallpaper. "You should go back before someone notices I stole you."

She narrowed her eyes. "Will *you* be coming back?"

Jasper nodded. "In a few minutes, once it's not obvious."

"All right," she said. "Don't make me wait too long."

They both knew she wasn't talking about the party.

The isolated sofa Julia and Amelia were perched on had an uninterrupted view of their hostess. Julia's eyes kept returning to Prudence as she waited for Jasper to rejoin them. "Did you know she'd married?"

Amelia glared at Julia. "Of course not. Do you think we would have come? I would have told you."

"Prudence bloody Northam." Julia looked up to the ceiling. "Why not just strike me with lightning and get it over with?"

"It is a little funny. The meanest girl from our childhood is throwing us a dinner party. What is *she* thinking? She had to have known."

Some days, her sister's naïveté was adorable.

"They're trying to pawn off Lord Hathaway's brother on Lady Ruby," Julia explained.

Amelia looked over to where Mr. Hathaway was leaning in far too close to Lady Ruby. Her mouth dropped open. "Are they mad? Her and him?"

"Some people are optimists."

"Like us, thinking this dinner would be anything but a disaster." Amelia sipped her drink and grimaced. "Even the champagne is bad."

One time, as children, Prudence Northam had actually thrown rotten fruit at Julia while she was running errands in town with her mother. And now she was the host of Julia's first real social engagement. Life's ironies were in rare form lately.

"How have you clever young women managed to secure a Hathaway-free island in this nonsense?" As promised, Jasper had delayed his returned to the party long enough to allay suspicion.

He approached them now as if nothing had happened, but Julia didn't miss the glance he slid her when Amelia wasn't looking. With Mister Hathaway earmarked for Lady Ruby, that meant Jasper was officially her escort for dinner. Perhaps they'd find another opportunity to sneak away. His eyes shone as he looked at Julia, and she wondered if he was thinking the same thing.

"As a scandalous Bishop, I have a great deal of experience as a pariah," Amelia said, oblivious. "It's a natural sort of insulation that cannot be trained."

"May I at least bask in its peaceful aura for a while?"

Julia lifted her chin, peering down her nose. "That depends. What have you brought as tribute?"

"I have…" Jasper searched his pockets. "One silk handkerchief, and—" He did an acrobatic sidestep that took him into the path of a footman, from whom he liberated a tray. "Approximately thirteen canapes."

Julia held up her hand. "Handkerchief, please."

Amelia considered. "I will accept no fewer than three canapes."

He handed over the payment and took the chair across from them. "I take it you and Lady Hathaway have a history?"

"She was cruel to us as children," Amelia said.

Julia said nothing. He didn't need to know the specifics. She didn't need him to pity her.

"If it's any consolation, Ruby is going to tear poor

Frederick to shreds. She has eviscerated far loftier hearts than the eager Mister Hathaway."

"Not much consolation," Julia answered. "But a little."

"Would you like me to punch someone?" Jasper offered. "I'm newly practiced, and feeling rather confident."

Amelia pursed her lips. "You do have lovely form."

"Unless the person you intend to strike is Lady Hathaway," Julia countered. "I'm not sure it will give the desired satisfaction. Neither Lord Hathaway nor his brother have wronged us."

"We're nothing, if not just," Amelia agreed.

"I'm afraid I have to draw a line somewhere, and I've chosen to draw it at striking women."

"Admirable," Julia said.

Amelia's face lit up. "Julia could do it."

"Excuse me?"

"Jasper punched Montrose at my engagement party, and I slapped Charlotte Chisholm at her coming out ball. You're the only one of us that has not yet become a violent offender during a social event, and Prudence Northam has had it coming for years."

"Not to mention, it would probably put a quick end to the evening," Jasper added.

"I thought you objected to striking women?"

"I object to *me* striking women. What you do amongst yourselves is your own affair."

She wanted to. God, did she ever want to. She thought of every time Prudence had sneered at her, screamed insults down the driveway and run off, thrown things. She thought of all of them—every horrible child and all their horrible parents. But if she struck Prudence once, she might not be able to stop. And Julia still had designs on sneaking off with Jasper again. "I'm afraid I'll have to pass."

"You're a better person than I." Jasper took a sip of champagne and coughed. "God. That's awful."

Before too long, dinner was announced and they were dragged off to the dining room. Julia was placed between Nicholas and Amelia, across from Frederick Hathaway. Lord Hathaway monopolized Amelia's attention so that his brother could menace Lady Ruby. Given the choice between speaking with Jasper or Nicholas, Lady Hathaway chose to devote her attentions to Jasper. That left Julia and Nicholas to make conversation with each other.

"Are you and Lord Hathaway going to elope together?"

Nicholas scowled into his soup. "That man is an idiot. Did you know he thinks we should bring back the feudal system? As if that were even possible with the legislation from—"

Julia held up her hand. "Nick."

"Right." His expression fell slack. "You don't care about the law."

"Not even a little bit."

"You ought to, you know."

"So you keep telling me."

He leaned back to let the footman clear away his dish. "Traditionally, a good dinner companion will at least pretend to be riveted by their partner's interests."

"Oh?" Julia sipped her wine to remove the taste of whatever that fennel monstrosity had been. "So you would like to feign interest in the latest news about Victoria and Albert's marital strife? Or the proposed names for their children?"

Nicholas looked like he might be ill. "Well played, Bishop."

The next course arrived and Julia realized they had a dreadfully long way to go before dessert. "All right. Tell me about feudal property law."

"Really?"

"I can't promise I'll look interested, but I'll listen." Heaven help her.

On Nicholas's other side, Lady Hathaway had taken on an insistent tone. "But surely you don't intend to refuse a dukedom. All of London has been talking about it."

Jasper looked thoroughly bored. "My grandfather was a great man. I don't think we should be in such a hurry to replace him."

"But he's dead."

He blinked at their hostess.

"It's rather remarkable, really. Dukedoms rarely go to someone so young—so vital. Though I suppose if your parents hadn't drowned, it wouldn't have."

Drowned. Jasper's parents had drowned.

Lady Hathaway continued, oblivious. "Dreadful business, being trapped like that. I was too young at the time, but my mother was scarred for life after the articles about it. My whole childhood, she worried whenever our carriage went over a bridge."

Their hostess showed no sign of shutting up, even though Jasper had gone completely rigid. At the other end of the table, Lady Ruby was similarly frozen. Julia thought of all the times she'd shaken with rage while some ninny prattled on about her limitations, like they knew anything about her.

Julia pushed out her chair and stood up.

"Julia?" Nicholas moved to rise, but she put her hand on his shoulder.

Prudence was *still* talking, unaware that Julia had come to stand beside her. If common decency wouldn't shut her up, Julia would.

"Prudence?"

"Yes?" She turned, and was startled by Julia's closeness. Her upper lip curled in disgust—whether from Julia's absent dinner etiquette or just from her general person, it hardly mattered. Prudence's eyebrows raised in a wordless question laced with superiority, and years of sneering taunts from that same smug face welled up in Julia's memory.

"You are an abominable hostess and a detestable human being." With a prayer that she wouldn't lose control and accidentally murder the woman, Julia slapped her.

Chapter Twelve

Jasper loosened his cravat and undid the buttons on his shirt, sending up silent thanks to finally be free of them. After Julia struck Lady Hathaway, there was no sense pretending any of them wanted to be there. Even Ruby had looked quietly relieved to have an end to the evening, and she detested scenes of any kind. Julia had come to his defense—his rescue—once again. When Lady Hathaway had started talking about the accident, all he could hear was the rushing of water. Coming through the windows of the carriage. Rushing over the floor boards. He'd imagined it a thousand times, alone in the dark, thinking of how terrified they must have been. How cold.

He didn't remember how he'd gotten from the dining table to the coach. The room had faded into nightmare, and then he was bouncing along on the way back to Nick's house with Ruby beside him.

The rest of his clothes dropped to the floor. He climbed between the sheets, but sleep didn't come. When he was the duke, he wouldn't be able to come apart like that in a social setting.

When he was the duke.

He would have to accept it eventually. There was no one else with whom to trust his grandfather's legacy. But Jasper wasn't ready. When he thought of his grandfather, he thought of this solid anchor in the middle of all their lives. An immoveable fortress. An iron will. Jasper DeVere, damaged playboy reprobate, could not fill those shoes.

Not yet. Maybe not ever, but certainly not yet.

There was a soft knock on his door, followed by the drag of a door's edge across carpet. There weren't many people who would enter his room without waiting for an invitation. "Ruby, if you've come to lecture me, you should know—"

"It's not Ruby." Julia closed the door behind her.

Not at all. Even in a high-necked nightdress that dragged the floor with a dressing gown tied tightly around her, she set his pulse to racing. Her hair was down, tied in a braid. She looked impossibly sweet.

"Julia."

She stepped closer, closing the distance between the door and the bed. "Jasper."

He pushed himself up on the pillows, trying to gain some semblance of dignity. Julia climbed onto the far side of his bed, pulling her feet up underneath her to sit. "It's time for us to talk."

"Actually talk, or…" He had so many things he'd like to forget tonight. If she wanted him, he was through with refusing her.

"You don't swim because your parents drowned," she said. "That was the unhappy answer you didn't want to tell me during our drive."

Jasper's body froze, like it always did when he thought

of his parents. "Yes."

"But you went on a boat in a lake with me, anyway."

"Yes."

She inched forward on her knees across the covers. "And you didn't make love to me in the phaeton because you think I deserve a real romance."

"Yes."

She was close enough to touch him now. She reached out, tracing her fingers over the ridged muscles of his chest.

Jasper held her wrist, securing her hand against his heart. "I still think you deserve romance. As much as you can stand."

"Do you know what I think I deserve?"

"What?"

"Passion. As much as I can stand. Maybe more than I can stand."

Jasper groaned. His hold on her arm tightened, and his eyelids fell closed. The words echoed deep in his core.

"Unfortunately, that's not why I'm here."

His eyes opened. "No?"

"No." She let out a deep sigh. She sat back against the headboard and dragged a pillow across her legs like a shield. "I'm here to talk. I just couldn't help myself when I realized you didn't have clothes on."

In all his years as a famous debaucher, nothing resembling this had ever happened. "What did you come to talk about?"

"You. You're not all right."

He opened his mouth to deny it, but no words came out.

"Not just about swimming, or your parents. Your grandfather, too."

"I'm—"

"Hiding. I know a great deal about hiding." She sent

another longing look at his chest. "I wish I didn't, because then I wouldn't see how it's hurting you, and I could be seducing you instead of talking to you."

There were a hundred ways for him to deflect her concern. He had used them all at one point or another. But just this once, he didn't want to.

"We care about each other—you and I."

Julia nodded. "We do."

He'd known it, but it was something else to hear it confirmed. This thing was not just attraction. Their hearts were involved. "I'm not ready."

"For?"

"To have to become him—my grandfather. I'm not ready. I can't do it."

She touched his arm, squeezing reassurance. "It's going to happen whether you're ready or not."

"I know."

"Do you?" She settled under his arm, warming his side.

"I do—because it's what he wanted." He knew it sounded ludicrous, but… "Every time he was sick, he would wait until I arrived to get better. It was a trick to get me to come home. The doctors swore he wasn't pretending. He just had that kind of will. The kind that could stop death."

"Until it didn't," Julia whispered.

"Yes." He rubbed a hand across his eyes, exhausted by the day and every other day since his grandfather had passed.

Julia slipped her arms around him and held tight. Jasper brought his arm up to cover hers. She leaned her head against his chest and nodded. "You're not supposed to be all right. Not right away."

"Dukes have to be. They have to be impervious."

"Right now, you're just Jasper."

He sank down, bringing her with him. She curled in against his chest, under his arm. His grandfather was gone. No matter how badly he wanted it, Jasper would never hear him laugh again. He'd never ride up to the house and see him smiling on the steps. The smells of pipe tobacco and cognac would fade from the study. The memories would fade, too, until Jasper had to struggle to recall what his grandfather's voice sounded like. It would be as if Edward DeVere had never existed at all.

Julia held on to him, murmuring reassurance into his chest. Telling him about her fears—of living an unexceptional life, being a burden to her family, being forgotten.

In the darkest part of the night, they ran out of things to be afraid of and it was just peaceful silence. When sleep finally came for Jasper, it was brought by the rhythm of Julia's soft, even breaths against his chest. It was a different feeling than any he'd ever known before—and one he was determined to keep.

*J*ulia woke up with a naked man underneath her.

She must have crawled beneath the blankets, or he'd put her under them, because she was definitively under them now. The belt of her dressing gown had come loose while they slept. Her nightgown was bunched up around her hips. Jasper's bare chest rose and fell beneath her cheek, and his naked thigh was wedged firmly between her legs. And like an idiot, Julia had been *sleeping through it.*

She let out a groan of self-pity. Jasper moved underneath her, flexing his thigh in his sleep. It was everything Julia could do to lie very, very still. If he woke up, he would likely put a stop to it. If she just lay still, surely there couldn't be any harm in enjoying the feel of him for a few moments. She shifted her hips as slowly as she could manage, trying to find the ideal position from which to appreciate her good fortune.

It was too much. A rumbling noise vibrated through his chest, and suddenly Julia was pinned very happily between the mattress and Jasper. He buried his face in her neck, and his hands began to wander her body. When his palm closed over her breast, another happy rumble sounded—this time against her ear. His mouth traveled down, kissing his way across her neck. Down past her collarbone. When he reached the linen-covered bud of her nipple, he took it between his teeth and pulled.

It didn't hurt—far from it—but it was surprising enough that Julia cried out. She buried her fingers in his hair, encouraging him. Jasper answered her with a throaty hum. He swirled his tongue before pulling with his teeth again. It was…she was…*goodness*.

His other hand was not idle. He'd cupped her waist, kneading and brushing his fingers across the skin there, but when she cried out it began to travel again. Down her hip, across her thigh, up and back against the hypersensitive skin of the inside of her leg. When he touched between her legs, she jumped and let out a yelp.

Jasper froze. His teeth released her nipple and his head lifted. The fog of sleep slowly cleared from his eyes as he looked at her.

"Good morning," Julia said. There was zero hope her face wasn't bright pink with embarrassment.

"Good morning." His hand retreated back to her thigh. "I owe you an apology. I thought I was dreaming."

Julia would tell him what he could do with his apology. "Jasper."

"Yes?"

"If you stop, I will never forgive you." She pulled on the hair trapped between her fingers. "Ever."

He dropped his chin to her chest. His lips curved against her sternum. His palm was still cupped around her breast. "I thought you just came to talk."

"We talked." She shifted her hips. "Now, seduction."

"More passion than you can stand."

"You were listening."

The room was quiet for a moment. Then the hand resting on her thigh moved. His fingers drew a spiral against her skin. "Tell me something."

"What?" The spirals circled up, in. Making slow progress toward her center.

"Do you ever touch yourself?" He was still looking at her, resting completely comfortably between her breasts. "Here?"

Pink flamed into crimson, but she wouldn't lie to him. "Sometimes."

Her answer elicited a smile. He scraped his teeth across her nipple again, just for a second. "How? Like this?"

The tips of his fingers brushed the curls between her legs. They teased, little whispering touches that sent hums of pleasure through her like fingers on a harp string.

"I—yes."

"How about this?" He drew his finger through the damp cleft at her center. When he reached the top, his finger pulsed softly against the bead of nerves there.

It was maddening. She needed him to go faster. Use more pressure. Her whole body ached for it.

"Tell me. Is this what you do?"

"Yes." She gasped it. Cried it. She moved her hips, seeking out what she wanted.

He tortured her with his teasing touches while his lips kissed a trail back up to her mouth. "What else? Show me."

Julia reached down and grabbed his hand, holding it in place while she moved against his fingers. The rumbling growl vibrated through him again. His teeth scraped her neck, her earlobe. He let go of her breast and pinned her free hand above her head.

"Go on. Show me. Show me what you want."

She pushed his fingers inside her, raising her hips off the bed to rock with them while the ache coiled tighter and tighter. He cursed, captured her mouth with his, and copied her movements with his tongue. Their hands clasped tight against the pillow in a grip that whitened their knuckles.

His weight on her chest pressed her into the mattress while she pressed back against his hand. She found a frantic rhythm that spoke to her, promised to take her where she wanted to go, and she gave into it. He abandoned her lips to murmur against her ear.

"You're holding back, Julia. Let me hear you. Tell me how good it feels."

She was so used to being quiet, she wasn't certain she could give him what he wanted. But then he took control, doing things with his fingers she'd never dreamed of. When she finally erupted around his wicked, clever fingers, it was because he'd insisted—growling it into her ear like an order.

As she came down, he held her, kissing her and stroking gentle designs into her skin while she tried to remember who and where she was. Eventually Julia's heart slowed back to a normal beat. Her mind took longer to come around. "Do you still want to apologize?"

His laughter shook the bed. "No. I'm not sorry at all."

"Good."

"You are a constant surprise." Jasper nudged her leg. "Not just because you're still wearing your slippers."

Slippers! Julia scrambled to pull her nightgown down, dragging it over her feet. How could she have forgotten? How long had they been uncovered? What if he had seen? He hadn't seen—he would have said something—but he could have.

"Are you all right?"

"Yes. I am. I just"—she slipped out from under his arm and off the bed—"I should get back. Nora will be looking for me."

He sat up, confusion furrowing his brow. "Julia?"

She couldn't stay—or explain. *I'm terrified that you might see my foot, and then become completely repulsed by me.* Not that he was like that, but…she could never be certain how someone would react until they did. She had to get out of here. "I'll see you at breakfast?"

"I—"

She didn't wait for the answer; she just rushed out the door.

Straight into Lady Ruby. "Lady Julia."

Not again. There was no way Julia was equipped for the situation that was about to occur, so she mumbled an apology and kept walking.

Chapter Thirteen

ecent events had not gone according to Jasper's plan. He had not planned to spend the evening baring his soul to the most extraordinary woman he'd ever met. He hadn't planned to wake up between her legs or spend the morning hearing her moan. And he hadn't planned to watch her literally run from him as if he'd grown a second set of arms.

Only one of those things constituted a problem in Jasper's mind, and it was a problem he meant to fix. However, experience had taught him that sometimes Julia needed space. He went down to breakfast as if everything was business as usual.

"Nicholas. Amelia. Good morning."

"It is, isn't it?" Amelia's smile was especially bright.

Nicholas just nodded and went back to his paper.

Jasper sat down with a cup of coffee and waited for a footman to fill his plate. While he did, Amelia picked up her plate and moved seats. He looked from the now-empty place setting across from him to her new position between him and Nicholas. "Amelia."

"Jasper."

Nick looked up. "Do I want to know?"

"No. Go back to ignoring us."

He nodded to his wife and did as she asked.

"I take it you would like to speak to me?" Jasper asked.

Amelia nodded, still grinning.

His food arrived. He speared a piece of roasted potato. "Do you intend to use words, or should I start guessing?"

Amelia looked around and leaned close. "Was my sister in your room last night? Or this morning?"

"I'm sure I don't know what you mean."

She gasped. "She was!"

Jasper gestured for her to keep her voice down. "I didn't say that."

"You didn't say she wasn't, and you would have, if she wasn't."

He had not gotten enough sleep for this kind of interrogation.

"Wherever Julia was last night and this morning, I'm sure she was there under the purest of intentions."

Amelia snorted. "Is that why the maids are whispering about hearing some very distracting sounds coming from your room while they were lighting the fires this morning?"

For the love of— "Does Nicholas know?"

"No."

They both looked at Nick out of the corner of their eyes. He continued to read the paper.

Amelia knowing what transpired posed both a troubling complication, and an unexpected solution. Out of respect for Julia's privacy, he hadn't wanted to ask Amelia's advice on Julia's odd behavior, but since Amelia already seemed to know, he wasn't revealing anything by discussing it with her. "All right. She was with me."

Amelia's grin practically split her face.

"I'm flattered you're so pleased about it." Especially since he intended to be spending a great deal of time with her sister. Jasper had no intention of letting his and Julia's attachment stay temporary—not after last night.

"Of course I'm pleased. I adore you." Amelia's practicality regarding the sensual pursuits was refreshing.

"I adore you, also." *And I adore your sister even more.* "But there's a problem."

"A problem?" She looked around again. "During the—"

"No. That part—and we didn't, by the way—but…what we did, no problems. Flawless. The problem was after."

"What happened?"

"I'm not even entirely certain. One moment, she's fine, and the next she's jumping out of bed at a run." Jasper had been basking in the overwhelming feeling of rightness, having her there in his bed when he woke up, when she'd just bolted. It didn't make any sense.

"Did she say anything? Did you do anything? What time was it?"

Time? "I didn't exactly check my watch, Amelia. Why would the time matter?"

"There are things—never mind. That's probably not it. She seemed happy, and then she jumped up suddenly?"

"Yes."

She frowned down at her plate.

Jasper forked a tomato slice and watched her ponder.

"Did you say anything?"

"Nothing outrageous." Nothing like what he'd wanted to say, about wanting her in his bed every morning. Jasper had the impression Julia might need a little more coaxing before that kind of declaration. "I made a joke about her slippers, but—"

Amelia went very still. "Her slippers?"

So. It *was* something he'd said. "She was still wearing them. I commented on it, but I didn't think I said anything that would hurt her. Not after last night. We talked for hours, about everything."

"Not everything," Amelia mumbled.

Jasper narrowed his eyes. "Is there something I should know?"

She sighed. "You didn't do anything wrong. My sister is very particular about not letting people see her feet."

"Her feet?" He thought back, trying to remember if he'd ever seen them. Under normal circumstances, of course he wouldn't, but they'd decimated traditional social boundaries over the last few days.

"She's sensitive about the way they look."

He was so careless. The limp. "It's part of her condition?"

"Yes."

"Are there other things that are part of her condition?" If it affected Julia's life, he wanted to know about it.

Amelia smiled at him. "There are, but I think you should ask her about it instead of me."

Right. He didn't imagine Julia enjoyed having people talking about her difficulties, even when it was with good intentions. Come to think of it, there were a lot of things he ought to know about Julia that he didn't.

He would learn them. Everything there was to know, and everything that might stand in the way of her wanting to wake up with him every morning. Jasper stretched his arms out, settling into his muscles. There was something very satisfying about having a purpose to accomplish. Particularly when success meant more time wrapped up with Julia's naked limbs.

"Am I allowed to be part of the conversation again?"

"You are." Amelia leaned over and kissed him on the cheek. "Did you know you're my favorite husband?"

The small smile Nick gave her as he reached out and covered her hand with his resonated within Jasper. That was how he felt. That was what he wanted—open kisses and private smiles over breakfast.

"Jasper." Ruby entered the dining room with her shoulders back and her chin high. "I need to speak with you alone. Immediately."

Jasper's grandmother referred to the stance as Ruby's difficult posture, and getting trapped with her when she was in one of those moods was sure to ruin *his* mood. Besides, he had a mission to accomplish. "So sorry. I can't right now. There are things I have to see to."

"What kind of things?"

"Important things." Like devising a plan to make Julia Bishop fall in love with him. "We'll talk later."

"Jasper, stop."

But he was already out of the chair and on his way out the door.

$\mathcal{I}$t was cowardice, but Julia skipped breakfast—again. She didn't argue when Nora read her the riot act on the dangers of being late for her morning routine. She didn't even tell Nora to mind her own business when she demanded to know where Julia had been all night.

"I was with Jasper."

Nora gasped. "You've finally done it, then. You've gone and ruined yourself."

That made Julia lift her head. "I don't feel ruined. I feel wonderful."

"Then why do you look as though someone has died?"

"I think I love him." She tried the words out in her mouth. They were strange to say, but they felt right.

"No need to ask how it went, then." Nora landed on the chair with a thud. "You don't love him, you're just—"

"I think I do." She knew about lust, and this was something different. She cared about what he thought, and she hurt when he was hurting. It was different than what she felt for Amelia and Nicholas, but it would be, wouldn't it? Parts were the same. Still, how could she know for sure? And what would be the point? "He's a duke and I'm…me, so nothing can ever come of it."

"Nothing more than's already come of it, which could be a child for all you know," Nora grumbled.

"We didn't—it wasn't like that. I know enough to know that's not a concern."

"Oh." Nora frowned. "But you love him."

"Yes." The tightness started in her throat. She squeezed her eyes shut to keep it from turning into tears. "And I wasn't supposed to, because now I want so much more than I'm allowed to have."

Nora's skirts rustled as she crossed to Julia's bed. "Don't you worry, my lady. There's no reason to cry."

There was every reason to cry. She was tired, she was sad, she was hungry. It was a bloody miracle she'd lasted this long. But before she could properly immerse herself in pity, a knock sounded on the door. She couldn't even have a proper cry without being bothered.

It took Julia a moment to realize Nora intended to open it. "What are you doing? Look at me. Don't answer—"

"Lord Bellamy. How may I be of assistance?"

"Please tell Lady Julia I would like to have a word with her, to continue our conversation from earlier."

Nora looked back at her.

Julia shook her head. She couldn't. Not until she figured out how to get this feeling under control. Otherwise she'd make a fool of herself.

"I'm afraid my lady is indisposed."

"Not a problem," Jasper answered. "I'll wait."

Nora looked back again.

"You can't really expect her to let you into my room," Julia called.

From the door, Jasper called back, "It's only fair. You were in mine."

Thank God she hadn't lied to Nora about where she'd been, or all hell would have been breaking loose in her bedroom. As it was, Nora looked far from happy.

Julia sighed. She checked her eyes in the glass to make sure they weren't puffy. "Let him in."

"Lady Julia—"

"You're welcome to try to keep him out, but I'm too tired." And the chance to see him, even when she was miserable, sent anticipation racing across her skin.

"If he's anything like you, there's no point," Nora grumbled. "If you need me, I'll be downstairs—far away from this indecency."

Jasper was already making himself at home in the chair Nora had abandoned.

"Is everything all right?" Julia asked.

"Perfectly fine. I just needed to talk to you."

"About?"

"Why you ran off this morning."

She wasn't ready to talk about that. She didn't yet know how she could explain it—or if she even wanted to. "Jasper—"

"There's a great deal I don't know about you. I'd like to find it out."

She raised her eyebrows.

"What's your favorite color?"

He'd lost his mind. "Blue."

Jasper frowned. "Why blue?"

"I don't know?" Because it was. Who asked a thing like that?

Jasper leaned in, looking for all the world like he was deeply interested. "What do you like about it?"

Suspicion tugged at Julia's mind. "What is the point of this?"

"I want to know you."

Warmth bloomed in her chest. Julia squashed it down. "You think a color is going to bring that about?"

"Why do you like blue?" He was insistent.

Julia sighed. "It reminds me of the sky, and the ocean, and the deep part of twilight when the shadows get long."

"That is an excellent reason." His smile shouldn't matter. It shouldn't send excitement swirling through her abdomen. "Do you like to read?"

"You can't be serious." If he wanted to know about her, there were better things to ask. Not that she would answer them, but that was beside the point.

"Is that a no?"

"It is not. I just…" Julia found her dressing gown, pulling it on and angling her legs out of Jasper's view as she got out of bed. "This can't be what you want to do with your morning."

"It is."

"Really? Hearing about Jane Austen is what you had planned?"

"If Jane Austen is who you like, yes."

Julia paced the space in front of her window, trying to understand him. "Why are you doing this?"

"Last night, we said we care about each other. I meant that. I think you did, too." Jasper left the chair and came to take her hand. "I want to know the details of your days. I don't know if you prefer early mornings or late nights, tragedies or comic farces, and I think you'd like to travel, but I don't know where."

There was that warm feeling, spreading through her again. He wanted to know her.

"Late nights. Love stories—no matter how they end." Julia pleated the dressing gown with her fingers. "And I would like to start with China."

"You'll love Canton. I'll take you there."

And then she was right back on the edge of tears. The world would never let them keep each other, no matter how good it felt to be with him. He was a duke, and she was the disabled daughter of a disgraced country lord.

Julia pulled away from him and turned to the window. It was the same Berkshire countryside she'd looked at her entire life. No grand adventures, no Canton skyline. Just a stretch of grass and a line of trees. That was her world.

"No, you won't." Her shoulders slumped. "I don't want to talk about myself anymore."

"Julia."

"Don't. Please. You don't understand."

"What don't I understand?" It was a challenge.

"Anything! The way people whisper, stare, and point." Julia started to pace but her left foot caught the edge of her dressing gown, and she toppled forward, catching herself against one of the bedposts. *Perfect.*

His hand touched her shoulder. "I am sorry about the fair."

"It's not just that."

"Then what else?"

"Nora has to massage my legs every morning! There are foods I can't eat and things I can't do." She looked him straight in the eye. "I have to relieve myself on a bloody schedule, otherwise I'll fall ill and die."

God, what on earth was wrong with her telling him that? Well, that would be the end of it. Any moment now, he should find a reason to make his exit.

But he didn't run. His hand stayed on her back, warm and sure, tempting her to lean into it. Tempting her to need him. "What else?"

She couldn't. Every sweet gesture made her want to keep him that much more, but he was only here to hide. Once he wasn't hurting anymore, he'd leave.

"I'm sorry. I'm not doing this. This is just temporary, and I don't want to ruin it."

"What if I want more than temporary?" Jasper turned her around to face him. There was a soft look in his eyes. "I know what we said, but after this morning…"

After this morning, he probably felt guilty. Because she'd come apart in his arms and nice young ladies weren't supposed to do that without promises. "There isn't a future for us, Jasper. People like me and people like you don't end up together."

"People like me do as they please—and so should you."

"That's easy for a duke to say, but I'd be a terrible mistress, and an even worse duchess. I'm selfish and I'm brazen and I wouldn't be helpful to you at all. I'd distract you from the things you need to do." No matter which version of permanent he was offering, she wasn't the right woman for it.

"I like all those things about you, and I certainly like

being distracted by you." He reached for her hands.

Julia looked down at their interlaced fingers. "Being with me would make it harder for you to be the man your grandfather wanted."

"It won't."

"It will. People shun me, and some of them will shun you for choosing me."

"Then I'll shun them back. I'm a powerful man, after all. I hold all the cards." His grin made her ache, but she couldn't give in to it.

"I'm sure that's exactly what's best for the dukedom."

He tipped her chin up until she was looking at him. His jaw was set and his eyes were clear. No one could mistake him for anything other than what he was—a peer of the realm. "I *am* the dukedom, and you're what's best for me."

Julia closed her eyes and rested her forehead against his chest. They couldn't be together. They might be good together, but she wasn't good for him. "It's a sweet thought, but not a realistic one."

"Will you let me keep trying to change your mind?"

She should say no. It would be torture to have him tempting her, but she couldn't bring herself to shut him out. She desperately wanted him to find a compelling enough argument so she could say yes. "You can try."

And if she gave in she would ruin the man she loved, which would ruin her.

Julia hoped to God she could resist him.

Chapter Fourteen

He'd set out to learn things about Julia, and the mission had not been a failure. The woman standing in front of him was a romantic. She could have told him to go away. She could have told him not to try, but she hadn't. Julia's objections were based on what she thought society would allow. Jasper could give a damn what society thought. He wanted Julia. Waking up this morning, he'd felt a peacefulness he hadn't known in years. He would not allow asinine prejudices to rob him of that—or of her. He was prepared to fight unfairly and use every weapon in his arsenal, now that the challenge was out in the open.

Jasper took her trailing dressing gown ties and pulled her closer with them. The warmth of her thighs pressed against him. "The world answers to us, Julia. Not the other way around."

"Maybe to you."

"To us." He sat down on the bed, dragging her onto his lap. He lifted her arms until they wound around his neck. When her fingers began sifting through his hair, he sighed in relief. "Kiss me."

She leaned in, her mouth hovering just short of his.

The tease of her was exquisite. When she played with him like this, stopping just shy of giving him what he wanted, it set his pulse racing. Having her in his arms was quickly becoming just as much about easing the brutal ache that had begun the moment he first saw her as it was about an attempt to convince her to be with him.

"Julia," he begged.

She closed the distance. The moment her lips touched his, the tightly coiled tension in Jasper's body responded. This was right. This was how it should be. He was hers to command.

Jasper wrapped her up in his arms, angling her chin and kissing her with the promise of their future together. Her hands roamed his chest and shoulders, making him stretch under her touch like a cat. She paused, fingers hovering over his chest. Jasper waited, pulling back on the kiss until they barely touched. She leaned in. He leaned away, keeping them right on the edge. With a moan, Julia pushed his jacket off and attacked the buttons on his shirt.

The dressing gown fell off her shoulders, pooling around her hips in his lap. Jasper explored her full curves through the thin linen of the nightgown. When his hands traveled down her spine to the indent of her waist, moving lower, she flinched forward.

Jasper froze. "Did I hurt you?"

It was the last thing he wanted to do. If he'd done something wrong…

"No, it doesn't hurt. I just—" She didn't finish the sentence. Instead she moved his hands out, onto her hips and thighs, and returned to kissing him.

Jasper was slow to resume his exploration, not wanting

to make the wrong move, but before long he was dragging his palms down her thighs, over her kneecaps, down her calves.

She flinched again.

Again, Jasper stopped. "Julia?"

"It's not—I just—I don't want you to touch my feet."

"Does it hurt?"

"No. It feels wonderful, but…" She straightened her spine. "They're not pretty."

Not pretty. Jasper frowned. "I think everything about you is beautiful."

"You haven't seen my foot."

"May I?"

"No!" She realized that she'd raised her voice and calmed herself. "No. I'm sorry. No."

The problem was compounding. Her surety that they couldn't be together wasn't the only difficulty. Not only did she not believe in their future—she didn't trust him, either. "Julia, what are your intentions right now?"

"Right now?" Her smile was edged with wickedness. "I thought we might make love."

The temptation called to him. "I would very much like to make love to you."

She leaned in to kiss him, but Jasper stopped her.

"You don't trust me." If she didn't want him to see parts of her, that was her business. They could have a great deal of fun with blindfolds and darkened rooms, but Jasper couldn't make love to someone without trust.

Her face fell again. "I trust you, I just don't want you to see my feet."

"Or your back." Surely, she could see what he was getting at.

"There's a scar there."

"All right."

"It's ugly."

Nothing about her was ugly. Even this insecurity was endearing in its way, but he couldn't move forward with inhibitions. Inhibitions led to regrets, and he didn't want either of them to regret anything about being together. "Julia, do you think I care about a scar or what angle your foot has?"

"It's not that."

"Isn't it?"

"No." She scrubbed a hand across her forehead, as if she could scrub away his questions. "I want to feel beautiful, but I wouldn't if you could see…you wouldn't care, but I would."

"You don't trust me," he repeated. He kissed her palm. "You want to, but you don't."

They looked at each other for a long moment. A fireplace log crackled in the silence.

"It will change the way you look at me," she admitted. "When you look at me, your eyes light up like I'm some kind of treasure. I don't want to lose that."

"You won't," he promised. "Even if we never make it past this, I'll always see you that way."

"What are you saying?"

Jasper kissed her knuckles. "If you're worrying that I might see or touch something I shouldn't, you're not really with me in the moment."

She frowned, shaking her head. "I'm with you, I'm just…"

Not really with him. The trouble was, he needed her to be. When he lost himself in her, he wanted her to be lost right alongside him. He wasn't giving up, but he wasn't the sort of man who compromised, either. He wanted to spend the rest of his life with her. He wanted to know everything there was to know about her, and be completely known by her.

He hoped she would want that, too, eventually.

Julia reached for him, but he caught her hands and moved her off his lap.

He stood up, squaring his shoulders. "When you're ready, I am more than willing. Until then, I think we should spend more time getting to know each other."

"Jasper."

"I'll wait, Julia—as long as you need me to—but those are my terms."

If he was very lucky, he'd manage to earn her trust before the waiting killed him.

The boathouse was empty except for Julia, which suited her perfectly. She'd come out to think without interruption from Nora, Jasper's sister, or whatever fresh misery decided to crop up next.

He'd done everything right. The things Jasper was offering, the words he was saying—they were exactly what she'd always wanted to hear. So why couldn't she just let him see her? She wanted to. God, did she ever want to.

Just once, she wanted her spine and foot to not be a factor.

Julia looked around to make sure she was still alone. After removing her slippers, she rolled down her stockings with steady, determined gestures. Stretching her legs out in front of her, she looked at her feet side by side. The arch of her left foot was unusually high, making an angled bump on the top of her foot. Her toe joints had a severe cant to them as well. She stared at them, willing herself not to care.

It was just a foot. People had all sorts of things they didn't like about themselves. Nicholas thought his nose was too long. Amelia had always lamented that her legs were too stubby. *It was just a foot.* Angry tears welled up in her eyes. She was going to lose her chance at having a lover, lose countless precious moments spent with Jasper, all because she couldn't come to terms with it. But if she couldn't, how could Jasper? She'd had twenty years to accept herself. And she'd thought she had, until it came time to prove it.

Steps sounded on the boards, and Julia jerked her feet back under her skirts.

"It's just me," Amelia said. "What are you up to out here?"

Julia swiped at the tears, putting on a weak smile for her sister. "Nothing in particular."

Amelia sat down next to her, stripped off her own slippers and stockings, and dangled her feet down into the water. "You used to be a better liar."

Julia dipped her feet down into the lake. With the ripples distorting them, they looked the same.

"Are you going to tell me what happened, or do I need to push you in?"

She swiped at another tear that slipped out. "Jasper won't make love to me."

Amelia sat silent for a moment. "I know that's disappointing, but…surely it's not that dire."

Julia shot a glare at her sister. "He says I don't trust him, and until I do, we can't."

"Ahh." Amelia picked up Julia's slipper, turning it in her hands. "So, why don't you trust him?"

"I do trust him. I just—" The kind of trust he wanted from her was too much. It was so far beyond their live-in-the-moment promise beside the lake. "He's not staying. Eventually, he'll leave, no matter what he says. We're just temporary. I shouldn't have to…I can't let him in, and then watch him walk away."

"I thought you *wanted* an epic love affair."

"This is different. I wanted to laugh and be scandalous and make memories. I didn't want to miss him."

Their reflections wobbled in the ripples of the lake. Amelia wrapped her arms around Julia, resting her chin on her older sister's shoulder. "My sister never thinks of the risk, only the reward."

"She sounds delightful. You must be dreadfully jealous of her."

"She's a pain in my backside. I try to drown her every chance I get."

Julia laughed, but it died off far too quickly. She rubbed a hand over her eyes. "I don't want to get my heart broken, Mia."

"Nobody does," Amelia answered. "Would you rather you'd never met him?"

No. The rejection was immediate. A life where she'd never gotten to row on the lake with him, or have him feed her fruit in front of the fire, would be too tragic to bear. She wasn't ready to give it up *now*, when it hurt half the time. She couldn't possibly wish it never to have existed at all.

Julia nudged Amelia with her elbow. "When this goes horribly wrong, and I'm a mess, you have to help put me back together."

"Of course." Amelia took a strand of Julia's blond hair and started braiding it with strands of her own. "You should know, though, I don't think that's what's going to happen."

"If it does—"

"If it does, you can kick Nick out of bed as many nights as you need to."

Julia grinned. "The other day he told me I was his best friend. I bet he regrets saying it now."

Amelia scoffed. "He'd better. With some of the things he's convinced me to try in our bed lately, I'm the best friend he has."

"Ugh." Julia pulled her feet from the water. "I think I'm fine now. There's no more need to cheer me up."

"Are you sure?" Amelia's grin was impish. "There's this one thing I think he heard about from Jasper…"

"No! All my problems are solved. I'm ready to face the day."

Amelia nodded. "Good. That's the Julia Bishop I know."

Now all Julia had to do was figure out how to *be* that Julia Bishop.

Chapter Fifteen

"This time, why not just open by tipping your king?" Nicholas set the board for the next match. "It would save us both the trouble of playing it out."

Jasper sipped his whiskey and stared at the checkered marble squares, but it did no good. He couldn't see what move he wanted to make any more than he could see his and Julia's futures. Waiting was not one of Jasper's talents. "How have I known you this long, and never known you're the sort of cad who kicks a man when he's down?"

Nick snorted. "This is hardly equal to what you've put me through during our friendship."

He supposed it was what he deserved—Jasper hadn't given Nicholas any quarter when he was heartbroken over Amelia—but he might have if he'd known what it felt like to want someone who wasn't ready to want him back.

"What problem has presented itself that you cannot buy or charm your way out of?"

Jasper pinched the bridge of nose, toppling his king in the process. "Julia."

Across from him, Nick went still. "Am I going to end up in another brawl?"

"No—but you might end up drinking too much while I lament my fate."

Nick cleared the pieces away, rightly suspecting there wouldn't be any point in another game. "I thought you two were getting on like a house fire."

Jasper's laugh was humorless. "We were…we are. Sort of. I care about her. It's not going to go away, but she doesn't believe me."

"Tell me, Jasper." Nick frowned down at his hands. "Have you actually done anything to prove you're serious?"

"Apparently not, or we wouldn't be having this conversation." He'd tried to give her romance and adopted a previously unheard of self-imposed celibacy, but it wasn't enough.

"You do realize, to make an honest offer for her, you have to get your own house in order." Nick's grimace was almost an apology. They were in the habit of being honest with each other, but they both knew that wasn't what Jasper wanted to hear.

Still, he couldn't deny it. An honest offer was the least Julia deserved, and he couldn't make it hiding from his family and his title. He had to face it, if he wanted any chance of convincing her.

"Are you going to?" Nick asked.

"Make an honest offer?" Countless affairs decorated Jasper's past. Almost all of them were pleasant memories he thought of with fondness, but that wouldn't be the case now. He needed Julia. He wanted to build a life with her. "Yes, I am, but there are things she and I need to work out first, though."

Like the fact that she didn't trust him. Or the fact that

he was still grieving. They both had things to overcome, and none of them were small.

"Well." Nick poured them both glasses of warm-amber whiskey. "A preemptive toast, then."

"To?"

"To your finally becoming responsible."

They clinked glasses and Jasper took a swallow. "Will I end up as boring as you are? Is that something they hand you alongside responsibility?"

"Absolutely," Nicholas smirked. "You'd better write to your tailor and break the news that it's all brown tweeds from here on out."

"Percival would rather see me dead than wearing tweed."

"My lord." The butler's interruption saved Jasper from Nicholas's impending lecture on the patriotic nature of boring textiles. "Lord Bishop is here to see his daughters. I couldn't find Lady Amelia."

From behind him, Lord Bishop's deep baritone rumbled. "I'll wait in the parlor with Wakefield until my daughters turn up."

Winslow cringed.

Nick just smiled and stood—his patience for all things Bishop was a lifelong achievement. "Bring in some brandy. Lord Bishop, it's a wonderful surprise to have you stop by."

"I'm just passing through on my way to Cardiff and thought I'd check on my girls—I won't be staying." The father of Jasper's tormentor clapped Nicholas on the back and then turned to Jasper. "Bellamy! Or, my apologies, Your Grace. It is the Duke of Albemarle now, isn't it?"

The question of the month.

"It's not official yet, but I don't think they have anyone else to give it to." Jasper stood to shake the older man's hand. There wasn't much resemblance between Lord

Bishop and his daughters, but there was a sharpness to the way he took in the room and everything in it that reminded Jasper of Julia. She was very perceptive, and so was her father.

"It's a rough business, the passing of a title." Lord Bishop nodded his condolences. "It's a happy occasion to run into you, though. I never properly thanked you for punching that brigand that tried to blackmail my Amelia."

"It was my pleasure." He hadn't realized he'd be defending the honor of his future family member. The idea of it brought a smile to his face.

The brandy arrived and they passed glances around before taking their seats. Lord Bishop chose one of the sofas, stretching out in the wide-legged posture of a man at ease.

Jasper did his best to make conversation. "Are you headed to Wales on business?"

"There's a doctor there that published an interesting paper on the treatment of spinal conditions. I've arranged to speak with him about Julia." Lord Bishop sipped his brandy. "There's no promise that anything will come of it, but I've got to try."

"Our father leaves no stone unturned where Julia's medical care is concerned," Amelia answered from the doorway. She kissed Lord Bishop on the cheek, pushing his knee to make room for herself beside him. "We didn't expect to see you today."

"Especially since you promised to leave off chasing any more doctors." Julia followed her sister in, but chose to claim an armchair rather than squeeze in on her father's other side.

Jasper's breath caught at the sight of her. *Patience*. He'd promised to be patient.

"I know what I said, but there's potential for some truly interesting developments. With a little bit of funding—"

"Papa, do not give that man any of your money," Julia insisted.

"The benefit of it being *my* money, daughter, is that I can give it to whomever I choose." The set of Lord Bishop's jaw reminded Jasper of Julia in her more stubborn moments.

"Nothing ever comes of it."

"Nothing ever will if I don't go and see if there's anything worth pursuing."

Julia's chin went up. "Am I that bad, Papa? Are you really so desperate to fix me?"

A different woman would give up the argument, or at the very least demure, but not Julia. She wasn't cowed by anyone, not even her father. She would make an excellent duchess.

"Julia. Papa." Amelia stepped between them, hands raised. "Perhaps this isn't the place for this discussion. Are you staying? Maybe in the morning…"

"I just popped in to see you on my way. The carriage is waiting in the drive."

"Running the horses to death in his frenzy to make me normal," Julia spat.

"Enough!" Amelia insisted. "Nicholas, Jasper. Would you give us the room for a minute?"

"Of course."

On his way out, Jasper passed behind Julia. He gave her hand a small squeeze. "Can I see you a moment?"

Julia nodded, stepping out with him. The muffled voices of Amelia and Lord Bishop reverberated through the door as they waited for Nicholas to clear the hallway.

She breathed deep. "My father is frustrating."

"You're maddening."

"What?" She leaned back from him, scowling.

Jasper closed the distance, pressing their foreheads together. "You drive me mad. I want you near me every second."

She relaxed against him, running her hands over his lapels.

"You're wonderful," he told her. "You know that, don't you?"

She sighed. "Sometimes I'm not sure my father thinks so."

He placed a quick kiss against her lips. "You know he does."

"Well, he has an odd way of showing it." She leaned in, resting her head against his chest. "Can I just stay like this a moment?"

A quiet contentment moved through him as he wrapped his arms around her. "As long as you like." *Forever, if you want to.*

They stood quietly in the hall, leaning against each other. It brought a calm to him that had been missing for weeks.

Eventually, though, she had to step away. "All right. I have to go back in, or my father will end up bankrupting us with his misguided philanthropy."

Jasper grinned. "Give him hell."

"What has gotten into you?" Lord Bishop demanded. "Petulance is beneath you, Julia. You've never doubted that I love you exactly as you are."

Petulance! "Why are you racing off to Wales, if not to fix me?"

Amelia sat down on the empty sofa, her face strangely expressionless. "He's not just going to meet a doctor."

"What? Why would he—" *No.* "You're going to see Mother? That's what this is all about?"

Lord Bishop was suddenly very interested in the carpet. "The doctor and your mother are both in Cardiff, but I haven't decided yet if I would see her."

Obviously, he couldn't see her. She'd locked Amelia up and tried to ship her off to Canada in a horrendous forced marriage. "I'll decide for you. Don't. Don't go at all."

"He can go if he wants to, Jules." Amelia's voice was pitifully small.

"No, he can't." Julia sat next to Amelia and held her hand. "She did awful things to you."

"She's still your mother," Lord Bishop insisted.

"Then she should have acted like it," Julia threw back.

Once again, it was Amelia trying to be the voice of reason. "She is our mother, and she is your wife. Do you have reason to think she's had a change of heart, Papa?"

If she even has a heart. Julia might have forgiven their mother for trying to hide her, but she would never, ever forgive her for trying to send Amelia away.

"It's been months. I just—surely she's seen sense by now."

"Sense has never been Mother's strong suit." Julia picked up Nicholas's abandoned brandy and downed it.

Lord Bishop looked between his daughters. "If it still hurts you that much, I won't go. But I don't see how any of us are going to get past this staying as we are."

It seemed getting past things was the theme of the day. Julia sat down and took Amelia's hand. "What do you want, Mia? You were the one who was wronged. I'll go with whatever you decide."

Amelia nodded slowly. "Go, then. But Papa?"

"Yes?"

"Make absolutely certain, if she says she's changed, that she truly has."

"Of course."

"I mean it," Amelia insisted. Her fingers clenched around Julia's. "If she chooses status over her children a second time, there won't be a third chance."

Lord Bishop nodded his agreement. "I'll be sure. The prospect of a titled son-in-law overwhelmed her, but all that's past now."

Amelia coughed. Julia sent her a glare and a not-so-subtle elbow to the ribs.

Lord Bishop saw it, his brow crinkling into a frown. He looked to the door Jasper and Nicholas had left through, and back at Julia. "Is something developing between you and Bellamy?"

Of all the times for parental instinct to kick in. The situation was complicated enough between her and Jasper without trying to explain it to her father. "Maybe. I don't know. There's a lot to think about."

"Meaning," Amelia jumped in. "My sister is a ninny who keeps trying to get in her own way."

A smile spread across Lord Bishop's face. "My Julia, a duchess."

"He hasn't asked, and even if he did, I wouldn't say yes." They couldn't be together. It was all well and good to fantasize about being a duchess, but everyone in the room knew it could never happen in real life. Or they ought to, if two of them hadn't abandoned all sense.

"Should I stay?" Lord Bishop asked. "Is it even proper for you to be here with him?"

Julia groaned. "Nothing is going to happen, good or

bad, so you needn't concern yourself."

Amelia rolled her eyes, but she didn't abandon Julia completely. "I'm a married woman now, Papa. It's completely proper."

Perhaps not completely—or even remotely. Not that her father's presence would have stopped any of Julia's behavior up to this point. She would just have had to lie more.

"It's not that I don't trust you to keep an eye on your sister, Amelia, I just—"

"Don't trust me to keep an eye on my sister." Amelia smirked. "Does it help to know Lady Ruby, Jasper's sister, is also here?"

"Not to mention that Nicholas has the temperament of a scowling dowager," Julia added.

One of those did the trick. Lord Bishop slapped his knees and stood up. "All right. I'll trust you girls, but you also have to trust me. If I come back with your mother, will you promise to give her a chance?"

"We will," Amelia answered.

When Julia didn't say anything, Mia elbowed her.

"Fine," Julia agreed. "One chance."

They stood up and Lord Bishop kissed each daughter's cheek. "About the other thing—you know I'm not trying to 'fix' you, don't you?"

"I know." It wasn't entirely the truth, but it was one more thing that would be too difficult to explain. She knew he loved her as she was. That was what he was really asking.

"I couldn't forgive myself if there was something we could have done, opportunities we could have given you, that we missed."

"I know, Papa."

They walked him out of the parlor, into the foyer.

"I should say my good-byes to Nicholas." Lord Bishop waggled his eyebrows at Julia. "And Lord Bellamy."

She put her hands on his back and pushed him toward the door. "Get in your carriage, old man."

Chapter Sixteen

The smoke from the cheroot wafted around Jasper's face before being whisked across the lawn by a midday breeze. He was not in the habit of having to be patient, but on the few occasions when it had been called for, the cheroots helped. He'd promised to earn to Julia's trust—and he would keep that promise—but the argument between Julia and her father in the parlor made him realize it might take longer than he had anticipated.

Jasper had always known he was born privileged, but he'd never stopped to consider *how* different things were for him. Jasper organized orgies and walked out on the queen, but the *ton* was always happy to see him. No matter what travesties he perpetrated, society embraced him with open arms. Because he'd been born a DeVere, destined to be a duke. He had never done anything to deserve his welcome, and she hadn't done anything to deserve her exile.

The swish of skirts caught his attention, and Jasper snubbed out the cheroot to avoid smothering his guest with smoke. Amelia joined him at the terrace railing, looking out into the distance with him. "Deep thoughts?"

"A few."

"I should tell you—I've just given my father the impression that you're courting my sister."

An unexpected nervousness raced across his skin. "Did he seem amenable?" If Lord Bishop thought he was worthy of Julia, perhaps she would give him a chance.

Amelia laughed. "Of course."

"I suppose I should write to Victoria."

"The queen?"

Jasper nodded. "Victoria has to approve my future spouse before I can marry—that ridiculous Royal Marriages Act."

If declaring his intentions to the queen wouldn't convince Julia of his seriousness, Jasper wasn't sure what would. He also wasn't above using Julia's affection for Victoria to help his cause.

Beside him, Amelia had gone still. "What if the queen doesn't approve?"

"Why wouldn't she? I'll ask, Victoria will agree because we're cousins and no one ever says no to the Duke of Albemarle, and then Julia will realize there's nothing temporary about the way I feel about her."

Amelia smiled, but it dropped away as fast as it appeared. "I hope you're right. Not everyone sees us the way you and Nicholas do."

He looked down at her with a raised eyebrow.

"The Act is meant to protect the royal bloodlines from corruption. The scandalous Bishop family, and especially Julia, is—"

"That's ridiculous." Jasper didn't let her say the rest of it. "The queen knows better than that nonsense."

"Like I said, I hope you're right."

Jasper hoped he was, too. It had honestly never occurred to him that Victoria *could* say no—no request had ever been denied. Still, there was far too much at stake to leave it up to chance. Jasper left Amelia in search of the most qualified person he could think of to help him entreat a queen.

He found Ruby in the library, sitting at a table with papers spread out around her. A few of them looked suspiciously like summaries from estate agents. Guilt tugged at him, but he pushed it away. He was going to take care of all of that, he just needed to take care of this first. "I need your help."

"With more than you realize, I assure you." She didn't look up as her pen scratched against the surface of the page she was writing.

He ignored the dig. "I need to write Victoria and request permission to marry Julia."

Ruby blinked at him. She set the pen down on the blotter.

"I'd do it myself, but I suspect she may hold a grudge after being stood up at Parliament."

"She would have every right." Ruby leaned back, looking him from head to toe. "Is Lady Julia pregnant?"

"What? No!" Jasper scowled at his sister. "And if she were, that would be none of your business."

Ruby pressed a finger between her eyebrows, smoothing out an invisible line. "I'm just trying to understand your sudden haste to become a bridegroom."

"I need Julia to know I'm serious."

"Are you?"

"Obviously I am. Regardless of what else I've done, I wouldn't ask for the permission if I didn't intend to use it."

Ruby's brow furrowed. "She is an earl's daughter, and

she has the confidence of a duchess. If it weren't for her leg—"

"She's not a horse on the auction block, Ruby. We're not considering her assets. She's the woman I want to marry."

"I'm merely weighing the pros and cons out loud. She won't be a very popular choice."

"I won't be a very good duke," he threw back. "We're perfect for each other."

Ruby sighed. "Oddly, I think you might be. None of your previous dalliances ever inspired a letter to the monarch before."

Hope flared. She wasn't screaming, and she wasn't saying no. He just needed to make her understand, and he was certain she'd help.

"Julia's the one, Ruby. I don't want anyone else, and if there's a chance the queen might deny the request…" He sat down next to her, taking her hands. "I need to know."

Ruby studied his face, searching for something. After a moment, she nodded. "I will help you on one condition."

"What?"

"I will accept Julia as your wife, *only* if she becomes the Duchess of Albemarle."

Meaning he would have to be the Duke of Albemarle when he asked her. *Bloody hell.* With half his sister's single-minded determination, Jasper could be the monarch and he wouldn't have to ask anyone for permission to do anything. "She'll be the duchess either way, Ruby."

"Not if you run off with her to the continent, and keep avoiding your duty."

"I won't do that."

"Then you should have no difficulty agreeing." Ruby went back to her letter. "Those are my terms. They're not negotiable."

He knew he had to deal with it sometime, to prove he could be the sort of man who deserved Julia—he just hadn't expected to have to do it this soon. Still, if it helped him convince Julia to marry him, then it would be worth it.

"Fine," he told her. "Once I have the queen's answer, I will accept the title."

Ruby's eyes sparkled. "Tell Winslow to hold the outgoing post. We can send the request and ask for another summons at the same time. It should help repair some the damage you did if we show her you're settling down, and accepting your duty to the dukedom."

Jasper wasn't sure reminding the queen that he'd walked out on the first summons was in his best interest, but Ruby was the expert in matters of state.

"Hurry, if you want this to get to London today," she called as he went in search of the butler.

*A*bove the stable, the sky was overcast. The wind had gone completely still and there was a quiet in the air. It was perfect weather for a ride; something Julia desperately needed. A sprint would be the perfect thing to clear her head and shake off the last vestiges of irritation that thinking of their mother always brought to the forefront. Once she was relaxed and her mind was empty, she could set her mind to the task of Jasper.

"Good morning, Lady Tryphosa." She bowed to her horse with perfect formality.

Lady Ruby's voice sounded behind her. "I've heard your sister does the same thing. It seems like an odd custom."

"Sometimes we *are* odd." The groom gave Julia a leg up. She was about to wheel off toward the meadow when Ruby put her hand up.

"Wait." The word was dangerously close to an order. "I'll accompany you."

Julia sighed. She didn't want company. She wanted open hillsides and a breakneck pace. Tryphosa stamped her hooves in irritation while they waited for Ruby's mount to be saddled.

"It's a beautiful day for a ride." Ruby adjusted her seat and took the reins from the groom. "Shall we?"

If she was going to share her ride with Ruby, it would be on her terms. "A quick warmup and then we gallop."

Ruby's eyes went wide, but she didn't argue.

Once they cleared the outbuildings and the horses had gone through a walk and a trot, Julia shouted and dug her heels in. Her horse shot off like a bolt of lightning. The ground flew past below them, with chunks of mud flying up from Tryphosa's hooves. Julia looked back to see if Ruby was being caught in the spray and was surprised to find her keeping pace.

She urged Tryphosa faster. Ruby's horse matched speed. Julia gave Tryphosa free rein, and the little mare finally broke ahead, but not by much. When they'd finally run the horses out, both animals and riders were panting from the exertion. Julia rubbed Tryphosa's neck, praising her. They settled into a meandering walk.

"Your horse is exceptional." Julia wasn't used to people keeping up with her.

"Thank you." Ruby smiled down at the bay stallion. "He was a gift from my grandfather."

An unusual mount for a lady. Even Lord Bishop had insisted on restricting his daughters to smaller breeds, though the ones they'd chosen were anything but docile.

"I wanted to thank you for the other night," Ruby said. "At the Hathaway dinner party. I heard that horrid woman tormenting my brother, and what you said before you slapped her."

Julia's fists clenched around the reins. "Prudence and I have a history."

"So I gather. Still, thank you. My brother is very dear to me."

And to me. Julia stayed silent.

Eventually Ruby said, "Am I correct in assuming you are not an opportunist, Lady Julia?"

"Excuse me?" Julia had been called many things, but opportunist was a new one.

"My brother is considered quite the catch, but as I understand it your family is plenty wealthy and you don't appear to have any social aspirations. You seem to care for Jasper." There was a haughtiness to Ruby's tone that begged to be antagonized.

"I assure you, my intentions toward your brother are entirely dishonorable." Julia lifted her chin in challenge. "And largely physical."

Lady Ruby's eyes narrowed. "So if he asked you to marry him, you would decline?"

What was it with today? Everyone was anxious to marry them off. "He hasn't asked and, if he does, I believe he should be the first person to know my answer."

"Lady Julia, at the risk of sounding calculating—"

Julia choked on a laugh. "I'm sorry. Go on."

"What can I offer you to make sure your answer is no, if he asks?"

Julia tapped the reins and Tryphosa stopped. The little mare stamped her feet in response to the tension radiating through her rider. Julia was a fool. She'd thought Lady Ruby might grow to like her if they had a chance to get to know each other, but that wasn't how the world worked. When someone like Julia associated with a duke's heir, it was all hands on deck to get her out of the picture.

"My brother is not naturally suited to being a duke. I think he may take to it in time, but he needs someone by his side who has been bred for that kind of role."

What a shame he can't marry you. Julia met Ruby's imperious stare head-on. "There isn't anything you can offer me, and while we're on the subject of Jasper—you're wrong about him."

Lady Ruby's spine stiffened. Her mouth went pinched and pale, and her entire body radiated irritation. "I think I know—"

"You don't," Julia interrupted. "Jasper will make an excellent duke. He's a natural leader that people love to be around, and he brings out the best in those people. You think you know him, but you don't even know why he doesn't want to take the title."

Lady Ruby stared at her for a long moment. "Jasper has never been fond of responsibility."

Julia searched the gray sky for patience. She didn't want to help Ruby with anything, not after the insulting bribe she just tried to offer, but Julia did want to help Jasper. In the end, that beat out any animosity she felt toward Ruby. "Your grandfather was a great man. A once-in-a-generation kind of man, the way Jasper speaks of him. The sort of man that changes the world."

Ruby nodded. "He was."

"You're all mourning him, but only Jasper has to live up to *who he was*. If Jasper were as irresponsible as you seem to think, he would just take the power and squander it. He doesn't want to become the Duke until he can live up to your grandfather's legacy."

Ruby shook her head. Julia thought she'd missed the mark—hadn't said it right—but then Ruby took a shuddering breath. "Oh, Jasper."

"He's a once-in-a-lifetime man, too, but he's grieving right now and you're not helping."

The other woman wiped her eyes, removing all evidence of emotion. "I don't push him for my own amusement. A duke must be infallible. As must his wife."

It stung because it was the truth, but Julia would be damned if she would let this woman see her weakness. "Well, as I said, he hasn't asked."

"He will, you know. Once my brother gets an idea in his head, he doesn't let it go—no matter how foolish."

"Lady Ruby, this conversation is inappropriate. Whatever relationship Jasper and I have, it's between us. Please remove yourself from it."

She'd gone out to the stables for peace, quiet, and some time to think. Instead, she'd gone from confused to angry. Tryphosa was responding to all of it, eyeballing Ruby's horse with malicious intent. It would serve Ruby right if she got thrown in the process, but her horse didn't deserve it, and there was no point in continuing the ride. Julia turned back toward the stables, keeping a close eye on her mount.

They'd almost reached the outbuildings when Ruby said, "Under different circumstances, I think you would be an excellent match for my brother."

"Under any circumstance, he or anyone else would be lucky to have me." Julia dismounted and set off toward the lake, hoping the boathouse would offer the quiet she'd tried to find on her ride.

Chapter Seventeen

Sending the letter filled Jasper with a desperate need to see Julia, and reassure himself that he wasn't being a complete fool. There was something real between them. He just needed to show it to her. He'd set for the stables on Nora's advice when he saw Julia cutting across the grass toward the lake. He covered the last bit of distance at a run.

When she saw him, she stopped and waited for him to catch up. In that moment, it didn't matter what the queen said or who might see them. He kissed her, in the open air, where anyone could pass by. It was gentle, but they were both breathing heavily when they came up for air.

"I was looking for you," he said softly.

"You found me." She sounded tired, and she leaned into him, taking his hand. "Can we go somewhere? Somewhere quiet, where no one will find us?"

Jasper would like nothing more. "There's a place I saw, not far off. A bunch of boulders around a tree."

Julia nodded. "I know it."

He took her hand, and they walked. Jasper set a slow

pace so she could find her footing.

"Which do you like better, London or the country?"

Julia smiled. "I don't know. I've only ever been to London a few times. I love the bustle of it, but I couldn't say for sure if I'd like living in it all the time."

They reached the secluded spot at the base of the hill and the lake. The boulders were waist-high and the entire view of the lake, with the sun glinting off its surface, stretched out before them. When he first saw it, he'd imagined stretching Julia out across the boulder tops and bringing her to climax while the sun set around them.

"I want to spend the next few hours not thinking about anything at all." She stared out over the lake with a sigh. "Can we do that?"

"Talking first, then passion." He said it mostly to himself. It was a good precedent for them to set, otherwise they might go days without ever speaking to each other.

Julia looked around, over her shoulder. "Is passion on the menu? Because that seems like an excellent diversion."

"It always is. I just don't want either of us to regret anything."

She nodded, looking back to the water. "I do want to be open with you, Jasper, but it's not easy for me to trust."

"Whatever you need from me, it's yours."

"In that case." She looked down at her feet, then back up at him. "Will you help me forget?"

He was confused. "About?"

"Everything."

There was a challenge in her eyes that set his blood on fire. There was something about her that made the devil in him stretch out and unfurl. It was something he'd never expected to find in someone he could imagine himself marrying.

That was the beauty of Julia. She was sinner *and* saint, all at once.

He spun her around, catching her by the waist so she wouldn't fall. He pressed her back to his chest and placed his lips against her ear. "Oh, I certainly can. Are you paying attention?"

He knew she was. Her lips had parted in a gasp, and she was leaning into him. Jasper began by raining kisses and bites down on her neck while his fingers went to work on the buttons of her riding jacket. Julia angled her neck, silently asking him for more. No one could ever be more perfect.

The jacket peeled free of her shoulders and fell to the grass. His fingers went to the buttons of her shirt, making quick work. The white silk dropped to the ground. When he started undoing the fasteners of her skirt, he felt her tense.

"Don't worry. I won't go too far."

The burgundy velvet slipped free, landing in a pool around her feet. Jasper ran his hands over her shoulders, pushing off the straps of her corset and shift. He felt her pulse racing beneath her skin. His palms dragged down her arms, across the flat boning where her corset covered her stomach. His lips brushed against her ear again.

"Breathe out."

She had a dazed expression, and her lips were parted.

Jasper stepped closer, pinning her between his body and the boulder. His hand slipped lower, pressing against the juncture of her legs. "Breathe. Out."

She exhaled.

Jasper gripped the bottom of the corset and pulled. The thick fabric jerked down, releasing her breasts from its confines. Julia gasped.

"Are you paying attention?" he asked. His palms slid up,

covering them. His fingers pinched and pulled her nipples as he cupped the bare skin of her breasts.

"Yes."

He kissed her neck. Paid homage to the curve of her shoulder.

"Jasper."

His fingers circled her wrist. He laid her palm out flat on the boulder top, covering it with his. Their fingers wove together. His other hand returned to her thighs, found its way through the break in the fabric there, and began stroking her with wicked purpose. He rocked against her, pressing the heel of his hand in time with the press of his hips.

Julia moved against him until everything took up the pulsing rhythm he set. Her heartbeat. Her breath. Even the lapping of the waves on the lake. She let her neck go slack, dropping her head down and closed her eyes.

Jasper's teeth scraped her shoulder. He wanted her there with him, feeling everything. He wanted her to get swept up and overwhelmed. In front of them, the water of the lake shifted and shimmered in the sun. A groundskeeper walked out toward the boathouse, laying rope and tools beside it.

"Jasper."

The second syllable cracked as he altered the curve of his fingers. "Hm?"

"There's someone. A groom. At the boathouse." Her words broke off into a moan. Her knuckles went white as she gripped the rock and tried again. "If he looks over here, he'll…"

Jasper didn't stop. He didn't even slow down. His lips touched her neck. He murmured "Then you should be very quiet."

"I—"

The pace sped up. He curved his fingers, working them into her in a quick, shallow staccato. "Can you, love? Can you stay quiet?"

He felt her react to the game. Felt the shiver run through her, and her hips move faster as the thought of being discovered inspired her to new heights. A cry broke from her throat.

"I don't think you can," he told her. "I don't think you want to."

*W*icked man. He was made for her.

She was made for him, too. No matter what anyone thought or said. It was time she showed him how much he belonged to her. Julia reached back, putting her hand between them. She stroked the rigid length of him, squeezing. "Can *you* stay quiet?"

He swore, grabbing her hand and trapping it with the other on top of the boulder. She pushed back against him with her hips. Her curves, his angles. Julia felt depraved, and for once she'd earned it.

She threw her head back, face pressed against his they rocked together, his body curved around hers. "Do you touch yourself, Jasper? Do you think of me when you do?"

The sound he made was agony.

It was hers, and she loved it.

"Show me." She threw his words back at him with a laugh, feeling every bit the temptress. This was what he liked. He needed her to see him, feel him, want him. Needed her smooth hands wrapped around the length of him. Julia needed it, too.

Jasper put his back to the rock and undid the buttons of his jacket. She moved to watch, trapping her lower lip between her teeth to keep from going to him. His jacket shrugged off and he pulled his shirt from his trousers.

Julia moved close, flattening her palms against his abdomen. She traced her finger along the edge of his waistband. "Do you take your time?"

"No," he answered honestly.

"Well, I'm going to." With deliberate leisure, Julia undid the first button on his trousers. "Take off your shirt."

Jasper pulled his cravat from his collar. She popped the second button loose. He unfastened the buttons of his shirt in double time. Julia leaned forward and pressed her lips to the column of his throat as the skin was revealed. Her tongue flicked out.

"Is this how you think of me? Is this what you imagine me doing?" Her palm slipped into his pants, between fabric and flesh, and caressed the length of him.

"I — " It came out as a groan.

She explored the textures of him with curious fingertips. So smooth, and yet so rigid. Her hand closed over him. "Is this what you do? Is this what you think about?"

His hips pushed forward against her hand in answer.

"Show me. Show me what you do."

Jasper's hand wrapped around hers. He thrust a slow rhythm and showed her what he liked. "Julia."

She kissed him, cutting off his gasp.

They moved together while she learned the secrets to his body. She'd never been a particularly diligent student, but this was a subject to which she could certainly apply herself. Before long he was gripping the edge of the rock, accepting her touch with an expression that was half pleasure, half pain. "You're killing me. Keep going."

She'd do more than continue. She'd up the stakes.

"This isn't the only thing you think about, is it?" Julia kissed his chest. Her teeth scraped a line across his skin. "Do you think about my mouth? What if I wrapped my lips around you right now? Right here?"

It was the right thing to say. Jasper groaned and went over the edge, shuddering into her hands. Julia couldn't help but feel immensely pleased with herself.

Until Jasper sank down to his knees.

She frowned down at him. "Are you all right?"

"Very." He took her hips in his hands and pulled her forward. The pressure of his lips against her pelvic bone sent her eyes wide. "You *will* think about my mouth."

He parted the fabric of her linen riding pants and tasted her. Julia's knees buckled and her hands gripped his shoulders. She would never, ever tire of this. If he spent the rest of his life with his tongue buried inside her, it would be enough. Forget titles and families and the bloody *ton*. This was all she needed.

She buried her hands in his hair and let him work, crying out and not giving a damn who heard. His fingers joined his mouth and together they pushed her up to the limit of what she could bear.

"Jasper. Jasper!" She called out his name as the feeling overtook her in waves.

He caught her, lowering her to the ground.

She blinked up at him from the grass with a lazy smile on her lips. "You're very good at that."

"Just with you."

"Liar."

It felt like she had died. As if she were no longer attached to her body. She had floated away somewhere into the ether.

"Do you think the groundskeeper heard us after all?"

Jasper wrapped his arms around her, resting his head on her shoulder. "Shall we ask him?"

She nudged his chest with her elbow. "Wicked man."

"Always."

They couldn't stay like that forever, but they stayed for a while. When it was time to go back, Jasper helped her dress. Julia did her best to hinder him getting dressed. Eventually, though, it couldn't be helped. They had to go back or they would be missed. Julia was tempted to stay, just so Ruby could be the one to find them.

Instead, they were met in the hall by an extremely irate Nora. One look at the maid's face and Julia knew what was wrong. "I lost track of time."

"Oh, well then, I'm sure that will make everything all right." Nora started pushing her toward her bedroom.

Jasper kept stride with them. "Is something wrong?"

"I haven't kept my schedule for the day. Everything will be fine."

"You hope," Nora grumbled.

"Do you want me to—"

"No! No. It's fine. I'll be down in a bit. You go on." She smiled at him and he smiled back. For a moment, they were right back against that rock—until Nora shoved her through the bedroom door and the moment was gone.

Nora handed her the chamber pot before putting water on the fire to heat. While Julia saw to the most pressing task, the maid kept up a steady stream of griping. "Didn't get a proper night's sleep. Haven't been eating nearly enough. Then you run off for hours on end with that rogue."

"He's a duke. I don't think they can be rogues."

"Of course they can. That one's the worst of the lot." Nora spirited the chamber pot away and came back to press a hand to Julia's forehead.

"Please, Nora. I don't have…"

All color leached out of the maid's face.

"…a fever. No. Nora, I can't."

There was no mistaking the fear creeping in to Nora's eyes. "I'll undo your buttons, and have Lord Nicholas call the doctor."

"Maybe I'm just warm," Julia pleaded. She'd certainly done plenty to warrant an uncharacteristic flush.

"Maybe so. If you are, the doctor will say so, and I'll only have one or two new gray hairs to pluck out."

By the time Nora came back from alerting Nicholas and Amelia, Julia knew she wasn't going to be that lucky. The dry, warm feeling had intensified and muscle aches were beginning in her lower back. Within hours, she was shivering and sweating, unable to keep her eyes open. Someone brought her water. Pressed cold cloths to her head. Every once in a while, they tried to make her eat, but then the violent retching would begin.

They were whispering, out on the edges of her comprehension. Worried words. Words of fear.

It was a kidney infection. She'd had them before. It was nothing to worry about.

Julia rolled over, clutching a pillow to her chest. Violent chills shook her body. Unseen hands piled blankets on top of her. Stuffed hot rocks under her sheets. Mia's warm shape crawled in beside her.

"If you think this is going to get you out of letting Jasper see your feet, think again."

Julia laughed, but it was a weak chuckle that had no sound. "If I die, do I still have to?"

"Yes, but there will be no dying."

"If you insist."

"I do."

She drifted in and out for a while after that. At some point, she kicked off all the covers, suddenly too warm and sweating profusely, and Mia left her side. Then later, someone held her hand, and she didn't need to open her eyes to know it was Jasper. He had the best way of touching her. Even now, when she felt wretched, the soft pressure of his thumb kneading against her palm felt like heaven.

"Impatient man. I said I would be down in a bit."

His hand closed around hers, squeezing. When he spoke, his voice was thick. "You know how I hate to wait for anyone."

She smiled. "Too bad."

His lips pressed against her knuckles. "Did they tell you what the doctor said?"

Julia didn't answer. She knew what the risks were, but she was too exhausted to want to waste words on that. Instead, she rolled onto her side, bringing their joined hands up to her cheek. "Tell me something nice."

"Something nice?"

Julia nodded, eyes closed. "Something that has nothing to do with doctors or fevers or fluids."

He shifted, running his fingers through the hair at her temples and the nape of her neck. *Heaven.* "When I was a boy, I once put a giant toad in Ruby's chamber pot. Somehow, it stayed in there until she pulled the pot from under her bed, and then it leapt out and startled her half to death."

Imagining Ruby's face made the mattress shake with her laughter. "That's not nice."

"Well then, how about this?" He leaned in close, so only she could hear. "I love you, Julia Bishop."

Love. Not want. Not need. *Love.*

"Jasper, you can't—" The chills started again, and suddenly it was too much, trying to care why they weren't supposed to be in love with each other. He made her happy, even when everything else was miserable. To hell with what they couldn't do. "I love you, too."

She felt his exhale of relief across her cheek, and it made her smile. He hadn't been sure she loved him back.

"Will you stay?" she asked.

"As long as you'll let me."

Julia drifted off to sleep to the feeling of his fingers combing through her hair.

Chapter Eighteen

His grandmother was every inch the duchess, even in grief. She sat on the edge of the Duke's bed, holding his hand and smiling down at him. Tears ran down her cheeks, but her spine stayed straight. Her shoulders never hunched.

"It's all right, Edward. It's all right, now. Everything will be all right."

The wheeze of his grandfather's breath filled the room. It was an ever-slowing metronome. They all subconsciously counted the beats between.

"Jasper," his grandfather rasped.

Jasper stepped forward, leaning in over his grandmother's shoulder. "I'm here."

"Remember what I told you." The words were a struggle. Each pause seemed like the next word would never come. "I'm so proud of you. Both of you. My remarkable grandchildren."

Behind him, Ruby began to cry. Soft, muffled sobs.

"Lillian?"

His grandmother lifted the Duke's hand. "Yes, my love."

"I will count every minute without you, but don't hurry. I've never minded waiting for you."

Sitting by Julia's bedside was a unique agony, but he stayed. Even though he wanted to run off to a pub or the continent, and do anything but sit still and watch her suffer—he stayed. He told himself this wasn't like the last bedside he'd sat next to. Julia would be all right. Everyone said so. She was strong and stubborn, and she'd come through this before. He knew that, but it didn't stop the memories from toying with him in the silence of the night.

It didn't stop him from thinking about Ruby, either, or the way she used to beg him not to go before he set off on one of his wild adventures. She had stopped begging a few years ago. Now she just glared, or lectured. The truth was—Ruby never did anything dangerous, so Jasper had never had to spend an anxious night worrying over her. If it felt anything like this, he owed her an apology. Or twenty.

Nora's coming and going broke up his reminiscing. Eventually she stopped bustling about and took a chair by the fire. Jasper watched Julia, sleeping restlessly. Nora watched him.

"I can't quite figure you out," the maid said eventually.

"How's that?"

"You're a rake through and through—that much I know. But rakes don't stay when it stops being fun and easy."

Jasper didn't owe her any explanations, but he was growing tired of everyone making assumptions about his character. "I believe in living life to its fullest potential. Taking pleasure where you find it."

Nora scowled.

"And embracing love with an open heart when you find *that*."

"Is that what you've found with my lady?"

"Yes." He loved her. He wasn't going to change his mind. There were certainly less complicated women for Jasper to love, but this was the one who had stolen his heart with quick wit and reckless inclinations.

Nora blinked at him. "If she couldn't give you children, would you still want her?"

The question hit him like a jolt. He hadn't thought as far as children, for himself or for them. He thought about it now, but it didn't change anything.

"Is Julia barren?"

"Don't know. Maybe. Could be."

"I don't need children. Pregnancy would be harder on her than most, wouldn't it?"

"A duke needs an heir."

"I need Julia. My sister's children can have the title." In fact, that wasn't a half-bad plan. Ruby needed some sort of motivation to get her to the altar, and she was abysmally dedicated to being responsible.

Nora's eyes narrowed. "What if the time comes that Lady Julia can't walk?"

Another thing he hadn't considered. "We'll figure something out."

Nora wasn't finished. "She can't go flying off on spontaneous adventures. There is a schedule she has to follow."

"I'm learning it."

"Traveling is difficult." Nora pinned him with the intensity of her stare. "It might kill her."

Looking at Julia, pale as the sheets beneath her, he knew he would do everything in his power to keep that from happening. He couldn't lose her. He wouldn't. But she liked being cooped up about as much as he did. He knew from experience there was far more to life than being safe. No amount of security would satisfy her if she never truly got to live.

"We'll take it slow, and I'll hire excellent doctors to travel with us. And you, if you'll come."

Nora's eyes narrowed. "You wouldn't stay in England? It's safer for her here."

"If she wants to travel, I'll take her, and we'll make it as safe as we can."

Nora sighed. "Of course I'll come. It'll take years off my life, but no one else can manage her sass."

It didn't escape Jasper that Nora was no longer speaking in the hypothetical. Whatever test she'd been administering, he appeared to have passed it.

"Nora—" He wouldn't move away from the bed, so he tried to impart his words with the gravity he intended. "I will cherish her with everything I am and everything I have."

"Will you marry her?" The maid's pursed lips and narrowed eyes made him nervous.

"If she'll let me." She loved him. It was a start.

"I suppose that will do."

*E*ventually the worst of it passed. Her fever was coming and going in bursts, and her entire body ached like she'd been run down by a carriage, but there were hours where she felt significantly less miserable. It was during one of the wretched hours when Jasper came to sit by her bed, but Julia was not in the mood to be good company.

"Go away," she groaned. "I'm hideous."

"You're lovely. Shall I read to you?"

Her hair was plastered to her forehead with sweat, her head ached, and it felt like her eyeballs were on fire. "All of Amelia and Nick's stories are boring."

"It's fortunate, then, that I have a few of my own." His cheerfulness was abhorrent. "We have a story about a pirate, one about an unapologetic prostitute, and the memoir of a dashing young gentleman traveling the far east."

Unapologetic prostitute sounded promising, but Julia refused to be tempted. "No books."

The mattress dipped down next to her. He didn't say anything, but she felt the tie at the end of her braid coming undone and his fingers threading through the strands. He combed through her hair, tugging on the ends. His fingers massaged the column of her neck and the space around her ears.

Julia sighed and rolled over, into the space under his arm. "I'm sorry I'm awful."

"Don't be. I expect you to be gracious when I'm awful. I'm a terrible patient."

He likely was. They had a great deal in common; limited patience and a tendency toward drama. The implication that they would have the kind of future where she *could* take care of him made her snuggle in closer to his chest.

Nora cleared her throat. Julia groaned. Jasper's chuckle vibrated under her cheek.

"Come on. Ignoring the schedule is how we got here." He extricated himself from Julia's grasp and stood up. "Tea or broth this time?"

"Let's try some broth," Nora answered. "I'll crack the door when it's all right for you to come back in."

He kissed Julia's cheek and headed down to the kitchens.

The chamber pot ritual took twice as long when she felt

poorly, and it happened twice as frequently with Nora and Jasper pumping her full of liquids any time she stopped protesting for a moment.

"That man of yours is coming along, I think." Nora changed out the bedclothes with brisk efficiency.

"You shouldn't use him like a servant. He's a duke." The edge of her vision started to go dark. She grabbed Nora's arm for support.

"Have I ever asked him to do anything? He takes it on himself."

It was true—and strange. He'd woven himself so neatly into her and Nora's routine. No one except Amelia had ever seen so far beyond the facade she put up.

Nora tucked her back beneath the sheets, and then opened the door for Jasper. He came through carrying a tray with a steaming bowl on it.

Julia shook her head. "I can't."

He set the tray aside. Julia motioned for him to join her and made room for him on the bed as he took off his jacket. When she was settled back in against his chest, he picked up a book.

"Reprobate's log, day one."

Julia laughed.

"We've only just left port and already I feel better. London has lost its charm, so I am off to greener pastures…"

They'd made it through many pages of exaggerated observation when the author made mention of his sister— Ruby.

"Which book did you say this was?" she asked.

"The memoir of a dashing young gentleman." He tried to pick up where he left off, but Julia pinched him.

"You're reading me your diary!"

"It's quite riveting."

"You are an incurable egotist," she laughed. "Read me one of the other ones."

"Which would you prefer, unapologetic prostitute or pirate story?"

"Pirate story."

He flipped through the book he was holding, finding a new page. "Reprobates log, day seventy-five. I believe we are under attack."

Julia pinched him. "That's still your diary."

"I only brought one book, love." The man was incorrigible.

"So, the unapologetic prostitute…"

"Much later in the sequence of events. Well after the pirates. Her name was Delphine—I think you'd have liked her."

Julia wasn't so sure about that, now that she knew these were accounts of Jasper's actual adventures. "Read me that one, then."

He didn't get a chance. A footman came to the door to tell Jasper there was a messenger waiting to hand-deliver an envelope for him. She felt Jasper's body tense beneath her.

"Is it a *royal* messenger?" Jasper asked.

"It is, my lord."

Jasper kissed her forehead again and made his excuses.

She would have followed him if she weren't certain to end up face down in the hallway. Did he know what the message was about? He appeared to have been expecting it. Why hadn't he said anything? But one did not leave a royal messenger languishing in the foyer.

Instead, she let him go without comment and turned her silent questions to the ceiling. A royal messenger could not be good news for her. In the best-case scenario, it had nothing to do with her and the queen was finally getting around to dressing him down for his behavior at his summons to Parliament.

In the worst case, Victoria had heard about them—likely from Ruby—and was commanding her cousin to stay away from *scandalous Julia Bishop*. Julia wouldn't put it past Ruby, especially not after her failed bribe.

If the queen did command him to stay away, would he do it? He said he loved her, but you didn't just ignore a direct order from the queen. How could she hope to keep him if the crown was set against them?

She never should have let herself love him.

Chapter Nineteen

Jasper took the stairs two at a time, apprehension quickening his steps. The need for Victoria's approval was higher than ever, now Julia had admitted she loved him.

It would be yes. It had to be yes. No one had ever been refused before.

In the foyer, the queen's messenger bowed from the waist and held out the crisply folded sheet of cream vellum. The queen's seal was stamped on it in silver wax. Jasper stared at it for a moment, like it might leap forward and bite him.

You're being ridiculous.

He accepted the letter and opened it.

Dearest Cousin,

Unfortunately I cannot, in good conscience, grant your request.

Please accept my deep apologies, and even deeper wishes for your future happiness.

Sincerely,

Victoria Reg.

That was it. No explanation, beyond that nonsense about her conscience. She'd written two lines and destroyed his bloody world. Two lines.

"Ruby!" Jasper bellowed at the top of his lungs. When she didn't immediately appear, he did it again.

The door to the drawing room opened and his sister appeared. Her expression should have turned him to stone. "I do not appreciate being shouted for."

Jasper didn't care. He was going to get answers. "What the hell is this?"

With raised eyebrows, she strode forward and took the page from his hand. Her eyes flicked back and forth as she scanned it. It didn't take long.

"She refused."

"Yes, I know she refused." Jasper snatched it back. "I want to know why."

Ruby sighed. "You knew this was a possibility."

"A miniscule one!"

"Not as small as you thought, apparently."

Jasper crumpled the page in his fist. "Did you do this? Did you interfere somehow?"

"No." The word was laced with venom. "You did this yourself, but by all means, blame it on me. Everything is my responsibility, isn't it?"

His anger reduced to a smolder. It wasn't gone, but it didn't have a suitable target right now. Jasper's shoulders slumped, and the paper fell from his hand. "She refused me."

As his temper deflated, so did Ruby's. She took him by the arm and led him into the drawing room. There was no one else there, just a wooden circle with Ruby's latest needlepoint on it. She pointed him at an armchair, and gravity did the rest.

Jasper stared at his empty hands. "I have to do something."

"I don't think there's anything to be done."

There was always something to be done. A DeVere didn't give up, and he didn't take no for an answer. "We'll go to Paris, or New York, and get married there."

"Jasper, you can't." Ruby clutched his arm. "If you disobey the queen's edict, it's tantamount to treason. You wouldn't be able to come back."

"I don't care about coming back."

Her gripped tightened. "England needs you. It needs the Duke of Albemarle."

"I don't care." England didn't care about what he needed. He would be damned if he spent a moment worrying about it. For his grandfather's sake, he could hire the right people and leave instructions before he left, but there was nothing keeping him here.

Ruby knelt down, filling his vision with her face. "You wanted Julia to believe you're serious. *Be* serious. Serious men don't run. Grandfather never did, and he'd be ashamed to hear you talk about abandoning his legacy now.

"Victoria said no, Ruby. What else am I supposed to do?"

Ruby gave him an encouraging smile as she stood up. "Go home. Make nice. Play the dutiful servant to the crown, and in a year, you can—"

"A year?" Jasper bellowed.

"Yes, a year," she threw back at him. "You know how this works. In a year, you can petition the privy council to reconsider. And you will spend the next twelve months making certain they side with you."

"They won't go against Victoria."

"They will, if you learn how to use the title correctly."

A year. It was too long. It wasn't as long as *never*, but it was still too long. But if he won and Julia still wanted him, they could stay here close to their families and build a life. He could wait for her. He would go home. He would learn to be the best damn duke anyone had ever seen, and he would win the right to choose who he married.

"Pack your things," he told Ruby. "I want to be on the four o'clock train."

She probably said something that was meant to be bolstering, but Jasper didn't hear it. He was too busy trying to figure out how he would explain to Julia.

He couldn't ask her to wait for him. A year was a long time, and she'd never wanted things to become complicated in the first place. Not to mention—he hadn't asked her to be his wife yet, and she certainly wasn't ready to say yes. Telling her he had to leave for a year to go pretend to be a model duke would not go over well.

Neither would the reason. Julia adored Victoria. How many times had she said the queen was her idol? Her idol's refusal had infuriated Jasper, but it would devastate Julia. After the fair, the Hathaway dinner, the argument with her father, even Amelia's uncertainty when she heard he had to ask.

Julia would believe it was her fault.

There was no way Jasper could willingly hurt her like that, and he couldn't lie to her. Which meant he couldn't tell her at all. A dull buzzing filled his ears, as he realized what he had to do.

Once he came to terms with it—or as close as he was

going to—Jasper went in search of Nicholas. How fitting that he should find his host in the same study where Nicholas had lectured him about the dangers of letting Julia fall for him. Had it been a fortnight? Not even.

"I need to borrow a carriage to take Ruby and me to the train station."

Nicholas looked up from the book he was studying. "Going back to London?"

*H*e hadn't come back. Every minute he was gone was another minute Julia spent imagining the worst, so she sent Nora to find out what was keeping him. Royal messengers did not deliver inconsequential news. When *Nora* didn't come back, Julia's worst fears ran rampant. No one ever gave her a moment's peace when she was recovering from a bout of fever, and she'd been alone for over an hour. Something very important was happening, and Julia needed to know what it was.

It was time to push the limits of her recovery. She took a deep breath and swung her legs out of bed. She waited to see if the motion would bring any nausea. When it didn't, she stood up.

The room tilted alarmingly.

Getting dressed was out of the question. Her nightgown would have to do. If anyone chose to be scandalized over her wandering the halls in a state of undress, they only had themselves to blame for not attending to her. Julia hated being left in the dark.

She hated worrying.

With a death grip on the stair railing, she made her way

downstairs. Before she reached the bottom, she could hear arguing coming from the drawing room. Sweating and out of breath, she pushed open the door.

"What the devil is going on?"

Nicholas, Amelia, and Nora all spun around to face her. One person was noticeably absent.

Nora rushed to her side. "You shouldn't be out of bed."

"Where's Jasper?" Julia asked. Silence met her question.

All the way down stairs, she told herself she was being ridiculous. She told herself she would come down here, and everything would be fine. Mia and Nora would chastise her for overreacting and send her back to bed. But Jasper wasn't here, and no one was saying anything.

She'd been right.

"He's gone," she whispered.

"He's gone," Nicholas confirmed.

Gone.

The exertion of her trek hit her all at once, and her knees buckled. Nora caught her and Amelia rushed forward to help. They settled her onto the nearest sofa.

He didn't even say good-bye. One minute he was reading to her and playing with her hair, and one minute he was just…gone. "How long ago did he leave?"

"Perhaps we should talk about that when you're feeling better," Amelia suggested.

Gone. Gone where? Gone for how long? Forever? They couldn't just say gone like it was an explanation. "What did the messenger want?"

More silence. Amelia rearranged pillows. Nora couldn't meet her eyes.

Julia turned to the person most likely to tell her the truth. "What happened, Nick?"

His face settled into rigid lines. "He left. He and Ruby

took the train back to London."

"Oh." It shouldn't be a surprise. She'd known he would have to leave eventually. She thought, when it happened, he'd at least tell her he was going, but he didn't owe her anything. That was how she'd wanted it. Insisted on it, even. Something masochistic made her ask, "Is he coming back?"

"No." Nick's tone broke through her calm, scattering it like leaves in the wind.

Her voice shook when she spoke. "You're certain?"

If anything, Nick's face became even stonier. "I'm certain."

That was it, then.

Jasper had left her—without saying good-bye or giving a reason–and he wasn't coming back. Maybe it was Ruby. Maybe it was the queen. Maybe he'd just changed his mind, like he warned her he might. Julia didn't know what exactly had sent him away, but she had always known something would. She tried to tell him they weren't meant to last, but he kept insisting they were more than that. Rather than admit she was right, he'd slunk away like a coward.

She wanted to hate him. She *would* hate him—just as soon as his absence didn't feel like a gaping hole ripped straight through the middle of her chest. Every gesture, every touch, every devilish smile and earnest word raced through her mind. Gone. It was all gone. He was gone.

Julia barely noticed when Nicholas helped her back to her room.

She'd been foolish enough to let him convince her they had a chance, but it had all been lies. How long had he known he would leave her? Certainly while he was stroking her hair and telling her how she would take care of him one day. *Lies.* Had it cost him anything to say it, knowing it wasn't true?

There was murmuring around her, and then the door closed. Nora tucked the blankets in around her. "Can I get you anything?"

"Just leave me alone."

Silence stretched. Nora's voice was soft when she answered, instead of her characteristic snap. "You know I can't do that."

"Then your services are no longer required." Better to lose Nora now, while everything hurt anyway, than lose her later. She would leave eventually. She would resent Julia eventually. It was just a matter of time.

Nora was unfazed. "We've been over this before. You can't fire me."

A flash of anger managed to break through the gray. She just wanted to be left alone. Was it too much to ask? "I said, go away."

"And I said no. I'll sit quietly so you don't notice I'm here. I'll forgive you for the awful things you're bound to say, because I know you're hurting, but I'm not going anywhere."

Somehow, that made it even worse. Julia rolled over, staring at the joint between the panels of wainscoting. Nora wouldn't leave her—but Jasper would.

She'd meant nothing to him.

Chapter Twenty

*R*uby wasted no time getting the summons reissued for him to finally, officially receive the dukedom. They were parked outside of Parliament, but Jasper still hadn't left the carriage. His sister was poised on the edge of her seat. She refused to step out until Jasper did. As if he was going to order the driver to leave the moment she was clear of the doors.

It was difficult to blame her, all things considered.

"I'm not going to bolt, Ruby."

"All right."

"It's safe for you to get out," he promised.

"Of course it is." Ruby settled in against the carriage seat.

Jasper sighed. "I just need a moment."

"Then I'll take a moment, too."

"A moment alone?"

If anything, Ruby managed to give the impression of being even more solidly rooted in place. A benign smile graced her lips. "Once the title is confirmed, you can be as alone as you like."

Or as alone as he didn't like. It had only been a few days without Julia and he was miserable. He didn't feel like eating. Every time he closed his eyes to sleep, her face appeared behind his eyelids, haunting him.

I'm doing this for her. For us.

He kept telling himself that, but it wasn't helping.

In public, he was playing the part. Making the calculated transition from enviable playboy to likeable leader. Letting Ruby drag him to balls and functions meant to reintroduce him to all the *right* people. But when he went home, he sat in the dark and missed Julia.

There was no point. Staying in the carriage wouldn't change anything. He couldn't even tell her the real reason he'd left, and she'd see right through him if he tried to give her excuses. There was nothing to do but accept his fate and try to figure out some way he could go back to visit or a way to write her without her guessing the truth.

Jasper pushed himself off the bench and stepped out of the door.

Ruby let out an audible sigh of relief.

Atherton was waiting for them on the steps. "I'm not doing this a third time, Bellamy. The only reason I'm doing it a second time is because your lovely sister asked me very nicely."

That must have been difficult, given Atherton's designs toward Ruby and Ruby's lack of interest. Although, given the way she was smiling at Atherton now, they'd managed to put most of their past behind them, but either way — Jasper would handle his own affairs from now on. No more allowing his sister to smooth things over or call in favors for him. That wasn't what his grandfather would have wanted.

It was time to start standing on his own.

"Is the queen here?" Jasper asked.

"No. We're just bowing to the cloth this time." Atherton smirked at him. "I don't think she wanted to run the risk of being embarrassed twice."

Or she was wary of being face-to-face with Jasper after she'd needlessly ruined his life. It was probably better she hadn't come. *No one* had ever been refused under the Royal Marriages Act. One of Jasper's relatives had gotten his mistress approved after they had two children together, for God's sake, but somehow, Victoria couldn't bring herself to accept Julia Bishop. Jasper wasn't certain he could keep his temper in check if he had to stand in front of her and bend the knee.

Rage swirled deep in his belly, but he pushed it down. Dukes didn't lose their tempers. Dukes *didn't have* tempers. They had power and privilege. Tempers were unnecessary.

This was his life now. Asinine ceremonies, and pretending to be someone he was not. Pretending to be the man his grandfather had been.

Essex met them at the door to the antechamber, with the man known as the Black Rod. "They've decided to rush the fanfare this time. We'll get right to it, if that's all right with you."

"Fine." There was no reason to delay.

They draped him in the crimson and ermine cloak, walking him along in the procession. The herald presented his letters patent, and Jasper bowed to the absent monarchy. His voice caught a few times during the Oath of Allegiance, but he forced his way through it. Then he was signing the roll and being led to a bench for a lot of rising and sitting and the taking on and off of his hat. It all finished with a bow to the Lord Chancellor, and then the procession was being led back out of the chamber.

The entire time, Jasper just thought of Julia. Her smile. The clever gibes she surely would have made about his peers. The way she would be proud of him, even though there was nothing to be proud of. All he'd done was be born and survive this long. He hadn't earned anything.

He hadn't earned her.

He would, though. If it was the last thing he did, he would bend the world to his will and become worthy of her in the process.

In the antechamber, Jasper spent the minimum necessary time accepting the congratulation of his peers, making sure to have individual moments with the men Ruby had indicated would be key to his success, and then he headed back to the carriage.

As he climbed in, Ruby asked, "It's done?"

"It's done."

"Did you spend a moment with Wesley, Norton, and—"

"I spent time with everyone you asked me to."

His sister's smile should have warmed his heart, but it barely registered. Jasper held one of the most powerful titles in the country, and he'd never felt more helpless.

A year of this. Julia wouldn't be waiting for him, because as far as she knew, there was nothing to wait for.

Oblivious, Ruby launched into a list of things that needed to be done, now that he was the Duke of Albemarle. "…the gala Lord Wesley is throwing to launch that new painter, and I've arranged for an audience with Victoria so you can apologize and get back on the right foot."

The last part interrupted Jasper's litany of self-pity. There was one thing he hadn't yet tried—arguing his case to Victoria.

Maybe she could be made to see reason. Or maybe she needed to be reminded that no monarch had managed a successful reign without the backing of the Duke of Albemarle. Jasper was prepared to use whichever method would achieve the desired result.

"When is the audience?"

Ruby perked up at his interest. "Two weeks. I'm not sure what time—you know how those things go—so you'll need to clear your whole day."

"That won't be a problem."

He would meet with the queen, but not to apologize. Not even close.

*R*ain poured down outside her bedroom window, echoing Julia's mood. Sitting in this house, feeling sorry for herself, missing Jasper, was driving her mad. She tried to muster up the will to hate him, but it wouldn't come.

"Julia?" Lord Bishop came up behind her.

She plastered a smile she didn't feel onto her face. "Papa, you're back."

"I was just downstairs, filling Amelia in on my trip." His eyes crinkled with concern. "Your sister told me about—"

Julia held up her hand, stopping him. She didn't want to talk about Jasper. Not with her father, or with anybody. "I'm fine. How was Mother?"

His face fell even further. "We had a good visit. I think she might be better, but I...I couldn't tell for certain, so I didn't bring her back."

"Love can blind you to the truth sometimes." Like father, like daughter. They'd both chosen poorly. Julia returned her attention to the dreary scene outside the window.

The heavy warmth of his hand came down on her shoulder. "Julia."

"You do still love her, don't you?"

"Very much."

"How do you—" Julia cleared her throat, refusing to cry again. "How do you stand to be apart? Or to see her, knowing what she did?"

His deep breath filled the space. His hand felt twice as heavy. "What else can I do?"

"Hate her."

Lord Bishop's tone was strained, just like Julia's. "Some days I do. She hurt you girls with what she did, and I can't forgive that."

"But it's still difficult for you to breathe when you realize she's not here."

"Yes."

Julia nodded. "If you hear about a cure for that, you have my permission to pursue it."

He squeezed her shoulder.

Lord Bishop had never been very good with female despondency. Their mother was fond of the sort of overdramatic outbursts that were easy to discount, and the sisters had always endeavored to be pleasant whenever he was near. But this time, he was faring pretty well. Julia had never felt closer to her father than this moment of shared misery.

He gave her shoulder one last pat, and drew it away. "I have to go into London for some business. Would you like to go with me? A change might cheer you up."

More people. More reminders that she would never have the life she dreamed of. "No, thank you. I'd just like to be alone."

"If that's what you want."

It was as close as she'd get to what she wanted.

Lord Bishop hesitated at the door. "Are you sure you'll be all right?"

Julia smiled again. She made sure to put effort into it this time. "Perfectly fine, Papa. Have fun in Town."

Her father nodded, instructing her not to get up to too much trouble, and then he, too, was gone. Someday it would be just like this—everyone gone and Julia all alone.

Except for Amelia.

The door opened again, and her sister joined her at the window, a near-permanent presence the last few weeks. It was putting a strain on Amelia and Nick's marriage. They hardly spent any time together, with Amelia constantly by Julia's side, and Nick was too good of a friend to admit he missed his wife's attention. Julia had told her to stop. She'd even tried to leave to go back to home, but Amelia had gone so far as to instruct the staff not to ready any carriages or saddle any horses for Julia unless Amelia was with her.

"You should go to London," Amelia announced.

"So that was your idea."

"I think it would do you some good."

"And risk running into Jasper? I don't think so." What would she even say to him?

Julia left the window and slumped down onto the chair by the fire, leafing through a book in the hopes that her sister would take the hint and leave the room.

No such luck.

Amelia dropped down beside her and took the book, putting it out of her reach. "I can't believe you're taking this lying down."

"Believe it."

"The royal messenger came right before he left. Don't you wonder why?"

"No." Julia was done with wondering. All she wanted to do was forget him. She wanted to go back to being the Julia Bishop that had never known what it was like to be loved by Jasper DeVere.

To be left by him.

"He asked the queen for permission to marry you."

Everything in the room went still. Julia's breath caught and the feeling of her heartbeat came in slow motion. He'd wanted to marry her.

No.

It was just more cowardice. He had no business asking Victoria, when he hadn't bothered to ask Julia. She shook out her hands, taking a deep breath to keep her body from trying to start crying again. It wasn't romantic, because *he wasn't here*. Whatever Jasper and Julia might have been, he'd ruined it. He'd left. He didn't get credit for doing or feeling anything, because he hadn't been man enough to stay.

Amelia watched her closely. "Aren't you curious about what the response was?"

"Does it matter? If he left because she said no, he still left." It was time to put a stop to this. Julia had let go of the hope that he was coming back. Now Mia needed to do the same. This wasn't doing either of them any good.

"It'd be a reason, and—"

"He didn't want me, Mia! Not enough to make a difference." Julia squeezed her eyes shut to keep from breaking down into more useless tears. "Whatever the reason, he didn't stay, and he didn't care enough to tell me why he was leaving. He doesn't love me."

"I don't believe that, and neither do you."

She had to. You didn't just abandon the people you love with no word, no explanation. Whatever that was, it wasn't love. Someone who loved her wouldn't put her through this. Nothing he could say would change that.

Amelia took her hands, squeezing a little too hard. "You deserve a reason, Julia."

Julia closed her eyes. "If I ask him, and he tells me the truth—that he just didn't love me enough…"

It would destroy her.

Because she had felt loved. Right up until the moment he left her. She'd already lost him. She didn't want to add insult to injury by hearing him tell her how little she meant to him. Not when she still had a few good memories to cherish.

"Even if that's what he says, you know it's not true. We both know that's not true."

If they were having this conversation, whether Julia wanted it or not, then they would have it all the way. She opened her eyes and looked her sister directly in the face. "If he loved me, then why did he go?"

"I don't think he wanted to."

Not good enough. "Why did he go, Mia?"

"Maybe he was afraid."

He didn't get to be afraid. Not after the things he'd said, the life he'd tricked her into wanting. "What was his reason, Mia? What's the thing that makes it all forgivable?"

"I—" Amelia's voice broke. She looked away, pulling her hands back. "I don't know, but neither will you until you ask him."

Was that what everyone wanted? Was that what it would take for them to finally leave her alone? Her ripping her heart out by seeing him one last time and making him admit he'd run way because it wasn't worth it anymore?

Fine. If that was what had to be done, she'd give it to them. When it didn't change anything and she was still impossibly miserable, they would let her sit by herself and feel however she wanted to feel, or she would burn this bloody house down.

Julia stood up, shaking the wrinkles from her skirts. "Go stop Father from leaving while I have Nora pack."

"You're going to London?" Amelia jumped up with a giant grin on her face. "You're going to fight for Jasper?"

"For him—no." Julia's eyes narrowed into slits. "But there will definitely be a fight."

Chapter Twenty-One

"Exhausted" did not begin to cover Jasper's mood on his way home from his audience with the queen. He'd decided to stay at his townhouse to avoid having to face his grandmother or Ruby, and it proved to be a wise choice. At some point, he would have to account for the things he'd said to his monarch, but he did not have the energy for it today.

It was his fault.

Sometime between Victoria refusing to change her mind and Jasper saying a number of things that might still end with him being thrown in prison, he'd gotten her to admit why she had denied his request. The queen regent was harboring a grudge. After his walk-out in Parliament, she "believed he needed a wife with impeccable experience navigating social mores." Someone who would be able to smooth over the detrimental faux pas he was certain to make as he embarked on his life as the Duke of Albemarle. She did not believe Julia Bishop was the woman for the job.

Needless to say, Jasper had not responded well. He was

not impressed with the biased matchmaking opinions of a person five years his junior who had spent her formative years locked away in a country house. He had said so—along with a number of other things that could reasonably be perceived as threats to the crown. There was only one opinionated woman Jasper wanted making decisions about his life, and thanks to the queen's vendetta, he couldn't have her.

He was an idiot for not telling Julia. The queen didn't deserve her adoration. He should have explained it. He should have found a way. He should have done anything except leave her the way he had. Now more than ever, this life of titles and audiences meant nothing to him, and Julia meant everything. Whatever else his grandfather may have wanted for Jasper, he never would have wanted him to be this miserable.

"Your Grace." The butler's rumbling tones hit Jasper when he finally made it through the door of the townhouse. "How many daughters does Lord Bishop have?"

Jasper blinked. "What relevance could that question possibly have, Thompson?"

"A second daughter has arrived, unchaperoned. I just wondered how many I might expect in the future." Thompson had never forgiven Amelia for the day she'd managed to gain entry into Jasper's study under false pretenses and stolen a rather risqué invitation.

Thompson's wounded pride would have to wait. Jasper's pulse had started pounding the moment the other man said 'arrived'. "This Bishop daughter—blonde, gorgeous, lights up a room?"

Thompson's thick eyebrows fell into a craggy frown. "She is blonde, and waiting in your study, despite my insistence that you were not at home."

She'd come after him.

"Bishop just has the two daughters, and I'm in love with this one. She is welcome under any circumstances." Jasper didn't wait for the apoplexy that was certain to follow.

There was no telling what their meeting would be like— she might be here to put a bullet in him, for all he knew. It didn't matter. When he stepped into the study and saw her, his smile was so wide he thought it would split his face.

Julia was lounging at his desk, sifting idly through its contents. At the sound of the door closing, she looked up. There was no answering smile on her face, just an expression like cut stone. "I deserve an explanation."

"I know, and I—"

"You left me!" She shouted, unwilling to let him answer. She held on to the edge of his desk tight enough to turn her knuckles white.

Jasper kept his voice soft. "I know I did."

She threw her shoulders back and lifted her chin. "I cried over you *for days*."

It cut him to the core, knowing he'd made her feel that way, but they were together now. Everything would be all right. "Julia, I can explain."

His paperweight sailed through the air, narrowly missing his head as he ducked.

She picked up a box of calling cards, poised to throw. "I didn't even want your ridiculous future! I tried to keep things just temporary, but you insisted. You *made me* believe it would last!"

He had. He was every bit the villain she was accusing him of. "Julia, I'm sorry."

"Are you? Are you really?" she spat.

"Of course I am." He would give anything to take back what he'd done. If he could just make her understand. He stepped toward her with his hands up. "I love you, Julia."

"Then why did you leave!" A storm of objects sailed across the space between them.

He ducked again, coming around the desk to grab her arms so he could survive long enough to explain. If she still needed to throw things at him after that, he wouldn't stop her.

"I asked the queen for permission to marry you and she refused. I didn't know what else to do. Ruby said—"

Julia shoved him away. "Leave your sister out of this. You did this. You didn't have the courage to tell me. *You* didn't say a word to me before you left. Not Ruby."

It was all true. He had no excuse for it.

"What do you want, Julia? Just tell me and I'll do it."

Julia glared at him. "Tell me why. If you had a reason, why didn't I deserve to know it?"

"I thought it would hurt you if you knew Victoria turned down the request. I didn't want you to think it was your fault."

"So instead you said *nothing*?" She shook her head, splotches of red rising up on her neck and cheeks. "Nothing Victoria could say would hurt me as badly as what you did."

It was like a punch to the gut. All he'd wanted was to protect her from this. Even now, with her shouting and throwing things at him, he just wanted things to go back to how they were. "I was a coward. I wanted to ask you to marry me, and then she said no, and I didn't know how to make it right."

Julia's teeth clenched. Her hands came up, closing around nothing—just empty air. She screamed without words until she found them. "I never needed you to marry me!"

"I did." He needed every morning and every night and

all the hours in between. "I still do."

"Well, good for you, you selfish bastard. I'm glad it's all about what you need." She wiped away tears with an angry brush of her hand. "How do you think that's working out for us? Are you happy?"

"I'm miserable."

"Good."

"Are you—"

"Don't," she snapped. "You don't get to ask me that."

They stood and stared at each other; Julia silently fuming while Jasper drank in the sight of her. As his eyes pored over her, her posture wavered and she gripped the edge of his desk.

Jasper was by her side in an instant. "Are you sick?"

"Don't touch me!"

"Are you sick, Julia?" He demanded an answer. It was more important than any fight.

She shook her head. "No."

He knew that stubborn look. "When was the last time you ate, or slept?"

Her lack of an answer was answer enough.

"Come on." Jasper took her hand, and she let him. He pulled her toward the door.

"Where are we going?"

"My bedroom."

Julia dug in her heels, stopping them in place. "You left me. You don't get to pretend that didn't happen. I *do not* forgive you."

"I'm not asking you to. You need sleep. Let me take care of you."

"No."

"Please, Julia." If anything happened to her, he wouldn't survive it. He needed to take care of her. He needed to do the right thing for *her*, like he should have done weeks ago. "I won't touch you, and it doesn't have to mean anything. Don't let this cost you more than it has."

She didn't move.

"You can resume yelling at me once you've had some rest."

The exhaustion was getting to her. She was swaying on her feet. "You're not sleeping with me."

"I will keep my distance, if that's what you want."

"It is." With a tired sigh, she asked, "Where's your room?"

He showed her to his bedroom. Without saying a word, she slipped off her shoes and climbed onto the giant bed that dominated the room, pulling blankets and pillows around her as she settled in. Jasper lowered the gas lamps, until only the light from the fireplace remained.

"You're an ass, Jasper DeVere."

He sat down in the chair on the far side of the room. "I know."

As her eyes closed and her breathing settled into a steady rhythm, a weight Jasper had been carrying for weeks slowly faded away. His eyelids drooped. A few times he would pop awake, desperate to make sure she was still there, but she hadn't moved. Eventually he lost the battle and sleep took him.

For the first time since he'd walked away from her, it was peaceful.

When his eyes opened again, it was with a jolt. Something had struck him in the chest. A woman's slipper.

"Wake up," Julia demanded from his bed. She was sitting up with her legs drawn under her, looking much less exhausted.

Jasper smiled. "Good morning."

Julia scowled. "It's still night."

It didn't matter. She was still here. "Julia, I just want you to know—"

"I didn't come here to reconcile," she interrupted. "I just wanted you to know that you're an idiot, and I didn't believe for a second that you weren't madly in love with me."

Something was happening. He could feel it. She wasn't glaring at him as intently and some of the volume had gone out of her voice.

"You don't deserve me." She wouldn't look at him, choosing instead to focus on something over his right shoulder. "At all."

"All true." He fought to keep the grin from creeping onto his face and ruining everything.

"The queen's an idiot, too. I'd be the best duchess anyone has ever seen."

A laugh slipped out. Julia's eyes widened dangerously, and he held up his hands. "I agree, on all counts."

She settled again, glaring imperiously around his room. "Did she say why she refused?"

"It had nothing to do with you." Julia wouldn't look at him, but he looked straight at her, trying to convince her of the truth. "She's punishing me for embarrassing her. She says I need a wife who can smooth things over in society for me, since I'm bound to foul it up."

The corner of her lips twitched. "She did not say that."

"She did, actually."

When Julia finally looked at him, there was a sheen of tears in her eyes. "You don't get to marry anyone who isn't me."

"I won't." He couldn't sit still anymore. He started to get up from the chair. "May I…"

She nodded.

Jasper crossed the distance between them. He sat beside her on the bed, and set his hand on the coverlet, palm up. She hesitated for a moment, before she reached out and took it.

"I'm sorry. I'm so very sorry," he said. "It didn't feel right to ask you to be anything less than my wife. Not when you deserve—"

"A lifetime of tears? That's what you chose for us, Jasper. That's what being apart means for us."

"I know." Jasper pulled her into his chest, wrapping his arms around her. "Please don't make me live without you. I know it's what I deserve, but please don't."

"We're not going by what you deserve anymore—or what you want. You've made a mess of it, and now I get to make all of our decisions unilaterally."

It was a slightly terrifying thought. Julia was anything but typical and her decisions wouldn't be, either. Still, Jasper would rather be terrified than be without her. "I'm at your mercy."

*W*hat did she want? She could hurt him as badly as he hurt her, but not without destroying herself in the process. She'd been a fool to think she could come here without falling straight back into love with him.

Damn you, Jasper DeVere.

"After you left, what happened? What have you been doing?" Part of Julia hoped he'd been doing the same thing she had—wallowing in misery.

"I've been trying to fix it."

"How?"

He sighed. "By being the perfect duke. Playing politics, so I can ask the privy council to overrule Victoria's decision."

Julia leaned back so she could scowl at him. "I'm sure your sister had nothing to do with that plan."

"She was involved," he admitted. "It was the only way I could see where we could stay in England and get married. Though, after the scene I just made in the throne room, I'm not sure that's still an option."

It wasn't about her getting sick or him not wanting her. It was because of these asinine ideas about what she deserved. If they were going to make a go of it, that had to stop.

"I need you to promise me something."

"What is it? Anything in my power to give, I'll—"

She put her fingers against his lips. The man talked entirely too much. "Promise me, from now on, what I want will matter more than your fool notions about what I *ought* to have."

"I promise."

"Sometimes, that's going to mean you have to ask me what I want."

"I will." His hand came up, tipping her chin. "Does that mean you'll have me back?"

I never let you go. "That depends. Are you going to object when I insist you get me an audience with the queen?"

Jasper laughed. He pressed a kiss to her lips. "I don't see why I would. I got to try—even if it just made things worse."

She leaned closer into his chest, running her hands over his forearms. It felt good to touch him again. "I'm sure you made an excellent argument, but you're used to being powerful. You don't know how to win your point from an inferior position."

Julia knew all about fighting at a disadvantage. No one, queen or otherwise, was going to stand between Julia and happiness anymore. On that note, she had another request.

"Will you take me somewhere tomorrow night?"

"Where?" he asked.

"Anywhere. A ball. The theater. Whatever can be arranged on short notice." Anything public would do.

Jasper pressed his lips to her temple. "I have a box at the opera. I think it's *Maria Padilla* tomorrow."

"Perfect."

Julia didn't want to let him out of her sight, but it was past time for her to be going. Any minute now the watch would come bursting in, sent by her father. Or Nora, preaching hellfire and brimstone because Julia was about to miss an item on the schedule. At the mention of the schedule, Jasper called up his carriage to give her a ride home. He insisted on riding with her, and when they pulled up in front of the Bishops' London house, neither of them was ready for her to get out.

"Tomorrow," she said.

"Tomorrow," he promised.

She climbed down without looking back, lest she change her mind and decide to stay with him indefinitely. There was no question that he would let her.

After returning herself to Nora's care, Julia went through the motions, but her mind wasn't on their nightly routine. It was on her conversation with Jasper, and her future audience with the queen. She hadn't lied—Jasper leaving hurt her far more than anything Victoria could say, but that didn't mean meeting the queen was going to be easy. Julia had never been presented at court. She wasn't prepared.

In the end, it wouldn't matter. Victoria already disapproved, so there was nothing for Julia to lose. It was a fatalistic thought, but oddly comforting, and it let her finally get to sleep after hours of staring at the ceiling.

The following day, she had to face a different fear. No matter how much the queen disapproved of her, Victoria was certain to be dignified and reserved. There were no such guarantees regarding the other men and women at the opera. Julia rolled every possible scenario over in her head. *You've got nothing to lose. If it goes as bad as you think it will, you haven't lost anything.*

If it went better, it would be a bloody miracle. "How do I look, Nora?"

Nora positioned the last of the feathers in Julia's hair while Julia pulled on her stark-white opera gloves. They'd never been worn before because every time she thought she might go, she ended up changing her mind. Not this time. No matter what anyone said or did, Julia was going to stand her ground.

"You look as pretentious as the best of them, Lady Julia." Nora was grinning when she said it.

She was ready.

Julia went downstairs, where Jasper was waiting in head-to-toe black with a peek of white showing at his throat. For a moment, all she saw was his slow smile as she walked into the room. Then she realized Nicholas and Amelia were waiting with him.

"What are you two doing here?"

"We're allowed to come to London if we want." Amelia kissed her cheek. "Besides, you need a chaperone, and Papa hates the opera."

"You're trying to steal my moment," Julia accused, but there was no one she'd rather experience her first opera with than Mia, Jasper, and Nicholas.

"It's not just your moment," Amelia said. "I've been waiting for this for years."

"And you?" Julia asked Nicholas.

He put an arm around his wife's waist. "Where Amelia goes, so goes my nation."

"Is there room for everyone?"

Jasper took her opera cloak, settling the beaded velvet over her shoulders. "I think we can manage."

"Then I guess we should be off."

The Bishop townhouse wasn't far from Covent Garden, so they were barely in the carriage for more than a few minutes before they'd pulled up in front of the towering columns of the Royal Opera House. Julia held on to Jasper's arm to keep her hands from shaking as they ascended the steps. She was pleased to discover that it was mostly due to anticipation.

Jasper leaned in, talking low. "I prefer the Italian operas. They have so much more passion than some of the others."

She knew what he was doing, trying to distract her nerves, and she loved him for it. "Let me guess—it ends tragically. Possibly with a double suicide."

"I have no idea what you mean." He suddenly found the sleeve of his jacket very interesting.

The lobby was full of milling nobility. The women looked like glittering jewels in their silks under all the lights. As they moved through the crowd toward the entrance to Jasper's box, conversations died off and then picked back up at a whisper. Jasper's arm tensed under her hand.

"It's all right," she told him. She didn't care what they thought. It was a beautiful night, she felt beautiful, and the most handsome man in the room was wildly in love with her. They had nothing she wanted—not even their approval.

Ahead of them, a man didn't bother keeping his voice low. "Apparently, they'll let anyone into the opera these days."

She might not want his approval, but she'd be damned if she'd accept his scorn. Julia pretended to trip as they passed him, backhanding his drink across the crisp white fabric of his cravat.

"Oh, my!" Julia let her love of the dramatic have free rein. "How clumsy of me. I hope you have time to change before the performance."

The gas lights raised and lowered, signaling that people should take their seats.

Jasper's crooked grin taunted her, and she moved past him to take her seat. "You are a wicked woman, Julia Bishop."

"I have no idea what you mean." Her smile was coy.

People continued to point and make a spectacle of themselves as the opening strains of music started but, for once, she barely noticed. She let them all fade away and focused on the story. It was about a girl who falls in love with a king, and they marry in secret because he's supposed to marry a princess. The girl's father comes to court and, believing the king has taken his daughter as a mistress, challenges the king to a duel. Meanwhile, the girl's enemies try to convince her the king married the princess anyway, but the king finds out and proclaims the girl as his rightful wife and queen.

As the opera unfolded, Jasper's hand snuck over to hers, entwining their fingers. She looked over at Amelia a few times, and caught her sister staring back. They shared a smile.

The whole thing would have been perfect—if the girl hadn't then inexplicably killed herself at the end. *Leave it to Jasper.*

When the last note finished, he asked, "Was that what you wanted?"

Julia looked down at the gallery, and out at the other boxes opposite theirs. A few people were looking and talking behind their fans, but they all seemed so much smaller than the people in the box beside her.

She smiled back at him. "It's a start."

Chapter Twenty-Two

$\mathcal{O}$n the day of the audience with the queen, Jasper was a wreck. Beneath his court jacket, his skin was uncomfortably warm and his shoes, which had always fit perfectly up until that moment, had begun to pinch.

It wasn't just that he was afraid they would be refused again. Or that he was nervous for Julia, who was holding up remarkably well under the circumstances. It was also the elaborate piece of jewelry weighing down the inside pocket of his jacket that he couldn't keep his mind off of.

"There's no way this ends favorably," Nicholas said for the third time.

"Likely not."

"And you're going through with it anyway."

"It's what Julia wants." Jasper pulled at his cravat without actually untying it.

Julia and Amelia finished their perusal of the Green Drawing Room, and Jasper saw his opening. Ruby had disappeared to discuss their place on the list of audiences with a clerk. He wasn't going to get a better chance before they saw the queen.

"Could I speak with you a moment, Julia?" He tried to keep his tone as neutral as possible, but he failed miserably.

Julia exchanged a look with Amelia and dragged him off to a corner. "What's wrong?"

"Nothing is wrong."

"Something is wrong. Jasper, I can't have anything go wrong right now. I'm—"

He dropped down to his knee.

Julia stared at him, mouth open.

He searched for the words he'd planned to say, but for the first time in his life he was at a loss. He'd crafted a whole speech and he couldn't remember it.

"Jasper?"

He shook himself. *Just say what you feel.* "I wanted to do this somewhere special, but then I thought—Buckingham Palace—there are worse places."

"Worse places for what?" She was looking at him like he'd lost his mind.

Maybe he'd be better off trying a different tactic. He gave it another shot, this time without words. Jasper reached into his pocket and pulled out the ring.

Julia gasped.

A halo of white diamonds, set in gold, surrounded a much larger yellow diamond that reminded him of the color of her hair in sunlight. When he first saw the ring at the jewelers, it made him think of the night she showed up in the drawing room wearing that outrageous black dress and dripping with diamonds.

"Julia Bishop, will you be my wife?"

She didn't take her eyes off the ring. "We don't have the queen's permission yet."

"I don't care what the queen wants." Despite where he

was kneeling, no lightning bolt arrived from the heavens to strike him down. "What do you want?"

The wait for her answer felt like an eternity.

Slowly, Julia took the ring from him and held it out in front of her. Her hand shook, and she kept her lips pressed together, like her answer might fly out if she didn't keep them clamped shut.

Please say yes. "If you say no, it doesn't change anything. I still love you. I still want us."

No matter how complicated things were, no matter what Victoria said, he still wanted to be with her—but he also wanted her to *want* to be his wife.

She slid the ring over the fourth finger of her left hand and held it up to the light. Her lips parted. Finally, *finally*, she looked at him.

"Yes."

It came out as a whisper but Jasper would have heard her even if they were in the middle of traffic on Piccadilly Circus.

"Yes," she said again, louder.

He jumped to his feet and wrapped her in his arms. She pulled his head down, and her kiss answered all the questions he didn't have time to ask. She wanted to marry him—entirely for herself. Not because he'd asked. Not because they were afraid of losing each other. They were in this together. They wanted the same thing.

When they pulled back, it was only enough to let each other breathe. His forehead rested on hers and he brought her fingers to his lips. "Nothing else matters. Just this."

"Just us." She kissed him again, quickly, catching her own fingers in the process. As they laughed, she peeked around his shoulder, and her lips spread into a wide smile. "They might matter, too, a little."

Jasper turned around to find Amelia practically bouncing with excitement, and Nicholas doing his best to contain her.

Nick grinned at him. "Welcome to the ranks of the hopelessly devoted."

Amelia was squealing in delight. "I knew it. I knew it! How many times did I say—"

"Nobody likes a sore winner, sweetheart." Nick winked at her.

Jasper tucked Julia in closer to his side, unable to keep from smiling.

She smiled back, before taking a deep breath. "Now I just have to face the queen, and convince her to like me."

"It's not too late to back out," Nick told her.

Amelia elbowed her husband. "You're not helpful."

"It really is too late," Ruby informed them all, over-hearing Nick's comment as she rejoined them. "Jasper has already walked out on one appointment with the queen, and that's one time too many for any family."

Julia leaned close, whispering under her breath. "Did your sister just refer to me as family?"

"I don't think she realizes," he whispered back.

"What don't I realize?" Ruby looked at each of them, going pale when she saw the ring. "Take that off."

If she were his brother instead of his sister, Jasper would have become the first person to strike someone in the Green Drawing Room.

But Julia proved perfectly capable of handling the situation herself. "No."

"I mean it. Take that off right now."

"I meant it when I said no."

Ruby closed her eyes and pressed at the crease between her eyebrows. "I'm not resisting your match, but you cannot go into an audience with the queen wearing the engagement ring of a man she has forbidden you to marry."

"I'm not taking it off." Julia's chin had raised a few notches.

Jasper squeezed her arm in support. His sister was probably right—she usually was where this sort of thing was concerned—but he was glad Julia had refused. Now that she'd put it on, he never wanted her to take it off.

"Why you both insist on making everything as difficult as possible, I will never understand." With her eyes still closed, Ruby inhaled and exhaled slowly. When she opened them, the dark-brown depths were sharply focused. "All right. Lady Julia, come with me. If we're going to get through this with a favorable result, you need a plan."

It was nearly impossible to walk in the heavy ivory court gown Ruby had loaned her, but Julia was too nervous to be still and sitting wasn't an option without crushing the unwieldy train. Instead, she and Ruby made slow laps up and down a nearby gallery.

"I'm not taking the ring off." They would have to pry it from her corpse if they wanted her to remove it. Jasper had proposed. Even if they could never marry, that ring proved how they felt about each other. She wasn't about to let anyone take that away.

"I've moved on," Ruby announced. "So should you."

"All right."

"Keep your right hand covering your left. It will look demure, and most women keep their hands clasped after they curtsy anyway."

"About that…"

Ruby stopped dead. She turned to face Julia. "You can't curtsy."

"I can try, but especially in this dress—it's not likely to go well."

She was almost beginning to feel sorry for Ruby. Almost.

"You're going to be the Duchess of Albemarle. We can't have you falling over in the throne room." Ruby resumed walking, and it didn't escape Julia's notice that it was at a slower pace. "Acknowledge your limitation gracefully, and then skip to the next thing. Don't linger on it."

"What is the next thing, according to your strategy?"

"You can go one of two ways. Express how devoted you are to Jasper, or enumerate the ways in which you are qualified to be his duchess." They reached the end of the gallery, and turned to head back down. "Normally I'd say stick to the qualifications, but Victoria is something of a romantic so professing your love for my brother might actually work."

Professing her love wouldn't be so bad, albeit a bit awkward in a room full of courtiers and stewards, but the qualifications would be trickier. Julia didn't imagine they counted chess mastery, excellent horsemanship, or a love of gossip among the desirable attributes for a duchess.

"What if I'm not?"

"Not what?" Ruby asked.

"Qualified."

They stopped again, and Julia had to hide her shock when Ruby took her hand. "Under no circumstances can you let them see you flinch."

Julia had never before wondered how many times Ruby had walked past a group of whisperers with her chin held high. She could desperately use some of Ruby's poise right about now.

"You're bold, and you have a superior intellect. Those will help you as a duchess, and they'll help you get through this audience."

They returned to the Green Drawing Room as the guard was calling their names. It was their turn. Julia clasped her hands, using the pressure of Jasper's ring against her palm to keep herself focused.

The whole court ceremony had been explained to her in detail, but Julia had zero hope of remembering it all. Fortunately, she wouldn't have to. Ruby was ahead of her in rank, so Julia just copied everything she did. At the door, Ruby dropped her dress train to the carpet and let the lords-in-waiting fan it out for her as she passed, so Julia did the same. Ruby presented her name card to the man standing in front of the queen and curtsied when he called it.

It was the moment of truth. She looked at Amelia, then at Jasper. They both smiled. Julia handed the man her card.

"Lady Julia Bishop," he announced.

Julia stood completely straight, with her shoulders back, looking into the face of her queen. "There are circumstances, of which I believe you are aware, that prevent me from curtsying."

A murmur went through the assembled lords and ladies-in-waiting. The slightest of sneers lifted the upper lip of the queen.

Julia's chin rose a notch higher, gathering every ounce of bravery she could muster. "I came today to tell you I reject your refusal."

Beside her, Ruby whimpered. "Oh, God."

"I will be marrying Jasper DeVere, Duke of Albemarle,

at my family home in Berkshire in one fortnight, whether or not the crown chooses to recognize it."

"Lady Julia!" A steward came forward, trying to stifle her.

Do not let them see you flinch.

"You cannot keep us apart. You cannot tell us who we can love."

Chaos erupted around them. Victoria never said a word. Guards hauled them all off to a side room while advisors argued over what to do with them. Presumably someone went to consult with the queen about whether she would like to revive the previously abandoned tradition of beheadings.

"That was not the statement we discussed in the gallery," Ruby hissed once they'd been left alone.

"I decided to improvise." Julia looked to Jasper. "Do you mind terribly about the fortnight and the wedding?"

He took her hand and kissed her knuckles. "Not at all."

Ruby threw her hands up. "You're both fools. It won't be legal. It will be treason, in fact, if you try to have a clergyman do it. We could have petitioned the privy council in a year, but after this debacle—"

She was interrupted by the arrival of the Duke of Buccleuch, Victoria's Lord Privy Seal. He looked over the group with a stern eye.

"They dinnae call ye the scandalous Bishops by accident, do they?" His Scots brogue held no warmth. "I've been instructed to let ye go with the understanding that none of ye are welcome back at court. Is that clear?"

It was Nicholas who answered for them. "Yes, your grace."

"Ye'll leave out a side door—your carriages have been instructed on where to meet ye—and I will not be reading about today's little drama in any of the papers, or ye can expect formal charges."

They all nodded and murmured their agreement. They were shown out a servants' entrance where, as promised, their carriages were waiting. Ruby took one on her own, fuming in murderous silence over her ejection from court, and the four of them piled into the remaining coach.

Jasper turned to Julia and asked, "What would the woman who just mouthed off to the queen of England like to do with the *rest* of her day?"

The answer was easy.

"If it's not too much trouble, I'd like to go home."

She'd told off the queen, and lived to tell the tale. Victoria had just sat there, looking at Julia like she'd grown a second head. So much for Julia's childhood fantasy of them becoming the best of friends, but her dream of spending the rest of her life with Jasper was back on.

They were going to have a wedding—albeit an illegal one, on her father's land instead of in a church—in just two weeks. There was something to be said for shirking all convention. They wouldn't have been able to secure Westminster Abbey on such short notice, and Julia didn't want to wait a moment longer than necessary to start her life with Jasper.

At the townhouse, Jasper held her hands against his chest while he smiled down at her with the same grin he'd been wearing since she said yes. "Will you be terribly disappointed if I take a later train? I need to make amends with Ruby for putting her on the queen's bad side."

"Of course." Julia didn't want to let him go, but she didn't want him at odds with his sister, either. Not after everything Ruby had done to help her prepare. "Tell her I'm sorry she got caught in the middle."

"I will." He kissed her with enough heat to melt her slippers.

"I'll give you a ride," Nick offered. "I've got to stay and sort some business for next term."

Amelia cleared her throat. "So, you're going to abandon me."

Nick kissed her cheek. "You know you were going to ignore me the whole trip anyway, so you could plot with your sister."

He wasn't wrong. On the train back to Reading, Julia didn't waste any time getting started on the planning.

"Do you think gold is too ostentatious for a wedding?" she asked Amelia.

"Would my saying yes stop you?"

Gold might be a bit much. Then again, only a few people would be in attendance and they already knew Julia's tastes. It *would* go beautifully with her ring. "You're right. I want everything done in gold."

"That's easy, then." Amelia brushed her palms against each other to indicate a job well-done. "We'll just transfer your bedroom to the back lawn, and voila. Gold wedding."

"You think you're very amusing, don't you?" Her room was not that gold. There were notable patches of ivory.

Nevertheless, Julia would have a gold dress made, with lots of netting and diamonds. She would look like a star plucked down from the heavens. She devoted a few minutes to waxing lyrical about her debut as a celestial body of light. It helped her keep herself anchored to the earth.

She was going to marry Jasper.

No matter what anyone said, it would be a real marriage. They would promise to cherish and obey each other, and never part.

"I don't think I truly appreciated the simplicity of being

married in a smithy," Amelia grumbled.

"You planned your wedding to Montrose," Julia reminded her.

"Mother planned that. I just stayed out of the way."

Mother. It was a topic they didn't discuss very often anymore—not after she'd done her best to ruin Amelia's life—but it was Amelia who asked the question.

"Will you invite her, do you think?"

Julia didn't *want* to need her mother there, but she couldn't help but feel a twinge. "Would you be upset if I did?"

The day with her father, talking about being apart from the people they loved, still weighed heavily on Julia's mind. She didn't forgive Lady Bishop, but if she could ease her father's pain without causing Amelia any, she wanted to.

"Even after everything she did, I still missed her at my wedding. I wish you'd all been there," Amelia admitted. "Just don't tell her until it's all planned."

Otherwise it would end up another debacle like Amelia's first engagement. It would be so much worse, because Jasper was a duke. If their mother had lost herself over the social prospects of the boring Earl of Montrose, who knew what she would do when she found out about Jasper.

"We'll give her four days," Julia decided. "It'll be enough time to come, but only if she leaves straight away. No time for meddling."

Hopefully. Now that Julia had allowed herself to want this, she wouldn't let anything take it from her. With the matter settled, she set her mind back to planning.

"Candles!" Julia exclaimed. "We'll need heaps of candles. How long do you think it takes to order a field's worth?" The concerns spilled out of her, each one a piece of tangible proof that she would actually be marrying Jasper. "I'm sure Papa can find someone, don't you think?"

"I—"

"Oh, Mia!" Julia flung herself back against the seat. "Can you believe it? Can you believe I'm really getting married? That we're in love? I don't even care that he's a duke."

"Very big of you," Amelia agreed. "Before your mind bounces off on a new wedding tangent, don't you think there's something you should take care of first?"

"What do you mean?" What else was there, except the wedding, and her and Jasper's glorious future?

"Did you ever resolve that issue, about trusting Jasper — completely?"

Julia pinned her sister with a flat stare. "I told the queen to sod off. I think my demons are conquered."

"Does he know that?"

She was about to tell Amelia that of course he did, but she stopped. Did he? Did she? Julia had no doubt that they loved each other, but she hadn't yet given him the one thing he'd asked of her. Amelia was right. There was something more pressing than the wedding to plan.

Chapter Twenty-Three

"She said I'm to go where?" Jasper was no stranger to unusual requests, but he had to have misheard. After getting Ruby to forgive him—for the most part—they'd gone to see their grandmother to break the news about his not-wedding. She did not take it well. Jasper had missed two trains trying to convince her that it was a good thing, and eventually he'd had to leave or risk Julia thinking he wasn't coming. Ruby had stayed behind, promising to bring the dowager duchess around if it could be done. Now, before the travel dust had even settled, he was being dragged up the drive and through the Bishop house by Julia's very insistent lady's maid.

"The Fairy Barrow," Nora repeated.

No, he'd heard correctly. The clarification hadn't helped in the slightest. "Do you have any idea where I would find such a thing?"

Nora pointed to one of the servants' doors. "Go down to the ground floor—don't go belowstairs—and then take two rights and a left. It'll be on your left at the end of the hall, but you'll know it when you see it."

"I will?"

"Oh, yes. You should be going. Lady Julia doesn't like to wait."

Apparently not. She couldn't even wait for him to unpack or be shown to a room.

Jasper followed Nora's directions to their conclusion, and he did indeed know he was in the right place.

THE ROYAL FAIRY COURT OF
QUEEN JULIA LE FEY & QUEEN AMELIA ELPHAME

The sign was painted by a child's hand, and affixed to a velvet rope which stretched across the archway over a set of steps receding into a sub-basement. Around the arch, branches and vines interwove with shining strips of fabric to create the impression of a glowing, shimmering portal. Where it led, Jasper had no inkling. He stepped under the rope.

Jasper followed the curved steps down. Along the walls, a child had painted fairies in every color imaginable. A few had been drawn by a more mature hand. At the bottom, strips of sheer cloth fluttered like fingertips, serving as a makeshift door. They tickled his face as he pushed through.

Pillows. It was his first conscious impression of the room. Hundreds of pillows covered the floor and piled up at the base of little tables around the room. They were heaped into mounds, some of them looking deliberately placed. More of the sheer fabric covered the windows near the ceiling, coloring the light in diffused rainbow patterns. Great sweeps of thicker metallic cloths curved down from above, distorting the ceiling and forcing him to crouch. Hanging down at different lengths, all of them dangerous to his height, were little lanterns on chains that twinkled throughout the room. He had to duck around two to take his first steps in the room.

"I was five when Papa made it for us," Julia said from her pillow throne near the center. "I'm afraid it's not designed with grown men in mind."

"So I see."

"The pillows are easier if you take off your shoes."

Who was he to argue with a Le Fey? Jasper pulled off his boots and made his way to where she was sitting cross-legged with her hands on her knees.

"Sit, please." When he was mirroring her, she smiled. "Don't tell Nicholas I didn't make you do the ritual of approach."

"There's a ritual for approaching?"

"Oh, yes. It's very involved. We borrowed it from a Japanese emperor."

Now that Jasper was at the level the barrow was meant to be observed from, he noticed objects from all over the world. There were an abundance of trinkets and creations from India. A few from the Orient. Some from Africa. "The fairy court is very well traveled."

"Many adventurers bring us tribute," Julia answered with mock seriousness. "And by many, I mean my father."

"Had I known, I would have brought something." It was obviously her and Amelia's place. There were signs of them everywhere. He was as delighted by the fairy court as he was by its ruler.

Julia straightened her shoulders and nodded, apparently returning to some sort of internal script. "This is where I come when I want to hide. You told me once that you'd wait, until I was ready to show you all of me. Well, I'm ready."

The urge to reach for her bloomed strong, but he kept

his hands on his knees.

Julia stood up. She was wearing a simple day dress that tied in the front. She closed her eyes, took a few deep breaths, and undid the tie. The dress dropped to the ground. She was not wearing anything else.

"It won't always be easy for me, but I don't want to hide myself from you."

He could be patient. He could be anything she asked him to be. She was breathtaking. The soft light spilled over her body, highlighting and shadowing the full arcs of her curves. It lit the proud tilt of her chin—a woman demanding to be seen. It smoothed the nervous lines around her eyes.

"You are so beautiful."

She held up her finger. "Wait."

While Jasper watched, she turned a slow circle. With her back to him, she took another breath that lifted her shoulders, and swept her hair out of the way. An uninterrupted view of her from shoulders to calves was in front of him. There *was* a rough patch of scar tissue the size of Jasper's palm at the base of her spine and a bump that rose slightly off her back. He saw it as he saw everything else—it was Julia.

If he didn't touch her soon, there would be disastrous consequences.

"Well?" Julia asked over her shoulder.

"You are no less beautiful. And if you realized what being eye level with your backside is doing to me, you wouldn't ask that with such a cavalier tone."

A typical woman would have blushed, or feigned shock. Julia was so far from typical. Standing there, in her fairy fortress, naked as a nymph, the smile she sent his way was pure delight—at herself. She'd accomplished something just then, and she celebrated it.

"Well." She turned back around, hands fidgeting against her stomach. "What happens now?"

"I would like to touch you, if you're interested."

No one should be allowed to smile so wickedly and so innocently at the same time.

"I'm interested."

He was looking at her the same. More intensely, even. Like he wanted to drag her down to the pillows and do deliciously wicked things to her. With her. The heat to his attention brought out the devil in her.

He wanted her. He wanted her more.

Julia stepped forward, navigating the pillows with a lifetime of experience. When she was in front of him, she pushed down the nerves and listened to the rippling thrill urging her on. She put her foot on his thigh.

She was exposed. If he looked down, he would see what she'd been so desperate to hide from him. It wasn't the only thing she was exposing to him. The answering flash in his eyes told her which had his attention. Her skin flushed. Julia was hit with a rush of excitement.

Jasper pulled her closer, balancing her with his hands on her hips. He looked up at her, placing a kiss on the inside of her lifted thigh. His lips lingered. He licked. His teeth scraped.

It was heaven. It was torture. The light calanges of his fingertips stroked down, exploring the lines of her thighs and calves. He traced the line of her buttocks, paying devoted attention to the way the curve creased her skin as it met the back of her legs. All the while, his lips were traveling closer and closer to her center.

When his tongue stroked the center of her, it wasn't the same as the day by the lake. Then, she'd been delirious with passion and he had answered her challenge. This time, he was teasing her. Taking her from interested to desperate. There was no plan in his rhythm. Nothing she could anchor her mind to and ride to that place where her body erupted. He swirled and rocked and made her feel impossibly good, but he never gave her anything she could hold on to.

"Jasper."

He hummed against her. The baritone vibrations weakened her knees. "Are you more than interested now?"

"I want you to be naked. I want to touch you. I want…" She wanted. All of it. Everything.

Another hum. Her knees buckled. He lowered her to the pillows, sweeping her hair from her face and laying her out for his view. "Don't move. I want to look at you."

He stood up, removing his cravat and jacket. His eyes stayed on her while he stripped off his shirt and dropped it to the floor. At his trousers, his hands stopped. "Julia, if I ask you to do anything you don't want to do—don't do it, all right?"

"All right."

"Promise."

"I promise. Only things I want to do."

Jasper nodded and the lines of his face deepened again. Wolfish, that was how he looked.

"Touch yourself," he demanded.

She didn't even consider refusing. Her body ached in ways that begged to be relieved. Her hands swept down, covering her breasts, pinching her nipples. His eyes were riveted to her every move and it made her feel like an irresistible temptress. He pushed the trousers from his hips.

Hers. He was hers. Every part of her body told her so. So did the look in his eyes. He was beautiful, and lean, and strong—and he was all hers.

Julia's fingers dipped between her legs, finding the rhythm he'd denied her.

He groaned, standing over her and watching. "You have no idea—"

"Yes, I do." She could see it as easily as if he were a mirror. She was irresistible. She was a torture all his own. "I need you, Jasper. Don't make me wait any longer."

The pillows shifted as he lowered himself down beside her. His fingers framed her chin, stroking her temple, angling her mouth. "No more waiting."

When he kissed her, that was different, too. They'd kissed as an exploration, and out of desperation. This time it was a recognition. He belonged to her and she to him. They wouldn't deny what this was anymore, and kissing him knowing he was hers alone—she could have toppled mountains with how powerful she felt. She rolled toward him, taking ownership of the kiss. She drove him with her tongue and her hands in his hair, demanding more from him. He gave it to her.

"Julia," he groaned.

"Again. Say it again."

"Julia."

It did something to her, her name on his lips while their bare skin pressed against each other. Like no one had ever said it right before.

Jasper pulled her thigh over his hip, bringing them closer together. His cock brushed against her curls, resting heavy and warm against her abdomen.

She moved against it. "Jasper."

He put his hand on her hip, stilling her. "We're not in a hurry."

"I am."

"Too bad."

He kissed her again, massaging the nape of her neck, calming her need. Meanwhile, the slow rocking of their bodies and the barest of friction where his erection pressed against her sent the need spiraling back up. She was trapped in a languid, sensory limbo. He kept them there for an eternity.

Their hands explored each other, taking the time they'd never had before to learn every freckle and every shiver. Julia learned how to make his muscles quiver by scraping her fingernails lightly across his abdomen. He begged her out loud when she swirled her tongue against his ear. He did eventually touch her feet, curving his hands over them and massaging the tension from the arches, but she was too far gone to care.

"You're mine," she said.

"I am." Jasper rolled them both, bringing her to rest on top of him while he lay back against the pillows. He folded his arms behind his head. "Do as you wish with me."

Julia pushed herself up, closing her eyes at the slippery shift of her spread thighs over his cock. She rocked against him, pushing the head against the aching cluster of nerves. There was electricity between them, and she could feel it with each brushing contact. Jasper watched her, and it made her wanton. She arched her back and pinched her nipples.

He put his hands on her hips, guiding. The next rocking shift slipped the head of his cock inside her, just barely. Julia gasped. It was…so much more than her fingers. So different.

His satisfaction came out in a hum.

She shifted back, bringing him in a little farther. He whispered her name.

Julia shifted forward, teasing herself with the feel of him at her entrance again. Back. Forward. She made infinitesimal progress, testing each and every new feeling as her body stretched around him. Jasper's hands fell away, gripping pillows with white knuckles.

"You will be the death of me," he groaned as she brought them back to the start again.

She sank back down, almost filling herself all the way. "Will you regret it?"

"Never."

She brought them together the entire way. Their moans sounded in tandem.

"Jasper, how do I—" It was so distracting, feeling him there, sending pleasure pulsing through every part of her body. "There's a way we're supposed to do this."

"Do whatever you enjoy."

"I want to be good at it."

His laugh was strained. "Trust me, you are. You're doing far too well."

That was thoroughly unhelpful. Julia leaned forward, pressing her breasts against his chest and her lips against his ear. "Help me."

"Help yourself."

Julia swirled her tongue against his ear again. His hips thrust up, hands flying to her backside. She kept doing it, and his thrusts didn't stop. He let out a moan that was almost a whimper and flipped them over. He buried his face against Julia's neck as he rocked in slow bursts that pulled breathy sighs from her.

"Julia." It was a plea.

She rocked against him, increasing their pace. "More."

He gave her more.

It was too nice — too gentle. She needed... "Harder."

Jasper groaned.

Perfect. Every thrust caused little surges of pleasure and they pulsed through her faster and faster until there was no space between them. They started mixing with each other, building on each other, sending her higher.

"Jasper!" She bit into his shoulder and dug her nails into his back, fighting it and welcoming it.

The crash came, and Jasper pulled away. He held her to his chest and whispered her name like a litany, the only sound she heard as she shuddered. She came back to herself with Jasper's head resting between her breasts. His chest was rising and falling in time with hers. Neither of them could get quite enough air.

"Jasper?"

"Hmm?"

"I love you."

He lifted his head. The gold flecks in his eyes practically glowed. "I loved you first."

Chapter Twenty-Four

Jasper stopped in to see Julia before his next cigar and whiskey session with Lord Bishop. The last one had involved an awkward discussion about the funds Lord Bishop intended to level on his eldest daughter. Apparently, Julia was an heiress. Jasper was vaguely familiar with the sum Nicholas had been awarded upon marrying Amelia, but they needed the money with Nicholas only being a second son and Nick's parents not being thrilled about his marriage to Amelia.

The situation for Jasper and Julia was much different. The queen might be against them, but Jasper was in no danger of being short on funds. Still, Lord Bishop would not be dissuaded. They'd finally settled on putting it in a trust to be disbursed back to Julia upon Jasper's death, or evenly amongst their children if she preceded Jasper to the grave.

Bridal contracts weren't exactly Jasper's idea of high romance.

He hoped his blushing fiancée would deliver a much-needed injection of engagement excitement before he had to dive back into the mercenary world of father-in-law negotiations.

"I hope you're not trying to plan it all without me."

"See this." Amelia pointed with the dip pen she was using to take notes. "You should have picked someone like Nicholas. He didn't have opinions about anything."

"I'm going to tell him you said that, and no, thank you. I'm very happy with my choice." Julia lifted her cheek for his kiss.

He sat down beside her with the ease of a contented man. "So, what's it to be? Are we traversing the aisle on the backs of elephants? Entering the ceremony on ostriches?"

"I hadn't thought of riding animals!" Julia's face lit like a lamp, before falling into a scowl. "Which one goes better with a fairy barrow?"

Just the mention of the barrow made him reach for her. For Amelia's benefit, he feigned ignorance. "What's this about a barrow?"

Julia sent him a sly smile. "I've decided to theme our wedding after my favorite room in this house."

He was signing up for a lifetime of delicious torture.

"Are you disappointed we won't be at Westminster?" she asked, suddenly serious.

Every DeVere for as long as he could remember had been married at Westminster Abbey. It was the sort of tradition that Ruby and his grandmother would have insisted on, under different circumstances.

Jasper squeezed her hand. "Not a bit. Without the queen's approval, the bishop would be arrested for performing it, and I've never put much stock in tradition."

"What about your grandmother?"

"She'll come around." Just likely not in time for the

wedding. Ruby had written to let him know the dowager duchess could not support his break with the crown by attending his 'sham ceremony'. His grandmother wasn't coming. He tried to tell himself it didn't matter, and in the end, it wouldn't, but it still stung. Ruby would attend, though, and that made him happy.

Amelia tried to shift the subject back to more pleasant subjects. "Julia, tell him about the settees."

His fiancée lit up like the dawn. "I thought we could use settees and armchairs, instead of pillows on the ground, if we set them up just right. I'd want them in all white and gold."

"That sounds lovely."

"It sounds like it's going to be almost as difficult to find as all these candles you asked me for." Lord Bishop stood in the doorway, smiling over his daughters.

With great exaggeration, Julia batted her eyelashes at him. "Papa, I know that you have been dreaming about funding an extravagant wedding our entire lives."

"Have I?"

"Of course."

"Ever since you were a little girl," Amelia added.

Lord Bishop scowled at his daughters. "Albemarle, please tell me you're ready for our meeting so I can escape these hoydens I've raised."

Jasper much preferred watching the sisters tease their father, but it wouldn't do for him to get on his bride's father's bad side. "Ready as I'll ever be."

They didn't have much left to discuss. The dowry had been haggled over, albeit in the opposite direction it usually took. He was hard-pressed to think of what else they needed to discuss.

In the study, Lord Bishop poured the now-traditional

afternoon whiskey. He swirled the glass between his fingers for a long while before he spoke. "I wanted to ask you, before it's too late, if there's any chance of your taking Julia to Boston and marrying her properly."

Ahh. "I could, but we wouldn't be allowed to come back to England after that, and Julia couldn't stand to be away from Amelia. She is dead set on challenging the queen."

Lord Bellamy chuckled, low and a little sad. "My daughter doesn't have any shortage of nerve, does she?"

"No, she does not." Jasper picked up his glass. "You've raised formidable women, my lord."

"Maybe too formidable," the older man murmured. He studied the bottom of his glass for a moment, before shaking himself. "All right. If this is what she wants, then she'll have it, but what happens next? How does all of this work, after the ceremony?"

Jasper nodded. It was a hard thing to discuss, but he was stealing the man's daughter away. He owed Lord Bishop at least that much for going along with everything. "We'll live together as man and wife. That's how I'll refer to her, and I'll not allow anyone to disrespect her. As far as the law is concerned…"

"She'll be your mistress."

"Only in the eyes of the law. I intend to petition the privy council as soon as I'm able next year, but…there's not much hope of that being successful."

The quiet settled between them.

It was a hard thing to ask a father to accept for his daughter. Before this experience, he couldn't imagine himself or his grandfather accepting such an arrangement for Ruby, but Jasper knew the strength of his feelings for Julia, and he wouldn't be asking if there was another way.

"You love her."

It wasn't a question, but Jasper answered it anyway. "With all that I am."

"What about your children?"

"If we are blessed to have any, they will be the heirs to everything except my title."

Lord Bishop sighed. "If she ever wavers, and considers letting you make an honest woman of her —"

"We'll be on the first ship to France, and she'll be my legal wife within the day." In France, at least. England would never recognize the marriage without the monarch's approval.

It was all Jasper could promise without going against Julia's wishes, but it seemed to be enough. Lord Bishop frowned in thought, and then nodded slowly. He held out his hand. Jasper shook it, sealing the promise.

*O*rganizing a wedding in a fortnight was how families became estranged. First the candles were on time, then suddenly they weren't. Three days later, everyone who upholstered furniture seemed to be out of gold fabric. Then, five days before the wedding, some farmer mentioned that it would surely rain on the day Julia had chosen.

Now she was standing in front of a mirror in her bedroom and the dress she'd commissioned did not look right at all.

"You look lovely," Amelia insisted.

Pure rubbish. "It doesn't float like it ought to."

"Perhaps because it weighs four stone?"

Julia shot her sister a glare in the mirror.

"Right." Amelia stepped away from the dress and

toward the door. "I'll get Jasper, then, since he's the only one who can get you to admit to anything sensible these days."

"No! He can't see me. Not in *the dress*."

"I thought this wasn't the dress. I thought you'd decided the seamstress hated you, and we were going to find another one who could create a miracle in the twenty-four hours you have left."

Julia swished the skirt side to side. "I just want it to be perfect."

"It is, and it will be, but you'll be getting married in it alone if you don't behave yourself."

"I'm not that bad, am I?"

"Yes!" Nora shouted from where she was buried under a mountain of tulle.

Julia just wanted everything to go well. "Do you think people will understand what this dress was supposed to look like?"

"All they're going to see are blood stains if you keep fussing with it," Amelia promised, but she tugged a lock of Julia's hair when she said it. "Everything will be wonderful."

"How do you know?"

"Because you and Jasper love each other. If that's all you have when it's over, it's still quite a lot."

It was more than a lot. It was everything.

Amelia leaned in, whispering next to her ear. "You have overcome far more than an improperly floaty dress to get to this moment. Don't start doubting yourself now."

Suddenly, the dress was perfect, and she became very certain that the candle merchant would be able to sort out his difficulties. All became right in Julia's world—except for the fact that their mother showed up early, with a day still to go until the wedding.

"She's where?" Julia demanded of the housekeeper, Mrs. Polk, who was still standing in the room after delivering the news.

"On her way from the train station."

Julia scrambled to get out of the dress.

"Stand still," Nora demanded. "If you rip it, you'll have only yourself to blame."

With Mrs. Polk's help, Nora and Amelia got her out of the dress and into a new one without any major catastrophes. Julia managed to be downstairs in the foyer when Lady Bishop swept in like a hurricane.

"Girls!" She stopped when her daughters didn't rush to her side. "No warm welcome for your mother?"

"We still remember how you behaved during Mia's engagement," Julia said.

Lady Bishop brushed the thought away with her hand. "All is forgiven. Julia is marrying *a duke.*"

Amelia turned to Julia. "You didn't tell her."

"It must have slipped my mind." A small part of her had been relishing this moment. For her father's sake, Julia had invited their mother back, but she did not entirely intend to let bygones be bygones.

Lady Bishop looked between her daughters. "What's the matter? What's going on?"

Julia took a deep breath. "I'm not exactly *marrying* a duke. He's a royal, and the queen wouldn't approve it."

"Then what is all this?"

"We're committing to live in sin together."

"What do you mean, live in sin?" Lady Bishop knew exactly what Julia meant, she was just trying very hard *not* to know it.

"Julia is going to be Jasper's mistress," Amelia announced. "We're throwing a party to celebrate."

The shriek echoed through the foyer, and no doubt the rest of the house and halfway through the county. Lady Bishop's ungraceful collapse was disrupted by a footman with quick reflexes. Julia didn't miss the smile that flashed on Amelia's face and then disappeared.

Lord Bishop stepped out from his office. "Did someone scream?"

"Just Mother. She's arrived." Amelia didn't seem to feel the need to say more.

Their father raised his eyebrows at the scene in front of him. "It's good to have you back, Felicity."

"I think this might have been a real fainting spell," Julia explained, when Lady Bishop didn't respond. The footman lifted her prone form and carried her to a nearby bench.

Lord Bishop peered at his wife. "What happened?"

The folds of Julia's skirt were suddenly very fascinating. "I failed to mention that the event she'd been invited to was not, in fact, a legal wedding."

He squinted at his daughters. "Menaces, both of you."

"Most certainly," Julia agreed.

"I blame our parents," Amelia added.

"You should probably find some unsuspecting men to foist us off on before it's too late."

"What's all this? Who are you being foisted on?" Jasper came through the front doors and kissed Julia on the cheek.

She kissed him back. "Men who are oblivious to our flaws."

"I'm the perfect candidate, then. Also, your candle merchant just drove around the back. I'm going to meet him." Jasper noticed Lady Bishop, who was blinking back to consciousness in a slump on the bench. "Good afternoon, Lady Bishop."

He left with the same jovial mood he entered.

Amelia leaned close to Julia, watching him go. "Does it alarm you a little how well he fits in with our ridiculousness?"

"Not at all," she answered distractedly. For once, Julia's attention was on something other than Jasper or the wedding. She was watching her parents and the veiled looks of longing they were sending each other when they thought the other wasn't looking.

"Papa, can you explain the wedding preparations to Mother? I'm sure she'll want to find some way to help."

"Wouldn't you know better what needs to be done?"

"No time, I'm afraid." She grabbed Amelia's arm and dragged her toward the stairs. "We're still trying to sort out my dress."

She left them behind, confident that they would find something with which to occupy themselves. There was no shortage of occupations for Julia, either. It was late into the evening before everyone cleared out of her room and she had a moment alone.

The window seat in her room was lit up with moonlight. She sat on it, watching the world outside, trying to reconcile herself to everything that was about to happen. This was her last night in the room she thought she would live in forever. So much was about to change. So much had changed already.

People could say it wasn't a real wedding, but for her and Jasper, it would be. It would mean the same thing. Even if she never stood up in her gold dress, Julia knew—she and Jasper were forever. It was such a strange feeling, to have a man be so much a part of her and be sitting here in the sanctuary of her childhood.

Her door swished across the carpet. Julia didn't need to look. She and Jasper had agreed not to see each again until they stood up in front of their families at the ceremony. It could only be one person.

"You're still the noisiest creeper I've ever heard."

"I don't put the same value on illicit talents as you do," Amelia answered.

Julia grinned. "How sad for Nicholas."

A pillow sailed across the room, bouncing off the window. Amelia followed behind it on a longer delay. She crawled up into the window seat opposite Julia, and they looked at each other.

"Don't," Julia insisted.

Amelia couldn't stop her smile.

"I said don't." But it was no use.

"I told you so."

Julia sighed.

"I told you he would love you, and I told you that you would not die a spinster."

"But you didn't know."

"I did know! Admit it."

"I will do no such thing." Just because Julia was emotional and vulnerable over the coming wedding did not mean she was so slack-witted as to concede an unproven point.

"Fine, don't admit it." Amelia crossed her arms. "We both know I was right."

"Shouldn't you be with your husband?"

"This is more important."

"Gloating was more important?"

Amelia nudged her foot. "You couldn't be with me the night before I was married. It was awful."

Julia felt her throat go thick and the prickling start behind her eyelids. "Damn you, Amelia Bishop."

Her sister scrambled across the seat, finding room to sit shoulder to shoulder. "Just remember—I'm the boring

Bishop, so you'll always know where to find me if you need me."

"Nose deep in a book." Julia nudged her. "Thank you."

Amelia nodded. "If you just want to be boring for a while, that's acceptable, too. What you're doing—"

"People are going to hate it." More than they already hated everything about her. Julia looked around at the menagerie that made up her room. Gold elephant statues, wire birds suspended from the ceiling—aside from Nick and Amelia, they'd been her only friends growing up. Julia had no doubt that some days would be very lonely, but she could handle it. She still had Nick and Amelia, and now she had Jasper.

"I think what you're doing is very brave."

"You mean foolish," Julia added.

"That, too, but it's your plan, so we can't expect it to be a *good* one."

"My plans are excellent!" Julia nudged her, causing Amelia to almost fall off the window seat.

"Of course," she sneered, righting herself. "That's why the queen of England went out of her way to put a stop to you."

The snicker came out of Julia as a snort. "She really did, didn't she?"

"Broke precedent, for the first time in seventy years. Well done, Jules."

"Thank you. I try."

Amelia grabbed her hand and squeezed. "You should get some sleep so you're not puffy and unbearable in the morning."

"I've never been puffy a day in my life."

"Keep telling yourself that."

The silence descended again when Amelia left. It was

just her, the moon, and this bedroom—like it had been so many nights.

Julia looked up at the moon. "I once asked you for a prince on a white horse. You didn't send me a prince, but the man you did send—he's perfect. Thank you."

Chapter Twenty-Five

Jasper stood proudly beneath a gazebo he had built himself—with a little help from the groundskeepers. From it, yards upon yards of shimmering cloth stretched out, finding poles set out amongst the settees and armchairs upholstered in very specific shades of gold and ivory that Julia had not been able to live without. Nicholas stood beside him. All around them, candles and draping lengths of cloth rippled in the breeze.

"You have to have an officiant," Nicholas said for the hundredth time. "Even if it's not a member of the clergy."

"I recognize no authority but my own in this matter."

Nick rolled his eyes. "I am utterly unsurprised that you would say such a thing."

Jasper grinned. "I stole that from Julia, actually."

"You're made for each other."

"We are." Jasper scanned the guests. Ruby was eyeing the seating choices. She'd even managed to smile twice. That was a sign of progress. "Did you invite your parents?"

"No."

"Why not?"

"Because I'd like to live to see the end of this day," Nicholas answered. "We've barely managed to get them to accept Amelia. This is not going to do me any favors."

It couldn't be helped. Jasper wasn't willing to live without Julia, no matter how many feathers it ruffled. Why so many people felt it was their business was still beyond him.

Instead of choosing a seat, Ruby walked up to them on the gazebo. "Jasper."

He smiled. "How do we stack up to Westminster?"

"It's quite…" Ruby looked around, focusing on a pair of footmen waving fans to make everything flutter. "Whimsical."

"Thank you, and thank you for coming. You didn't have to."

She stopped judging everything around them long enough to meet his eyes. "I wouldn't have missed it. I'm happy you're happy, Jasper."

Jasper nodded. He was happy to be happy—finally. Julia was everything he'd ever wanted, right down to the way she'd insisted on the giant swans that were only barely being kept from harassing the guests.

There weren't many guests. Nicholas and Amelia had been certain to attend. Julia's parents were there, and her mother had finally stopped fainting every ten minutes. They were more used to this sort of pageantry from their oldest daughter than most. Ruby had come. Beyond that it was mostly members of the Bishop household and a few friends from Europe that Jasper had been able to get word to in time.

Nora, who had been there from the beginning, was sitting in the second row, steadfastly trying not to cry.

"Only the two of you would have a yellow wedding," Nicholas muttered.

"Gold."

"What?"

"It's gold. Kindly stop griping through my wedding—you're ruining it."

"You griped through mine."

"Did I?" He didn't remember that at all.

He wouldn't, either. Today was his and Julia's day. Nicholas's wedding might have been abrupt and more rustic than either he or Amelia had intended, but they'd been able to enjoy it knowing that no one could deny their existence as husband and wife after it had finished. All Jasper would have was this moment and what it meant to him—what it meant to the woman he loved—but Jasper couldn't imagine it being any other way.

When they'd met, he and Julia had agreed to expect nothing beyond that one moment. They were still living for the moment—they'd just chosen to promise all of their moments to each other. As many *now's* as they had, over and over again.

"I think it's almost time," Nicholas murmured.

Jasper looked around. "How can you tell?"

"The swans are about to line up."

Jasper blinked at him. "Humor is not your forte. Please limit yourself to the law."

Nick grinned. "Amelia thinks I'm funny."

"Amelia loves you. Her opinion is notably biased."

For a moment, they didn't speak.

"It would serve you right if the swans did line up," Jasper whispered. "Don't mention that to Julia. She'll be devastated she didn't think of it."

A hush fell over the servants at the back. Nick opened

his mouth to respond, but Jasper silenced him with a gesture.

It *was* time.

Only, instead of his beloved bride, Amelia was hurrying down the aisle. An elderly gentleman was being towed in her wake.

"What's wrong? Who's this?"

Amelia presented the stranger with her brightest smile. "This is the archbishop of Canterbury."

Behind them, he heard Ruby say, "Praise the lord."

Jasper just stared.

"The queen sent him," Amelia explained.

The reality of what was happening broke through. He asked the archbishop, "Is it true?"

The clergyman smiled. "The queen wishes you to know that she finds your choice of bride exceptional, and hopes Lady Julia will dedicate herself to being Duchess of Albemarle with as much passion as she displayed at court."

He had to be dreaming. Amelia handed him a thick sheet of paper with Victoria's seal on it, and he realized he wasn't. It was written there, plainly and clearly. The queen's approval.

Jasper turned to Amelia. "Does Julia know?"

His soon-to-be sister-in-law nodded, with happy tears welling in her eyes. "Get ready. You're about to be married."

Julia was about to become a duchess. The queen might be a serious young woman, but she certainly harbored a secret flair for drama. She'd waited until the last possible moment to send her approval.

But she *did* send it.

They'd won. The only thing that could have made this day any better had happened. Julia was going to be the Duchess of Albemarle. Her children were going to have Jasper's name.

She stood next to Tryphosa in her gold dress, which turned out to float just the right amount. All of the nerves were gone. She knew it, because Tryphosa was calm as could be. They were certain of where they were headed, and they were certain it was where they wanted to go.

Beside her, Lord Bishop was a mess. He'd burst into tears at the sight of the archbishop, and he hadn't stopped crying since.

Julia patted her father's hand. "Papa, you have to stop crying or people are going to think you don't approve."

"Don't worry about me, sweetheart. I just need a moment." He'd said that five times now.

Julia kissed his cheek, wiped off as many tears as she could, and let him hand her up into the saddle. It was time.

Violins began to play when Tryphosa reached the designated marker. The music floated through the fantasy land that looked exactly how Julia imagined. She barely saw any of it, though. At the end of the long tunnel of draping cloth canopies and candles was Jasper.

He stood waiting for her in gold and white with his hands crossed in front of him. Every careful step brought them closer together. It had taken so many to get them this far.

If he hadn't told her he loved her. If she hadn't followed him after he left. If they had let the queen's rejection break them. Any one thing and none of this would have happened, but here they were, eye to eye, in the world they'd imagined, surrounded by people they loved, who loved them in return—even when they'd thought Jasper and Julia were embarking on something completely foolish.

Now the archbishop was standing beside Jasper, and there wasn't anything pretend about any of it. She was going to be his wife — in the eyes of each other and the law.

Tryphosa reached him. Jasper stepped close, squeezing her foot in the stirrup. "Will you come down, Rapunzel?"

She grinned. "I suppose I could. I don't have anything else planned."

He grinned back. "Good, because I do."

He helped her down, and they stood on the dais of the gazebo. Amelia had joined Nicholas beside them, witnesses to their intention.

The archbishop turned to their assemblage of loved ones. "Dearly beloved, we are gathered together here in the sight of God, and in the face of this congregation, to join together this Man and this Woman in holy Matrimony."

Lady Bishop let out a sniff and a wail. Amelia rolled her eyes, and Julia saw Nicholas nudge her.

"Which is an honourable estate, instituted of God in the time of man's innocence, signifying unto us the mystical union that is betwixt Christ and his Church: which holy estate Christ adorned and beautified with his presence, and first miracle that he wrought..."

Julia let the archbishop's words drift into the background. She and Jasper looked into each other's eyes, and their lips started to curve upward. Her eyes started to tear up.

"Therefore if any man can show just cause why they may not lawfully be joined together, let him now speak, or else hereafter forever hold his peace."

Julia had a moment of fear that someone would object — namely Ruby — but blissfully, the onlookers remained silent.

The archbishop took Jasper's right hand and placed it

on Julia's right hand. "Lord Jasper Augustus DeVere, wilt thou have this Woman to thy wedded Wife, to live together after God's ordinance in the holy estate of Matrimony?"

It was impossible to keep the smile from her lips.

"Wilt thou love her, comfort her, honour, and keep her in sickness and in health; and, forsaking all others, keep thee only unto her, so long as ye both shall live?"

Jasper opened his mouth to answer and had to clear his throat twice. "I will."

"And wilt thou, Lady Julia Elizabeth Bishop, have this Man to thy wedded Husband, to live together after God's ordinance in the holy estate of Matrimony?"

Always.

"Wilt thou obey him, and serve him, love, honour, and keep him in sickness and in health; and, forsaking all other, keep thee only unto him, so long as ye both shall live?"

It was her turn to be too choked up to speak. She'd practiced the words a hundred times, but never thought she'd have the chance to say them. "I will."

There were more words—a lot more; the archbishop of Canterbury was not in any hurry to relinquish his pulpit— but they'd said the ones Julia cared about. She stood still like she was supposed to, and she bowed her head when she was expected to, but through the entirety of the sermon she was only waiting for one thing.

"For as much as Jasper and Julia have consented together in holy wedlock, and have witnessed the same before God and this company, and thereto have given and pledged their troth either to other, and have declared the same by giving and receiving of a ring, and by joining of hands…"

This was it. This was the moment.

"I pronounce that they be Man and Wife together, in

the Name of the Father, and of the Son, and of the Holy Ghost. Amen."

They turned to each other, and Jasper raised her hand to his lips like he'd done so many times before. He looked at her like she was the most beautiful woman on earth, and said, "Amen."

"Amen," Julia repeated. It was everything she'd hoped for, and it was only the beginning.

Epilogue

After their wedding breakfast, during which they did more receiving of congratulations than eating, Amelia pulled Julia aside for one last moment.

"Your grace." Amelia dropped into a low curtsy.

They erupted into matching grins.

"Remember what I told you last night." Amelia took her hand and led her toward the drive. "You may not be a scandalous mistress, but you can still come hide with me for a while if you want a break from being a duchess."

Julia nodded. "I still want my room at your house. Don't change anything."

"Not even if we turn it into a nursery?" Amelia's eyebrows lifted.

"Your house has plenty of other rooms." As what Amelia said sunk in, Julia stopped walking. "Were you just teasing me, or are you really having a baby?"

"I'm not going to tell you until we meet you in Italy. You'll have to stew about it for two whole weeks while you're on your honeymoon." Amelia smirked.

"Enough," Jasper announced, swooping in and catching her around the waist. "I demand you give me back my wife."

"Amelia is trying to torture me by not confirming if she is or isn't pregnant."

"I can solve that. She is — Nick already told me." He kissed Julia's cheek while Amelia cursed him for ruining her surprise. "You'll have plenty of time to talk about it in Italy. Until then, I'm claiming my right as husband and abducting my wife."

He dragged Julia off to the curricle parked in the drive under protest.

"If you're in the mood to disclose secrets, will you finally tell me where we're going?"

"I will not. Any one of these nuisances could overhear, and I don't want anyone interrupting us. Not even Ruby will be able to find us."

It sounded delightful, especially considering Julia's mother was already trying to ingratiate herself with Jasper's sister. Julia did not want any part of that match-up. Amelia's news would still be news when they set off on their tour of the continent together.

She was half in, half out of the carriage saying a teary good-bye to Lord Bishop when Jasper pulled her the rest of the way in, shouting, "We're not going to be gone that long. I promise I'll bring her back in one piece!"

"I didn't realize you would start manhandling me so soon after we said our vows." Julia righted herself as they lurched into motion.

"I'd manhandle you some more, if I didn't have to drive this rig."

"You might have to feed me before we *handle* anything." With the archbishop officiating, the ceremony had gone on much longer than anyone planned. They'd had to cut the wedding breakfast short, and lunch would come and go while they were in the carriage. Julia was starving.

"I promise to feed you within the hour."

He wasn't exaggerating. Almost to the minute, they pulled up outside a cottage surrounded by rose bushes. Jasper hopped down, turning to help, and pulled a hamper full of delicious smells from the tiger seat on the back.

"You had that the entire time?"

Jasper winked at her, carrying the basket in one hand and leading her into the house and up the stairs with the other. He let go of her hand to turn the knob on one of the doors and kicked it open with his boot. Jasper set the hamper down on the table by the bed.

The fire was already lit, giving the room a warm glow. "Do you remember our first dinner, by the fire in Amelia's library?"

He wrapped his arms low around her waist. "It was unforgettable."

Julia put her arms around his neck, looking up into his eyes. "Do you still believe all the greatest love stories end in tragedy?"

She would never tire of the way his eyes traveled over her. He looked at her with reverence. With wonder. With *need*.

"I think the greatest love story is ours, and we"—he leaned in close, brushing his lips over hers—"are going to be shamelessly happy for the rest of our lives."

From now on they would do exactly as they pleased, when they pleased. And what pleased her in this moment was to have him very, very naked. She pulled the shirt from his trousers. "Take me to bed, husband."

"As you wish."

Author's Note:

While it's never specifically named in the series, my research and writing for Julia's disability was done on spina bifida. Spina bifida was identified and named in the mid-1600s by an anatomist named Nicolaes Tulp, but the milder form that Julia has—spina bifida occulta—didn't get its name until 1875.

The first piece of historical documentation I found (which, of course, I've somehow managed to lose in my research notes) was from a doctor in the late 1700s experimenting with iodine injections. Every example sketch was of crying toddlers being held by their mothers. Even though they were just meant to be medical diagrams, I was struck by how terrifying and painful the procedure must have been for a young child. I also realized the lengths these parents were willing to go for the chance at one or two more years with their baby, and the incredible risk of infection dealing with exposed spine treatments in the eighteenth century.

The fact is, spina bifida survival during that time was almost non-existent. The iodine injections were only successful in about one third of the cases, mostly in children between ages one and three, and each of those children eventually suffered complications because the past was not a gentle place to live. Having Julia survive to adulthood was a little bit of an author's liberty, but I believe in perfect conditions (wealth, lack of the need for an occupation, and vigilant parents with a dedicated staff) it would have been possible.

Since there aren't any historical accounts I could find from adults with spina bifida occulta, the rest of my research focused on modern day young women. I'd like to give special thanks to two fantastic youtubers: Andrea Lausell, who gives first-hand information through her #spinabifida videos, and Jorden at JordenMakeup. They're both very open about living with spina bifida, but their videos really drove home how much more their lives are about. Their combined exuberance helped shape Julia's personality and her enthusiasm for adventure.

If this is the first you've heard about spina bifida, I hope my book encourages you to find out more about it. And if you're one of the Andreas or Jordens of the world, kicking ass and being fantastic while managing a disability, I hope I did Julia justice for you. Any failings are mine as a writer, not hers as a character.

Thank you.

Acknowledgments

Once again, I've got to thank my brother Mark. He shoveled snow seven hours a day—by himself—through the craziest winter Tahoe has seen in a long time while I tried to get this book written. He also hiked through knee-high snow with a hangover to come rescue me.

My sister Amy deserves a very special thanks. She's been harassing Ellen to have me on her show since before my first book published (she refuses to believe I'm not famous) and if we hadn't shared a room through childhood, Julia and Amelia's conversations would be way less interesting.

Thank you to the members of #RWCHAT for reminding me that I'm kind of living the dream. Thank you to Chelsea, Robin, and Alexis for telling me to quit complaining and write the damn book.

Thank you to my agent, Rachel Brooks, for understanding the stories I want to write. Thank you to my editor, Kate Brauning, for not letting me shortchange them. Thank you to the entire Entangled Publishing team for doing such a great job.

Lastly, but definitely not least, thanks to my mom. She has supported me from day one, even though she's still not-so-secretly hoping I'll write a book without sex in it.

Q & A
Kimberly Bell

AUTHOR OF
THE IMPORTANCE OF BEING SCANDALOUS
Originally published on USA Today's Happily Ever After Blog

Please tell us a bit about your new release.

The Importance of Being Scandalous is a friends-to-lovers, boy-next-door story. Amelia and Nick have been friends since childhood, even though Nick's family disapproves. Nick has been in love with Amelia from day one, but Amelia has no idea.

Amelia gets engaged to someone else and realizes a little too late that her fiancé isn't the right man for her (and possibly not a good man in general) so she asks for Nick's help to try and cause a big enough scandal to get dumped. Nick is more than happy to sabotage her engagement, especially if it means he'll get a chance to finally tell her how he feels.

What's coming next, or what are you working on now?

I just finished editing the sequel, A Scandal By Any Other Name, featuring Amelia's sister Julia and Nick's friend Jasper. They stole the show a little in the first book, so they had to get a book of their own. That should be coming out early next year, and now I'm rolling around ideas for the next series.

What inspires your book ideas?

Most of my ideas start with the question "What if falling in love was the worst possible thing that could happen to you?" It might just be my personal experience, but when you're trucking along, trying to achieve your goals and be a healthy, self-sufficient individual, and then Love shows up… it's a massive inconvenience. That's probably why all my books end up funny—trying to stick to your plan when life has other ideas usually ends up comical.

Do you write by the seat of your pants, or do you carefully plot your stories?

I wish I plotted my stories. Unfortunately, I'm kind of at the mercy of the characters. They move into my head and I'm kind of just their chauffeur.

Would you like to share a favorite moment from your writing career?

Oh, man. At a conference in 2015, I got to meet Jo Beverly. I've met more than a few movie stars and other famous-type people and, historically, I've always kept my cool, but with Jo Beverly I went full spaz.

She refused to let me walk away in embarrassment. It took about twenty minutes, but she kept asking me questions and telling me borderline dirty jokes until I turned back into a human being who could have a functional conversation. I bumped into her a few more times during that conference, and she would always wink or made a joke. It made me feel incredibly special.

Jo passed later that year, and I wouldn't trade meeting her for anything.

Is there a TV show that you've recently binge-watched?

I recently made way through The White Queen and The White Princess in an embarrassingly short amount of time, and now I'm heartbroken that the other books aren't series' yet. I'm also super upset none of my books have magic or river goddesses in them.

Do you have a pet that hangs out with you while you're working? (Feel free to include a picture!)

What Willis does isn't so much "hang out with me" as glare at me while pondering his next spot to passive-aggressively vomit, because he doesn't think I take his warning's that we're under constant attack seriously enough. He is, however, a first rate cuddler, and when he gets super excited his eyes cross which is hilarious.

Do you listen to music while you write? What are some tunes on your playlist?

I try to add new songs to my writing playlist with each new book. Some of my favorite new additions from this last book were Painting Greys by Emmit Fenn and I Found by Amber Run. No matter what, all of my playlists have Retrograde by James Blake on them. It reminds me that the book isn't going to write itself, and that I can do this.

I don't suppose you'd want to share a picture of you with your '80s or '90s hair or perhaps a prom picture?

I didn't go to prom, but I do have a picture of me as a little kid from the 80's in the coolest coat I have ever owned, looking thoroughly unimpressed with everything and everyone. This picture is also unique because, in every other picture from my childhood, I refused to wear any clothes, regardless of how formal the picture-taking occasion. (My mom deserves a sainthood.)

Do you have anything to add?

I was a historical romance reader long before I ever wrote in the genre. With every book I write, I try to capture the way those 90's era Amanda Quick novels make me feel. If I can manage that, then I'll consider myself a success.

Don't miss these other thrilling reads from Amara Historical

The Importance of Being Scandalous
by Kimberly Bell

None of the society-shocking scandals and pranks Amelia Bishop has pulled off lately are scaring away her stuffy, egotistical fiancé. The only thing left is to entice childhood friend Nicholas Wakefield into a truly engagement-ending scandal.

Nicholas's parents have made it clear a wife from the Bishop family would be unacceptable. But he'd give up his family and his fortune if Amelia would ever see him as more than a childhood friend. He'll go along with her scheme, even if it means ruining them both, because he's got a plan that will change her mind about him being the boy next door.

Scandal of the Season
a novel by Liana LeFey

Five years ago, Lord Sorin Latham fled England's shores to avoid heartbreak and scandal in the form of one Lady Eleanor Cramley. On returning home, he finds the young miss he knew is now a stunning woman who fires his blood. Now that he's back, the man Lady Eleanor once thought of as an older brother makes her long to be anything but proper. She must make Sorin see her as worthy of his heart and his desire without losing his good opinion, or her Season will end in disgrace.

THE BITTERSWEET BRIDE
BY VANESSA RILEY

Widow Theodosia Cecil needs a husband to help protect her son. The former flower seller turned estate owner posts an ad in the newspaper, and no one is more surprised than she when her first love, the man she thought dead, reappears.

Ewan Fitzwilliam has been at war for six years. Now, the second son of a powerful earl is back but his beloved Theo needs a husband and will not consider him. She believes Ewan left her—in desperate straits—so she denies the feelings she still harbors for the handsome, scarred soldier. Theo and playwright Ewan must overcome bitter lies and vengeful actions that ruined their youthful affair. Theo must reveal her deepest secret in order to reclaim the love that has long been denied.

MY SCOT, MY SURRENDER
BY AMALIE HOWARD & ANGIE MORGAN

Brandt Montgomery Pierce is a bastard—and proud of it. Despite the mystery surrounding his birth, he has wealth and opportunity, and wants nothing more. Especially not a wife. Lady Sorcha Maclaren is desperate to avoid marriage to a loathsome marquess, even if it means kissing a handsome stranger. But after the kiss turns into a public embrace, Sorcha and Brandt get more than they bargained for—a swift trip to the altar.

an imprint of Entangled Publishing LLC